Putting Makeup on Dead People

Putting Makeup on Dead People

JEN VIOLI

HYPERION
NEW YORK

Text copyright © 2011 by Jen Violi

All rights reserved. Published by Hyperion, an imprint of Disney
Book Group. No part of this book may be reproduced or transmitted
in any form or by any means, electronic or mechanical, including
photocopying, recording, or by any information storage and retrieval
system, without written permission from the publisher. For information
address Hyperion, 114 Fifth Avenue, New York, New York 10011-5690.

Printed in the United States of America

First Hyperion paperback edition, 2012

10 9 8 7 6 5 4 3 2 1

V475-2873-0-12173

Library of Congress Control Number for Hardcover Edition: 2011284550

ISBN 978-1-4231-3485-5

Visit www.un-requiredreading.com

To my father, Alfred D. Violi,
with gratitude and love.
This is for you.

prologue

I'm mixing a can of tomato soup with a can of two percent milk for dinner that no one will eat. But I have to do something, so I make soup. Linnie's with Uncle Lou and Aunt Irene, eating the greasiest goddamn potato chips Uncle Lou said he could find. B is at a party, celebrating the end of summer with his buddies before they all leave for college. And I'm here with Mom and what's left of Dad. I lose myself in the rhythm of stirring, and the soup almost bubbles over before I turn it off and go to get Mom.

Thin, in her white cotton pants and sweater, Mom looks like a ghost standing beside the hospital bed, a clinical invasion into my parents' peach-and-cream-colored room.

Dad's eyes flutter, his face two shades paler than its usual rich olive tone.

"I think he's going, sweetie," Mom says, *so calmly that I ask, "Where?" It sounds so matter-of-fact, like he might be going to the store or out for ice cream or to meet Uncle Lou at the Kozy Korner.*

As soon as I ask, I understand, and shut my mouth. Dad's breathing gets rough, like he's snoring, and I cross my fingers, willing him to open his eyes and laugh and say, "Fooled ya, pretty girl."

Mom says, "Just let it happen." And, "Say good-bye to your father."

I can't say anything out loud, but I speak clearly in my mind. Good-bye. I love you. Don't go. Please, I'll do anything, but don't go.

Mom holds Dad's hand, and I hold hers. I rest my hand on the upper part of Dad's arm, close to his shoulder. "Bye."

one

Lila Cardoza is dead and wearing my earrings. Not mine, exactly, but the same ones B's girlfriend, Gwen, got for me three months ago at Christmas. Silver zigzags with little silver balls at the tips. I realize I was never this close to Lila when she was alive. We didn't have any classes together, and the only interaction I can remember is handing her toilet paper under the stall in the third-floor girls' bathroom, but even then we weren't face-to-face.

We don't usually start the school day at Brighton Brothers Funeral Home, and I can see the dazed look on my classmates' faces, some of them crying (Becky) and some fidgeting (Patty), like they'd rather be anywhere else but here. It's not normal for a seventeen-year-old to drop dead on the basketball court, and I'm pretty sure it's even less normal for me to feel so comfortable near her coffin and corpse.

I haven't been to Brighton Brothers since Dad's funeral, and standing just outside the doors this morning in the cool March air, I was nervous. Now that I'm inside, I'm surprised to find it feels almost like home. Or at least how home used to feel, before Dad got sick and died.

Dad was in Viewing Room Two, but Lila's in Viewing Room One, and there are so many flower arrangements that I tripped over tulips on the way in. Lila was going to graduate with the rest of us in a few months and had gotten a basketball scholarship, basically a full ride to some school in New Jersey. Until she had a heart attack in the middle of practice in Dayton, Ohio's Woodmont High School gym.

Lila looks almost like Sleeping Beauty—except that she's wearing her Woodmont Warriors jersey with the shimmery gold shield, and not a princess dress—and someone has put eyeliner and pale eye shadow over her closed lids.

Becky's standing so close to me that I feel her shudder. Becky Bell and I have known each other since grade school. We don't ever have much to talk about, but she's just about the nicest person I've ever met, which is as good a reason as any, I guess, to be friends with someone. She whispers, "This is creepy."

I nod like I'm agreeing, even though I'm not.

"Yeah, can we get out of here?" Patty Turner asks.

Becky's dating Patty's twin brother, Jim, so unfortunately that means Patty sits with us at lunch. Jim is as nice and easygoing as Becky, but I call Patty the Evil Twin in my head because I think Jim got all of the friendly genes.

Patty clicks her gum. "I don't do funerals."

I want to tell Patty that she's this close to getting one of her own if she doesn't shut up, but instead I tune her out and look at Lila, tranquil in her coffin.

At Dad's wake three and a half years ago, the summer before I started high school, he was the only one I wanted to be near. Everyone else talked too much and hurt my ears, but Dad was stationary and silent.

My heart broke when he died, split in half and fell down into my stomach or somewhere deep and muddy, and I'm still not sure where it is now. I hear it beating sometimes in my ears, or feel its fast pulse in my neck, like I do now; but in my chest, where it should be, it mostly just feels empty.

After the funeral, I cried on our old red couch in the basement until I thought I might drown. I imagined my tears filling up the basement, and me floating away on a thick seat cushion to somewhere that didn't hurt so much. I sat there for most of that Saturday until it got dark and I had no idea what time it was. Once it got dark, my brother B came and sat next to me, his legs crossed and folded underneath him. I think he was hoping for the same thing, but nothing happened while we sat there.

All freshman year at school, I couldn't stand the noise
—lockers closing and volleyballs bouncing on the gym floor
and everyone talking about some dumb game they all had
gone to. I would go inside myself and imagine sitting in the
small empty place in my chest, watching everyone, with
all the noise around me. And I'd imagine Dad lying still in
that white coffin, his skin cold. Everything on the outside
seemed to be there—his big Roman nose I still worry mine
might grow into, his thin lips, the long eyelashes Mom
always said she was jealous of—but frozen.

I wondered if he had gotten still on the inside, like me.
I wondered where he was, and if it was heaven, if there
were pearly gates or if they were actually made out of
something else, like cubic zirconia. Or if it could be like
Hubcap Heaven on Route 70, which I think would be a
real disappointment.

From inside, I could see people staring at me, almost
always not directly, and often when they thought I wasn't
looking. I guess like I'm doing now, watching Matt
Capinski, one of the biggest jerks in school, squirm just
outside Viewing Room One—hands in pockets, hands out
of pockets, hands folded, hand cracking knuckles on other
hand—in the corner. Or Liz Werner, the new girl with
the coppery hair, by the stand with the visitors' book and
the little container of holy cards, hugging Mrs. Cardoza,
although I'm pretty sure they just met.]

I fit in better now because I've learned how to talk a

little more and how to act like I'm happy. I've learned how to make noise so that I can ignore the quiet place. But it's like a magnet. It pulls me back in, and sometimes it does make me feel better. It's not like the questions go away. I still wonder where Dad is now, and if I'll ever stop hurting. I still wonder why I am the one who has to live without a father. But in my inside place, all the questions can just float around without being answered. And floating with them, somehow that's been the only spot I feel at home. Until now.

"This is where your dad was," Becky says, like she just discovered something. Junior funeral sleuth, Becky Bell.

What could be the right thing to say to that? Yep, you got me. Boy, I thought I was so undercover, but you must be some eagle eye. Here I was trying to pretend I was some other normal person like you, vice president of the student council and whose dad is vice president of some company with initials I can never remember. Or like Patty, who plays volleyball and who always has a boyfriend, even if it's a different one every three months, and whose dad works in advertising. But I'm not her or you. I'm me. I'm the girl without a club and without a dad, so even though I haven't actually forgotten, thanks for the reminder. Should I wear a name tag?

"Do you know what we do, Donna?" Becky's eyes are kind, and her voice shakes. I'm not mad at her, and I do know what to do.

"Go up to the casket and say a prayer." I make myself smile at her. "I'm going to get a drink of water."

In the hallway by the water fountain and next to the long container of cone-shaped paper cups, a tall, tan man in a dark suit leans against the wall. He gives me a little smile, and I notice he's wearing hiking boots.

"Nice outfit," I say.

He looks down at his boots. "Thanks. I think it's kind of sporty." He clicks his heels together once. "I'm sorry about your friend."

"I didn't know her very well." I pull out a paper cup and fill it with water. "You work here?'

He nods.

"My dad was here. Nicky Parisi. I kind of look like him." I finish the water in one gulp.

The man studies my face and nods. "I remember him. Good natural coloring. Only needed a simple base coat."

I crinkle my eyebrows.

"Sorry," he says. Even though he's as tan as Patty gets after a full summer of daily visits to Kissed by the Sun on Huffman Avenue, I can see that he's turned red. "I don't usually do this part, with the talking to the live people and such. I just work on the dead ones." He glances at Bob Brighton, who I remember from Dad's funeral and who hands a box of tissues to one of Lila's aunts in the other room.

Crushing the paper cup into my fist, I fold my arms. "Did you put that eye shadow on Lila?"

"And the blusher." He grins at me like Becky's dad does at her three-year-old sister Leah when she says something grown-up.

I don't smile back, and his grin fades. "Okay then, so what do you think?"

"Looks good. I liked the lipstick, too."

"Joe Brighton," the man says, and holds out his hand, smiling at me now like we're equals.

As I shake his hand, across the way I notice two people staring at me. One is Matt and the other is Liz. What goes around comes around, I guess. Liz looks curious, but Matt's got a smirk on his face that makes me nervous. I pull my hand back from Joe Brighton. "Nice to meet you. I better get back to my friends. The service starts soon."

"Well, chin up, Donna P. Everyone dies."

I'm not sure how that's supposed to keep my chin up. And even though I'd like to talk with Joe Brighton a lot longer, I don't want to do it in front of everyone from school.

Lila Cardoza, 17

Cause of Death: Heart attack

Surviving Immediate Family:
- Mother: Carmen
- Father: Sammy
- Brother: Junior
- Dog: Sunshine (bichon frise)

Makeup: Lavender shimmer eye shadow, black eyeliner, Mocha lipstick, Pink Seashell blush

Clothing: Woodmont Warriors basketball jersey

Casket: Cherrywood, ivory silk lining

Special Guests in Attendance: Tiki Cardoza, founder of Cardoza's Old Time Taqueria

Funeral Incidents:
- Woodmont girls' basketball team accompanied by members of the cheering squad perform Lila's favorite cheer/chant, "Be Aggressive."
- Lila's boyfriend, Kyle, places one yellow rose in the casket.

Dumbest thing someone says trying to be comforting: "Now she'll be dribbling on the best court there is … God's." —Dee Taylor, Woodmont girls' basketball assistant coach and Church of the Savior youth group leader

two

I'm sitting in my senior Spanish class, whispering to myself, "*Cuerpos. Cuerpos.*" I like the hard *C*, how the *R* rolls in my mouth, the punch of the *P*. And I like what it means. We're supposed to be reading about new verbs, but I went to the career section of our textbook to find something I saw once when I was reading ahead. And here it is. Francisco is an *agente funerario* and gets many *cuerpos* ready for burial. I never thought of it before today, but now it seems so obvious. Bodies.

I glance around the room. At Matt, who now sits next to me in Spanish because he was causing too much trouble sitting by his friend Pete Jones. Matt has long earlobes. At Jane Slate, who talks even less than I do and has chin-length straight blond hair. At Mr. Trauth, whose back is to us while he writes new verbs on the board. His shiny bald head comes to a little point on top. I notice that Liz wraps slender fingers around a dragon-shaped pen. Of course I've never seen bodies like Francisco or Joe Brighton must have seen, but I like looking at people and all of their different parts. Even Matt, who's mean to just about everybody except for Pete, but who does have really interesting earlobes.

Matt catches me looking at him and hisses, "Hey. Donna?"

I glance down quickly and draw a long spiral circle in the middle of my blank notebook page, pretending I don't hear him.

"Pssst." I feel Matt staring at me, and my cheeks are hot, probably getting redder than usual. That's one of my special features—it always looks like I'm blushing. I shouldn't have been looking around so much. I got distracted again and forgot everyone could see me too.

A wad of paper hits me on the arm, and I can't help but look up this time.

"Hey, Morticia, have a nice conversation with the weird dude at the funeral place?" Matt looks at me like Uncle Lou's beagle, Lucky, waiting for something. A walk, a treat, maybe?

Out of the corner of my eye, I see a flash and realize it's Liz, who sits behind Matt. She reaches up and swats him swiftly on the back of his head with her spiral notebook, a lot like when Uncle Lou swats Lucky with his Sons of Italy newsletter when Lucky puts his paws on the dining room table to get closer to Aunt Irene's meatballs.

I gasp and command myself not to laugh out loud.

"Ow." Matt whips around to look at Liz.

The skin on Liz's face is pale and creamy, like Snow White's, and when she smiles at Matt and cocks her head to one side, she looks like pure innocence. She unfolds her notebook in front of her, and her copper hair falls in long thick curls like a curtain in front of her face, in stark contrast to the silk turquoise shawl wrapped around her like I've seen on Indian women on TV. She writes something at the left-hand top of the page with her dragon pen. Without looking up, she says, "Sorry, my hand slipped."

Mr. Trauth turns from the board. "Mr. Capinski, do we have a problem?"

"No," Matt mumbles, and looks down at his textbook.

"Good, then why don't you come up to the board and help me finish these?" Mr. Trauth scans the room. "We've had a tough enough day already, so I hope no one else is planning any funny business? Good, then the rest of you can keep reading pages fifty and fifty-one."

As Matt shuffles and grumbles to the front of the room, I look at Liz and whisper, "Thanks."

She shrugs. "I'm typically a fan of talking to weird dudes." She smiles, and I feel like her smile is the kind that gets her an extra scoop of ice cream and cuts in line and asked out on actual dates to Mama DiSalvo's and not on group ones to the cheap movies on Stroop Road. Or one that gets invitations from people who don't usually offer them. Like me.

"Hey, um, you want to sit with us at lunch?"

"Oh God, yes, please," she whispers. "I can't take another minute explaining to the varsity cheering squad that I actually like sitting alone."

"Well, do you? Like to sit alone, I mean?"

"Yep." She smiles again. "Unless there's a better option."

"I just need to stop by my locker after class."

"Cool beans."

"Cool beans," I repeat, thinking I like the sound of that, even if I wouldn't want to eat them.

I wonder what it would be like to be Liz, starting at a brand-new place halfway through your senior year of high school. I've watched her sitting by herself, reading or writing or drawing with a charcoal pencil on a huge tablet with thick art paper at lunch, and honestly, it makes me jealous. It's like a free pass to be invisible and special, which it seems like she is. But she wants to sit with me at lunch, so I'm not sure what that says.

I look back to my textbook and Francisco's cartoon face and dark mound of wavy hair without a one out of place. He is one chipper *agente funerario*. It's so funny I've never thought of it before, because it seems so clear and so easy now at this moment, after wondering for all of high school what the answer is; after telling lies like "teacher" or "nurse" or even once "acrobat," in response to the big question: What are you going to be when you grow up? After listening to everyone at Woodmont talk about their plans all year long. Becky will study international business, Patty will study sports science out of town, and even Jim will study graphic design and work at his dad's advertising firm. Good job, everyone. You're going to do so well! And Donna, what about you? So you'll study Communications here in Dayton? What do you plan to do with that? Oh. Well, you'll figure it out.

Now, with a tiny grin, I say to myself, just loud enough for me to hear, "Donna is a mortician who deals with many bodies."

I'm chewing on a piece of garlicky bread stick, sitting between Patty and Liz at our chipped corner cafeteria table in the unusually quiet cafeteria. The girls' and boys' basketball teams are out at the post-funeral luncheon Lila's family is hosting at St. Charles's. And everyone here seems to be acting like they're still at Brighton Brothers—talking softly and looking somber—which works for me, since I'm also imagining myself in a funeral home.

Except I'm putting just the right blusher on a dead someone's cheeks, or solemnly greeting a family in mourning. I see my long brown hair twirled in a bun, like Dr. Laughlin's, our principal, and wearing Mom's pearls—if she'll let me

15

borrow them—and probably some sensible pumps; I just don't think hiking boots are the look for me. I'm standing next to filmy beige drapes and nodding and holding out a box of Kleenex. The thought of it is comforting, familiar.

I know the route down the hallway, past the ladies' room, with two wingback pink upholstered chairs with a small cream-colored table between them, like a place where some elegant couple might sit down to tea. Past the water fountains, to the little reception room where some of them serve coffee and pastries—like the one where we had Grammy's viewing. I'd like to work in a funeral home with pastries, maybe pizzelles like Aunt Irene makes from Nonna's recipe. I do know my way around a funeral home.

I almost jump when I hear Patty's sharp voice say, "Charlie, what is that crap?"

I glance over at Charlie McIntyre and his lunch. Most of us are eating chicken fingers and bread sticks, but Charlie has something in a Tupperware container that looks like it has tiny noodles and raisins and green stuff in it, and which I can't identify to save my life.

Charlie is sitting next to Jim, Becky's boyfriend. Sometimes I wonder if Charlie is friends with Jim for the same reasons I'm friends with Becky. They don't seem to have much in common, but they grew up next door to each other, and Jim's just as sweet as Becky. Anyway, Charlie's tall and skinny with curly black hair that never wants to all go in one direction, and he wears these great dark-framed glasses that I think make him look like the guy who played Ichabod Crane in that movie. Charlie doesn't talk very much at all, which I find soothing. At the moment, he's got his eyes on a book called *Planting an Herb Garden* and is not paying attention to anyone.

"Hello. Charlie, what is that crap?" Patty repeats.

The sound of her voice pierces the cafeteria air, and even hook-nosed Dave Davis, the president of the math team, turns to look, which is a pretty big deal since the math team isn't interested in much that doesn't compute. Charlie also glances up, and I see a piece of noodle on his lower lip. He notices it too, and licks it into his mouth. "You mean my lunch?"

"Whatever," Patty says more softly to Charlie, and glares at Dave until he turns away. "That stuff in the container."

"It's quinoa salad." I don't know what quinoa is, but I like how it sounds—*Keen Wah*. Neat. I also like that Charlie answers in a way that is perfectly calm and not defensive, which is how I'd respond if Patty asked me that question, at least in my head.

"His parents are hippies," Jim says, which sounds a bit like, *Oh, well, Charlie was raised by wolves, so, you know, he poops in the forest and stuff.*

"So what does that mean?" Becky asks.

"Socks with sandals, you know, that kind of stuff." Jim laughs.

"And they have lots of sex and don't take showers,"

Patty says, and makes a face that crunches up all of her facial features, and which I think more accurately reflects her personality. "Gross," she says, which I also find to fit her M.O.

Through all of this, Charlie remains silent, serenely eating his salad as everyone speculates about his parents' sex life and personal hygiene. Nothing seems to ruffle Charlie or keep him from doing what he believes in, like circulating a petition in the fall to get the Home Ec teachers to add composting training to the curriculum, which surprisingly worked. But he's never pushy, like Tami Ritter, who practically shoves right-to-life brochures into our hands twice a year and will corner anyone by the tampon machine in the girls' bathroom to go into great detail about God's will.

Charlie, however, just does his thing and lets other people do theirs. Other people's goals at Woodmont seem about as interesting as drainage systems to me, but I have to admit I'm curious to see what Charlie will, as Uncle Lou might say, "make out of himself." Now he shrugs at Patty and looks back down at his book.

"You know," Liz says, pointing a bread stick at Jim, "I read that Americans shower too much anyway. It's not good for our skin. And nothing's wrong with lots of sex."

"As long as you're married," Becky says quickly, and glances at Jim.

Liz smiles. "I'm not Christian, so I don't have to follow that rule."

"What are you?" Becky must not realize that people other than Christians attend Woodmont, because she looks awfully shocked.

"I was thinking of becoming a Pagan."

Jim leans in with his elbows propped on the table. "What does that mean?" His eyes are so big that I wonder if he's thinking of converting.

Patty rolls her eyes. "It means she's part of some weird devil cult."

"Oh, grow up." Liz dips her bread stick into a small container she's filled with mustard, rather than the pizza sauce the rest of us are using. "Everyone knows that the Christians just made up the devil stuff so their religion would be the most popular. It was like high school even in the Middle Ages."

Charlie laughs.

I've always wondered how much stuff Christians made up, because Bible stories sound an awful lot like fairy tales to me. At the same time, I heard all through grade-school religion classes that it's all true, even Communion turning into Jesus' body and blood. Which honestly, I have a little trouble visualizing without special effects and a really messy altar cloth.

"Well, Donna, you really invite some interesting people

to the lunch table," Patty says, with another scrunched-up face in Liz's direction.

Usually I ignore Patty or act like I agree with her; I just don't care enough to argue. But for the first time since I can remember, something matters—some*one* matters. I turn to Patty and look her straight in the face. I pretend Liz is contagious, that sitting next to her means I've caught the fearless-and-confident virus, and I shrug. "You *are* pretty interesting," I say to Liz, and smile.

"Likewise," Liz says.

Patty huffs. "Whatever."

Becky, whose eyes are still a little red from crying this morning, says, "I don't think we should be fighting today. It's not respectful. To Lila."

"No one's fighting, Becky." Patty folds her arms. "And it's not like we really knew her."

"We went to school with her," Charlie says. "And it makes you think. It makes me think about my grandfather. And I'm guessing it might make Donna think about her dad. And I think you know Donna. So maybe you could be respectful to her."

"Sorry, Donna. And thank you, Hall Monitor Charlie." Patty stands up. "I'm going to finish my physics homework before class. Becky, come help me."

Becky, who hasn't been comfortable since sex and Christians came up, and certainly must not be relaxed now, jumps to her feet and follows Patty. "Come on, Jim," she says.

"I thought we all weren't doing our homework anymore." Clearly Jim was not uncomfortable, and he's right: it seems like no one's been taking class seriously anymore, like this low-grade fever is circulating among seniors, one that can only be cooled by the sweet balm of graduation. "Remember we have senioritis?"

"Consider yourself temporarily cured," Patty says slowly through her teeth. "And right now, I'm going to do my physics homework."

Becky pats Jim on the arm. "You can be a slacker later, Jimmy."

Jim reluctantly picks up his tray and walks away.

I feel like my whole face must be the reddest it's ever been, and I glance down at my tray. I notice that Charlie is watching me. "I hope I didn't say something wrong," he says.

"You didn't." I want to say more, to say how thoughtful he was, how I don't mind anyone reminding Patty to be a human being, that I think his lips must be really soft, but I can't get out any more words.

"Okay." He smiles a little and points to his Tupperware container. "Want to try some?"

My stomach does a little flip. I feel something, but it's not hunger. "No." I worry that I answered too fast and sounded rude. "But thank you. I like the name of it."

"It's spelled with a Q." He writes out a word on the back of his herb book, right there on the cover, and turns it to face me. Q-U-I-N-O-A.

"That's even better. It's like Spanish."

"It is Spanish. The grain of the Incas."

"Nice," Liz says. "And thanks," she says to me. "We made a pretty good team today."

"I guess so." I look again at the word on Charlie's book, and I touch it. It's different, and I think it's beautiful.

After school, when I close my locker and turn around, Liz is standing there. She's wearing big movie star sunglasses and says, "Want a ride home? I think we live pretty close."

"Riding the bus happens to be one of my least favorite things."

"Then you're in luck."

In the parking lot, the sun shines so bright on my face that I decide to take off my sweater and stuff it into my backpack. The air feels cool through my long-sleeved cotton shirt, and I'm noticing springtime, which used to be my favorite season. I'd rejoice at the end of winter—a miserable time in Dayton, usually with a bunch of snow, a lot of wet icy rain, and gray day after gray day. But then, all of a sudden, everything would change, like it's changing now. The tulips are popping up out of the ground all crisp and sure and bright, and I can smell the ground getting warmer.

And springtime means that it's almost my birthday, which used to mean Dad waking me up singing Happy Birthday at the top of his lungs and sticking candles in my scrambled eggs because it was funny. Now for my birthday, Mom and I stick flowers in the dirt in front of Dad's gravestone, which isn't actually funny at all. I used to love springtime, to feel it on the inside. Since Dad died, it's more like watching a movie full of lush gardens while I'm sitting in the dark theater with the trampled bodies of Sour Patch Kids lying in flat gummy destruction below me on a dirty floor.

A week from today, it'll be April second, and I'll be eighteen. I was due to be born on April first, but Dad always said I waited a day because I'm no fool. Sometimes I wonder.

Liz stops us at a Jeep the color of metallic chocolate. Of course she has a car this cool. "Wow," I say.

"I'm the only child, and my dad likes to give big presents —you know how they do."

I don't say anything. I hate when this happens. I should be used to it by now. I should just say yes, I know, just agree so no one feels awkward. But the truth is I don't know how dads give big presents to their car-driving daughters. I doubt Dad would have gotten me a Jeep, but I'm never going to find out.

"I'm sorry. Shit. I didn't even. Shit." Liz tugs at the fringe on her enormous purple purse.

"It's okay," I say. Usually when this happens, I don't care how it turns out. I don't care how the other person feels, but I've never met anyone like Liz, and I don't want to mess this up. Liz feels like possibility, like the door to the magic kingdom, like, well, springtime.

She asks softly, "You still want a ride home?"

"Yes." I reach out and touch her arm, and it feels strange to touch someone not in my family. "Really, it's fine."

"Okay? Okay. Then climb on in." She opens my door for me and shuts it once I get in. Her car smells like cinnamon.

On the way out of the parking lot, she smiles and says, "Let's roll the windows down."

I nod, and we roll the windows down. All the way. The air makes my face tingle, and I wonder if anyone will see me riding in Liz's chocolate Jeep. On the dashboard, a little statue of a fat happy man bounces up and down on a suction cup, and I laugh at him.

"That's my Buddha," Liz says. "He likes to go for rides."

"Didn't he start a religion?"

"If that's not a ride, I don't know what is."

I laugh and nod my head as the happy Buddha bounces.

It turns out Liz does live pretty close to me. Her family's house is in Oakwood, and mine's just over the line in Kettering. I'm guessing Liz's house is probably as cool as her car. Oakwood holds the distinction of being Dayton's fancy suburb, with its own fancy supermarket and fancy shops where middle-aged women buy sequined walking outfits with their Gold American Express cards. Some parts of Kettering are fancy, but my part's pretty normal suburban land. We live on Sherwood, which always makes me think that more exciting things should be happening there, involving forested escapades and surprise attacks from trees, but the most interesting thing at the moment is Mr. Grant's new cherry-red riding lawn mower. Although, given the big smile on his face last weekend when he broke out his new ride, I guess that purchase did make him merrier than the average man.

As we pull onto Sherwood, Liz says, "Thanks a lot for today. I've actually been a little lonely since we moved."

"No problem." It feels so easy to be with her, and there are so many questions I want to ask, like, *How can I one day be as cool as you are?* Before I can stop myself, I ask a different one, "You want to come over?" And then I immediately regret this offer. What would someone like Liz do at my house? Watch Mom do craft projects or see how much black makeup Linnie can put on her face? I can't remember the last time I had someone come over. Maybe Becky in the eighth grade? I don't even know what people do at each other's houses anymore, so I'm not sure how to do it right.

Then a thought crosses my mind. Maybe she wants to hang out with me. Maybe she's new in town and wants a friend, and maybe there's not a right way to do it.

"Can I?" Liz asks, and by the brightness in her eyes and voice, I know she means it, and otherwise I'll be spending all of Friday night watching boring television with B, who's home from college this week on spring break, or the incomprehensible Linnie, who plans to secretly dye her hair blue this evening. I'm not sure how long it will be a secret from Mom, but that's Linnie's problem.

"Yeah," I say, trying to sound nonchalant. I point to my house, where Mom's in the front yard, holding a shovel and wearing a rolled-up bandana to restrain her blond curls. "That's it. Um, my mom isn't used to me having friends stop by, so I'm not sure what she'll think."

"I'm not worried." I'm pretty sure Liz doesn't worry about anything. What she doesn't know is that she's about to meet the Wonder Woman of worrying, someone who worries about everything from dynamite to dust bunnies.

Worrying may be the one thing Mom and I have in common, and mostly I worry that someone else in my family will die one day. I'm not so much concerned about the dust bunnies. So, otherwise, I'm not sure how we're related. When we're out and people don't know she's my mother, I like to joke that the Gypsies brought me. She looks more like, say, Heidi from the Alps, and I look more like, well, like Dad. Long brown hair, dark brown eyes, nose a little bigger than I'd like. And it's not just looks. Dad was the one who *got* me, while Mom doesn't seem to understand anything I do. Mom likes ketchup, and I like Frank's RedHot sauce. I like metaphors; she likes the metric system.

When Mom sees us pull up and catches the glare from the shiny Jeep, she covers her eyes.

As Liz and I step out onto the driveway, Liz says to Mom, "That's quite an impressive begonia bed you've got there."

26

Mom says, "Aren't you going to ask for my phone number, too?" Then Mom and Liz both start laughing. Mom even makes that little wheezing noise she does when she finds something especially funny.

"You must be Mrs. Parisi. I'm Liz."

As I watch Mom wipe her eyes and sigh, I start to feel like I'm on someone else's date. I clear my throat. "Liz just started at Woodmont."

Mom cups her hand over her eyes like she's looking off into the horizon, or staring at me and trying to figure out if it's possible that I might have a social life. She turns to Liz. "In the middle of your senior year? Wow, that's a big move."

"My parents finally retired, and Dad got an offer to be artistic director for the Dayton Ballet. Mom and Dad were both dancers with the Pittsburgh Ballet Theatre."

"Really?" I can tell Mom's impressed. "Well, come on in. Do you girls want a snack?"

"Mom, we're not twelve."

"Seventeen-year-olds also need to eat. Right, Liz? And I made lemon cookies from a new recipe I found in the *Dayton Daily News*." I guess I have to cut Mom some slack; it must be as exciting for her as it is for me to have company.

Liz follows behind Mom through the front door. "I will not turn down lemon cookies."

In the kitchen, Mom gets a plate from the cupboard and asks, "So how was today?"

27

"We went to the funeral home in the morning," Liz says, "for Lila Cardoza."

Looking past Mom, out the kitchen window, I think of Liz hugging Lila's mom, and I think of Mom greeting everyone at Dad's viewing.

Liz looks from Mom to me, but maybe Mom's thinking about Dad too, because she doesn't say anything either. Mom uses the spatula to lift cookies off the cooling rack, and sets them on the plate. I can hear each cookie sliding off.

"It was sad," Liz says.

"I'm sure," Mom says, and turns around to bring the plate to the table. Her eyes seem hazy and vacant.

It's quiet in the kitchen, like we're all back at the funeral home, and everything sounds hushed and far away, like when my ears are underwater at the pool.

Liz licks her lips and runs her fingers through the fringe on her turquoise shawl. "Um, also, Donna and I have Spanish together. We are both *muy bueno*."

Something bright and lively in Liz's voice pulls me back to the surface again, and Mom too. She laughs.

And then it's like Mom and Liz are new best friends, and I watch a little dumbfounded. I'm glad I have something good to eat—the perfectly round cookies are sweet and tart and crumbly—because I wouldn't know what to do otherwise. Mom asks questions about the ballet, and Liz describes her dad in *Swan Lake* and the costumes and the lights and how her dad would pick her up when she was small and spin her like a ballerina.

"My dad used to do that too." Mom looks at the cookie she holds delicately in her fingers. At the moment, she seems fragile, like she's a little girl, and it makes me nervous. She sets the cookie down and says shyly, "You know, I always wanted to be a ballerina."

Liz reaches over and touches Mom's hand. "I bet you would have been a beautiful dancer."

My brain is on overload. This intimacy between my new friend and my mother. Mom talking about her dad, who I rarely hear about, other than that he was very athletic. Mom wanting to be a ballet dancer. Mom wanting something, period.

"You never told me that," I say, and it sounds angrier than I mean.

"You hate ballet," Mom says.

"No I don't." Actually, I do, but I just met Liz, who happens to be the spawn of ballet people, and I'm not ready to alienate myself just yet.

Mom points a finger at me. "When I took all of us to the ballet last November, you said, 'I hate ballet. Why are you making us go?'" I guess Mom has decided that alienating me from Liz is an acceptable choice.

Linnie passes through the kitchen. She's wearing black-and-white-striped pajamas, and her dyed black hair hangs down to her waist. She has the same round perky kind of nose Mom has, but it doesn't seem to fit with Linnie. "You did say that, and you were wearing that ugly silver jacket." She looks at Liz.

Liz brushes cookie crumbs off the corner of her mouth and smiles. "Hi, I'm Liz."

Linnie pours herself a tall glass of orange juice, drinks half of it, and fills the rest with ice cubes. "Hey." She nods at Liz and walks out.

"Charming," I say.

"I wish I had a sister," Liz says, which makes no sense to me, given the example she just witnessed.

"Donna's got a brother too," Mom says.

Liz looks up, interested. "Really?"

"Sorry, he's taken," Mom says.

"But his girlfriend's seriously lame," I say. "So you might have a shot."

"Donna, Gwen's very nice." Which is Mom's way of saying she might not totally love Gwen either, but employing something she calls tact.

On cue, my six-foot-tall brother B comes up the stairs from the basement, where his bedroom used to be. Now it's technically my room, but Mom made me move back in with Linnie for the week so he could stay here. He rubs his eyes and yawns. "I was dreaming about cookies."

B has the same brown hair that I have and that Linnie has when she's not trying to look like a vampire, but it's curly like Mom's, and there's no doubt that he's her son.

He's got not only her nose but also her cheeks and the fore-head shape and something like her narrow chin.

When I was three and B—Brendan—was seven, he used to wear a yellow-and-black-striped shirt all the time, and I told him he looked just like a bumble bee.

Mom said, "Yes, and, his name starts with the letter B."

So I said, "Then he's just B to me." And he has been ever since. I can't help but smile when B walks in a room. Growing up, we spent a lot of time together—building forts in the dirt with twigs and rocks and leaves, and making up stories. Maybe mostly I followed him around, but he let me. When he left for college right after Dad died, I thought I might fall apart. He only went to the University of Dayton, and although it's literally just ten minutes away, it feels like he's been in another country. And especially since he started dating Gwen last year, I can't help but feel like he's not mine anymore.

Now Mom gets up and pours B a glass of milk. She looks at Liz and smiles. "Apparently napping is part of the university curriculum. I haven't taken a nap since I was four years old."

I laugh. "Does it count when you fall asleep in the living room chair while we're watching movies?"

Mom puts the glass in front of B and sits down again. "No."

"That's more of an accidental nap," Liz says, "so it doesn't count the same."

"Exactly," Mom says.

"By the way," I say to B, "this is my friend Liz."

B puts a whole cookie into his mouth and says, "Charmed, I'm sure," amid a spray of lemony crumbs. Liz cracks up.

I shake my head. "He's also part Neanderthal."

Still with a mouthful of cookie, he says, "I'm hungry." I am always amazed at how delightful my brother seems under any circumstances—mouthful of food, half asleep. And everyone loves him. I've never met someone who doesn't like B, and vice versa. Last summer, he and his roommates had a barbecue at their house in the Ghetto, what UD students call the neighborhood where they live. Mom and Linnie and I went, and I sat on the porch and watched him for three hours laughing and talking with literally everyone at the party. He was like a magnet with a crowd of people around him at all times. I watched him and wondered how, after Dad died, he kept it—all that joy —and why I didn't.

B reaches for another cookie, and Mom says, "Don't worry. We're having dinner soon. And I made chili."

B nods like he just solved the crime. "I thought the cookies in my dream smelled a little like dead cow."

"Ick," I say, and Liz giggles.

"Donnnderrrrrr!" B says in his deep radio announcer voice that used to make me laugh no matter what. I don't think he's called me this in years, so as I'm laughing I also feel a little like crying. "Is Liz coming to your play?"

"You're in a play? I'd love to come."

I shoot my brother a dirty look. At school, I don't really talk about my secret drama life with the St. Camillus de Lellis Players.

"Good. It's tomorrow night." B grins. "Donna's playing a bank teller. It should be riveting."

Once last year, Becky saw one of our plays and mentioned it after school when she'd roped me into helping her make student council posters. She said we could have pizza, and since she rarely asked me for anything, I said yes. As we sat around a table with thick, primary color markers, Becky had said, "You were awesome in your play last weekend."

"*What*?" Patty asked.

I remained silent, but Becky spoke up for me. "Donna does plays at her church."

"That," Patty said, "is so lame."

But here at our kitchen table, Liz says, "I'll be there."

Now I have something else to worry about, which is losing a new friend the day after I meet her because she realizes what a huge dork I am. But I manage to relax enough to enjoy Mom's chili and the Sasquatch documentary we end up watching, because Liz is there and seems to be having fun. And everyone seems to like her, too. Linnie even

33

comes out and peeks her head into the living room with her shower cap on.

When I walk Liz out to her car, she says, "You have a great family."

"They're not usually this great. Maybe it's you."

"I doubt it. Anyway," she says, "I feel comfortable here. Thanks." She gives me a quick hug, and I realize she smells cinnamony like her car, and also like vanilla.

"Can I ask you something?" Liz says.

"Sure."

"Is Charlie a good kisser?"

"What? How would I know that?" For that matter, how would I know what anyone kisses like? I've never even gotten close.

"You don't? I mean, I thought you two were an item."

I feel my face getting hot. "No. We're not. We study together sometimes, but that's it."

"You know he likes you, right?"

"Um, no." The thought that someone like Charlie might like someone like me makes me feel like miniature circus performers are doing aerial work in my stomach.

"It's pretty obvious."

"I guess I never thought about it."

"Well, think about it." She grins. "If you're into hippies."

I laugh and surprise myself with the sound of my own voice. I wonder if I am into hippies. What I do know is that I feel comfortable with Liz. And right now, in the cool air with my new friend, so much feels possible that I think it might just be okay to share my new discovery. "Can I tell you something?"

"Of course." She sets her purple purse down on the driveway at her feet.

I watch how the fringe spreads out like octopus legs on the pavement. "I think I know what I want to be. You know—do, like for a job." The words almost sound like I'm speaking another language, like I do sometimes in my dreams, where I'm in class and start speaking in some foreign tongue that I don't even understand, and everyone looks at each other and says, "Oh, she's the crazy one."

"What is it?" Liz says. "The suspense is killing me."

I cross my arms over my chest and wonder if it's okay after all. "Can you keep it a secret?"

"Are you going to be a hooker or something?" She laughs and then looks at me. "Yes," she says, in a calm, kind voice. "I'm an expert secret keeper."

"So, you know people who work in funeral homes?" I pull at a thread on one of my sleeves. "Morticians?" I glance up at Liz.

"You're going to be a mortician? Wild." She puts her hands on her hips and nods and smiles. "Like that weird dude you were talking to today. Wow. I've never been friends with a mortician before."

"I'm not one yet."

"Oh, you'll be one. I can feel it." She holds her hands

out to the sky, closes her eyes, and breathes in. "You'll be a good one."

"Thanks." I feel myself smiling, and I'm thinking she could be right.

She drops her hands to her sides and picks up her purse. "Okay, I want to get home so my parents don't worry if they get there before me. But we'll talk more tomorrow. I'll see you at your play."

I almost forgot about that. "You don't have to come, you know. Seriously. It's just a stupid play."

"I don't have to do anything. I choose to come, okay?"

"I'll see you there, then."

"*Ciao*," she says, and kisses me on one cheek and then the other. As I feel the tingle of where Liz's lips brushed the skin on my face, I have a flash of Angelo's Italian Grocery on Main Street. I must look as discombobulated as I feel, because she says, "That's how they do it in Europe."

"Oh," I say, "*ciao*, then." And I remember Saturday trips with Dad—just me and him—to Angelo's. Dad would always grab one of the small Italian flags Angelo kept in the front display and wave it, saying "*Ciao, ciao.*" And then Dad would ask if Angelo had any extra cannoli so he could give one to his little lady, and Angelo, who had two gold front teeth, would say with a metallic grin, "Of course, one for the *bella donna.*"

As Liz drives away, I look up at the sky. I can see a few stars and smell that spring smell again. Keeping my arms

36

at my sides, I open my palms just a little and imagine what it feels like to be Liz, arms stretched wide to the heavens.

When I go inside, I open the basement door a crack to see if B's still up. I hear him on the phone, and he's using his soft talking-to-Gwen voice. I shut the door. I'm glad I got to share my news with Liz, since B's clearly not available.

Mom's asleep in the living room chair, and in our old room, Linnie lies on her bed with headphones over her shower cap, still cooking a new shade of hair. Walking down the hallway to the bathroom in our suddenly quiet house, I feel lonely and nervous.

While I brush my teeth, I close my eyes and say in my head, *I'll be a good mortician. I will be.* I do my best to spit out my fear with the toothpaste foam into the sink and watch it wash down the drain under the running water. Just to be safe, I run my hand over the whole sink, wipe away every last bit, and decide that tomorrow morning I'm going on a field trip to somewhere I once thought I'd never want to visit again. And I feel something, just a little something, move right where my heart should be.

three

In the morning, I eat a bowl of cereal and tell Mom I'm driving to the library to do some research in quiet. The research part is true. I will be doing that. For the moment, I'm putting Mom on a need-to-know status in terms of my future plans.

I pull the Lark—the Buick Skylark that Linnie and I share—out onto Sherwood, make my way down Far Hills, and turn onto Falder Road. The sun hides behind a thick wall of gray clouds, so it's colder today, and I keep the windows up as I drive past the old Big Boy, past the Kozy Korner, where Uncle Lou and Dad used to play cards. I think Uncle Lou still does, but I'm not sure.

I turn off the road and down a short gravel driveway lined with those bright, self-assured tulips, like pageant contestants all in a row. Yesterday, Becky struggled to find a spot for her car in this parking lot packed with cars—just like it was three years and eight months ago. Now only two regular cars take up space in the lot, plus two long black hearses and two limos. An oval sign perched on the front lawn reads BRIGHTON BROTHERS FUNERAL HOME, and below that, a simple PEACE.

I've got that nervous feeling again, here outside. So I sit in the car for a minute, reminding myself to breathe. I remember dressing up in my favorite purple sweater and new black dress pants that first night, and standing close to Mom and holding B's hand. Then I remember Mom looking for Linnie later and my finding her out here, actually, near the side of the building, smoking with our cousin Olivia. I was so mad that she could even think of doing that while Dad was stuck inside in a coffin. Or maybe I was mad I hadn't thought to sneak out myself.

Now I open the big wooden door with the long brass handle, and inside, Brighton Brothers sounds even quieter than the classroom where I took my SAT. No listings are marked on the board in the lobby—they've already taken down Lila's name.

It's vacant except for the shadows of all my cousins and aunts and uncles, Mom and Dad's friends, Dad's coworkers from Sanford Steel, who seemed so straitlaced and out of place compared to all of our crazy relatives. I glance into Viewing Room Two and half expect to see Dad lying in there. I'm relieved he's not. Ahead of me, an arrow-shaped sign says OFFICE, and I follow it.

I take a step directly onto a creaky floor spot and suddenly have the feeling I might get caught, even though I'm not doing anything wrong. A second later, I see Mr. Bob Brighton step out of the room that must be the office. He limps as he walks toward me and buttons his gray suit jacket.

I raise a hand in a hesitant wave. "Hi."

Mr. Brighton always reminds me of a toy we had: a white-haired, round-faced plastic head of a dentist with a mustache poised over his big set of pearly teeth. The plastic man-head came with an array of dental tools, and we could take out the teeth. I decide not to tell Mr. Brighton about this.

"Donna Parisi?" he says.

"Yeah, that's me."

"Saw you here yesterday." He takes another step toward me. "Very sad about Lila. Everything okay?"

"No one else is dead."

"Oh," he says.

"I guess that's usually why people come in here."

"Usually." A lot like the dentist head toy, Mr. Brighton has something static and still about him, like he might not actually be real.

I wonder if he needs that quality to make room for all the crying or angry people he must meet. And yesterday, it didn't sound like Joe Brighton helped out much in that capacity. "Um, is your brother here?"

"Joe? No he left this morning to go camping at Red River Gorge."

I wonder if Joe has his funeral suit rigged with some kind of Velcro so he can rip it off to reveal shorts and a T-shirt to do a quick change into Outdoorsy Joe.

"Can I help you with something?" Bob Brighton winks. "I'm smarter than that guy anyway."

I was kind of hoping Joe would be here, but I remember how kind this Mr. Brighton was to my family, how he made sure all of Lila's aunts had Kleenex close at hand all morning, and how Lila's service ran like clockwork, even with so many teenagers around. This Mr. Brighton probably also knows a lot of things I'd like to know. "I just had a few questions. Of a general nature."

He studies me for a second, and I notice his eyes are amber-colored like a cat's. "Come on in, then, and have a seat. Right now I can't stand any longer on this darn hip."

I follow him into his office, and he settles behind his desk into a high-back leather chair that swivels. I sit across from him in one of two lower-back leather chairs that don't swivel.

Mr. Brighton pulls at a corner of his thick white mustache. "So what can I do for you? Of a general nature."

"Why is it so empty in here?"

"Question with a question, is it?" He smiles and seems

41

to relax a little. "It's spring. Lila's is the only service we've had during March. People don't usually die in the spring-time." He holds up his hands and shrugs. "Just wait until the fall. They'll be dropping like flies." He grins. "And we'll be in the green."

I raise an eyebrow. I hadn't thought so much about mortician-ism as a business, but I guess it is, and I hadn't thought about when death's busy season happened either.

Now Mr. Brighton definitely looks like a real person, one who's realized he may have just said too much. "I'm sorry. I forgot my manners." I see that both Brighton brothers are a little awkward and unlike anyone else I know, which just makes me like them even more.

"I'm not upset. I just never thought about it, is all." And I really don't mind; it's interesting to me—death as a business. "So how would someone become a mortician?"

"Don't you have a boyfriend?"

I'm not sure what that has to do with my question. "Can morticians not have boyfriends? I mean, you're married, right?"

"Yes I am, but you're so, well, young."

I lean forward on my chair. "You weren't always this old."

"No." He groans a little and leans back to stretch his bad leg out. "I was not always this old."

"Is it like royalty or something? I have to have been born into it?"

42

He laughs. "Not exactly, but often it works that way."

As far as I know, no one in my family is in the business, and I'm not descended from any kind of funerary line. Dad sold steel beams, and Mom's a secretary at St. Camillus Elementary School.

He sighs. "So you're really looking to get into the business?"

He makes it sound like the Mafia, so much that I almost giggle, but I realize that wouldn't be professional; and I am, after all, a person seeking a profession.

"I guess so. I mean, yes I am." I sit up straight in my chair. "What do I need to do?"

"School's the first step. And Chapman's the closest one to here. Chapman College of Mortuary Science. I think I have one of their catalogs somewhere." He stands and limps over to a tall file cabinet and rifles in the middle drawer. "Here it is. We just got the new one." He hands it to me and sits back down.

On the cover of the catalog, young happy people with really white teeth smile as they walk down a wooded path next to an old brick building. I'm not sure what they have to do with Mortuary Science, and I didn't actually think about science as being a part of it. That sudden realization stops me cold. "So," I say, trying to sound casual, "there's a lot of science? Like physics and stuff?"

"It's not physics kind of science. It's about the human body, and really, the whole human person. If you can love the whole person, body and heart and soul, you can be a good mortician." Mr. Brighton leans forward onto the desk, and just then he seems like someone's grandpa. I don't have any grandparents alive myself, but I imagine this is what a good grandpa looks like, right here. Kind and smart and like he might have faith in me. "Do you think you can do that, Donna?"

Love seems like a strange way to put it—loving the whole person. "I don't know. But I do think I can be with a whole person, even the bloody parts. I didn't get freaked out when Linnie fell off her bike onto that glass bottle. And it was pretty gory." I ruffle the pages of the catalog with my fingers and then hold it still. "And I know what it's like to cry. I'm familiar with that."

Mr. Brighton nods. "That's a start."

I nod back. "So what next?"

"Why don't you take that home with you and give it a good read? Do some thinking. See if you can imagine yourself doing this work. Maybe write about it." He leans back in his chair. "And if you decide you're serious, I mean really serious about this, come back. You could help out around here this summer and see how that goes. It's not like I have people dying to get jobs here." He smirks.

I stare at him for a second. "Oh, I get it."

"Yeah, that's why I don't do stand-up. See you next time, Donna Parisi."

Walking back down the hallway and out, I can still feel

the shadows around me, the sense of who I was here once. But now it's different. Now it's like I'm in the between space, because I can see who else I can be here. I can see another possibility, even if I'm not there yet. I hold the Chapman catalog close to my chest and whisper the word "Peace" to myself when I pass the sign on the way to my car.

When I come through the front door, Mom asks, "How was the library?"

"Very informative. Very librarious."

"Okay," she says. "How about laborious?"

"Yep. That too." I feel the weight of the catalog in my backpack. I want nothing more than to read it cover to cover, and I have to think quickly how to do that undisturbed. "I think I'm going to take a bubble bath. You know, go over my lines for tonight."

"Fine, but remember we're going to Mass before your show. And we're leaving here at four thirty sharp."

"Got it," I say. In my old bedroom, I change into my bathrobe, hide the catalog underneath it, and walk fast to the bathroom without incident. Since I have to fill up the tub anyway, I figure I might as well take a bath while I'm here. I put in five lidsful of bubble bath instead of the recommended two, and sink down into the steamy water. I hold the catalog up high so I don't get it wet, and read about business classes and embalming classes and the experts who teach there from all over the globe.

At least according to Chapman, they're one of the best colleges in the country, if not the world. That seems a little arrogant, but I guess it's advertising. I read their mission statement: *The mission of Chapman College of Mortuary Science is to hold sacred the natural passage from life to death, to educate whole people in the art of funeral services, and to train funeral directors and morticians to be compassionate companions to both the deceased and those living in the wake of death.*

Living in the wake of death. I hadn't thought about that, but it makes sense. Being awake and knowing someone else will never wake up again. That's me.

I read their tuition policy, campus history, faculty bios, and student profiles—like stringy-haired Lars, who heard his calling to mortuary school while out at sea, when he and some friends saw a dead body float to the surface. I think Lars sounds a little weird, and if I ran into him on campus, I'd probably walk the other way. But stories about Betty, the once-librarian, and the very normal-seeming Sarah, the competitive swimmer who's only a year older than me, make me feel a little bit better.

By the time I come out of the bathroom, I'm a plump human raisin, saturated with water and information, and I don't have much time to get ready for Mass. At least we're going tonight, which I like much better than Sunday. It's like getting a free pass to sleep in. Also, something seems more holy to me about church in the evening. In the morning, it's all so bright and stark—like the surface of things. Nighttime seems like below the surface time, when it's darker and quieter and God can come out under some kind of cover. And so can I.

I grab clothes from my dresser in the basement and go upstairs to get ready. I put on my powder blue skirt and the white shirt I like because it has puffy sleeves. Brushing my hair in front of the mirror, I wonder if my eyebrows are too thick, which I'd never thought about until Patty got hers waxed, and said, "See, Donna, yours could look this good too."

Mom walks into the room. "Are you ready?"

Just for kicks, I say, "What if I didn't want to go?"

"For now, you live under this roof, and under this roof, we go to church."

I wasn't trying to pick a fight. I was actually just curious. But now that Mom's started it, I feel like maybe I'd like to fight after all. And I am actually curious. "So why do we go to church?"

Mom stands next to me in front of the mirror and wipes away a stray smudge of lipstick. "You sound like you did when you were five. Why, why, why, everything. Can't you just do something and not question it?"

"No."

"Don't be contrary."

The thing is, I'm not being contrary. I really mean no, I don't think I can. But I don't want to make Mom suffer. She's suffered enough. Still, I wonder why she does everything without questioning anything, at least anything important and not just what ingredients she can substitute in dessert recipes. Why everything must be a particular way. Wouldn't it make her feel better to dig into the big things and ask some questions?

Just then, Linnie walks in, and I get my first glimpse of her new hair color. I'm guessing it's also Mom's first glimpse, because she says, "Oh, dear Lord," and holds her hand up to her mouth.

Linnie's hair hangs to her shoulders in bluish green strands, more of a seaweed color than the electric blue she'd intended. She looks like a mermaid in exile. "Come on," she says. "It's not that bad."

Behind her, B steps into the room. "Hello, Green Goblin. I didn't know we were wearing costumes tonight, too."

"Shut up."

"You're going to wear a hat," Mom says. "You're not going to church like that."

Linnie folds her arms across her chest. "Maybe I just won't go to church."

"Do not start with me. I just finished that conversation."

"I don't want to wear a hat."

"You really should wear a hat," B says.

"Well, maybe you should try some of Mom's lipstick," Linnie says. "It matches your stupid magenta shirt."

B holds out his arm and checks his sleeve. "Red. My red shirt."

"Everyone cut it out, or we're gong to be late," Mom says. "And no one's borrowing my lipstick. You can all get your own makeup." As she heads out the door, she adds, "But Linnie, you will borrow a hat, and we will discuss your hair later."

At St. Camillus, we make our way down the sidewalk to the church—Mom and B first, me in the back, and Linnie marching angrily in the middle in black boots, black pants, black leather jacket, and Mom's impulse-purchase lime green beret, full of seaweed hair.

Father Dean Martin, the pastor of St. Camillus, greets us at the door. Father Bill, his assistant, usually does the Sunday afternoon Mass and also directs the Players' productions. Father Dean Martin, however, provides his own variety of entertainment. Father Dean Martin, who likes people to call him by all three names because he gets such a kick out of being called Dean Martin. After Dad died, I think Father Dean thought he was taking me under his wing by offering me the job of stuffing the parish bulletins every week. I still help sometimes in the parish basement office, which smells a lot like a hardware store and has these humming fluorescent lights that give me a headache. But luckily, there are some other kids helping these days, so I only get called in every few months.

Still, I got to spend a lot of time in the rectory observing Father Dean. He of the pale skin and the white-blond hair, who likes to belt "Volare" off-key into his letter opener. He with a complete lack of anything Mediterranean in his genetic code, but who likes to ask me at every chance where my family is from in Italy. "Calabria," I always tell him.

"Ah, the boot," he always says. And I never know how to respond to that other than a pensive and vaguely meaningful nod. I wonder if Father Dean became a priest because that's the closest he could get to being an Italian guy.

Now I smile and shake his hand.

Mom says, "How are you, Father Dean?"

"How are any of us, Martha?" Dean Martin has a philosophical bent, and when he bends that way, simple conversations suddenly extend in complexity. And duration.

"Hmm," Mom says, which is as good an answer as I can think of to that.

"Well, Parisi family, I just thought you should know, I'm going out for Italian with Father Bill tonight, and I'm hoping for the biggest bowl of pasta I can take in." He pats his belly, and I notice he's wearing a very large pizza watch. The minute hand ticks past a piece of pepperoni. "Rigatoni, macaroni, seashells, you name it." He smiles and asks, "Donna, what's your favorite kind of pasta?"

"Gnocchi, I guess."

Father Dean nods and sighs.

"Okay, Father," Mom says, "I think we're going to go find our seats now."

"Good idea," he says. "Say one for me."

As we walk away, Linnie mumbles, "Oh my God, he is such a nutter."

"But he's still a priest," Mom hisses. "Have some respect."

"Okay, Father Nutter."

We all laugh, even Mom, who tries to pretend it's not funny. "He's just a little different." She suppresses a snicker.

Once Mass starts, though, Mom's all business. Linnie gets pouty, and B gets easily distracted, looking around for and smiling at all the people he knows. I can't help but think of Dad in church, so Linnie's reaction makes sense to me, but B, I don't get. Sometimes I want to remind him that our Dad is dead, that living without him is hard, that he shouldn't ever forget what we lost. I couldn't if I tried, so at church I just give in to the inevitable and go to my quiet place inside.

I wish I could just sit there still for an hour and not get up and down and kneel and stand and sit again, but I tried that once, and Mom wasn't such a fan of that choice. My favorite time is during Communion, after I get it and go back to my seat and close my eyes. I think about Dad, or about nothing at all. Today, I think about what

Mr. Brighton said, and I say a little prayer that I am able to love the whole person and be a good mortician. I'm not sure God answers prayers like that, but I'm giving it a shot.

For a long time, I've thought God is supposed to look actually a little like Mr. Brighton, but with a big long beard and some sort of God toga. But I didn't always. Once, when I was in first grade, Mom and Dad took us to the Newport Aquarium in Kentucky, and I pointed to a sea turtle as big as me, swimming right above us. "She looks like God," I said.

"God isn't a she," Mom said.

"What about women's rights?" Dad asked. "Or turtles' rights, for that matter."

"They can still vote—or swim—but God is our father, last I checked."

Dad put a hand on my shoulder. "Well, Donna, when you find your sea turtle religion, I guess you can convert."

Since then, I've been keeping my eyes open for a group that worships a sea turtle and maybe holds services in the water or something, but I don't think it exists.

After Mass, B stops to talk with one of his high school friends and says he'll catch up with Mom at the car, and Linnie says she has to use the ladies' room and pushes down the side aisle. I know she just wants to escape walking down the main aisle like Mom likes to do and which always seems to take forever. I'd also like to escape, but I don't want to leave Mom alone.

When we finally reach the end of the aisle, Mary the usher lady hands Mom a bulletin. "So, Martha," she says, elbowing Mom lightly and leaning close to her, "are you seeing anyone?" She asks this like she's some kind of secret agent. "Singles Night Bingo next Saturday. We're having bean casserole. And the Berger brothers will be there."

"My husband died." Mom uses the clipped tone that means she's done talking.

"Oh, I'm sorry." Mary clearly does not recognize this tone. She crinkles her eyebrows, which, by Patty's standards, are well beyond needing a good waxing. "I thought —when did that happen?"

"Three and half years ago," Mom says.

"Oh, Martha." Mary smiles brightly, playfully, winks at Mom. "There are more fish in the sea."

"No," Mom says firmly, not smiling. "Just one for me. He was my only one."

"Well." Mary clears her throat, looks away from Mom. She finds me. "So Donna, how about you? Do you have a boyfriend?"

I shake my head no.

Mary clears her throat again, a high-pitched clear— "Okay, ladies, you have a good night. Break a leg in the play, Donna."

"You too," Mom says to Mary with a saccharine smile.

Mary purses her lips, perplexed. "But I'm not in the play."

"I know." Mom winks and steers us away from Mary.

We walk through the parking lot, past the headless statue of Saint Camillus standing on what looks like a pair of big marble dice. Father Bill likes to say that he lost his head in a bet, but it was really the hailstorm last October. Mom shakes her head. "The nerve."

I want an *only one*, I think. I also think, I don't want him to die.

I wait with Mom until B and Linnie make their way to the car. Then Mom and Linnie and B go to meet Uncle Lou and Aunt Irene for dinner, and I head over to the school gym to get ready with the rest of the St. Camillus de Lellis Players, hoping they can distract me from being sad and trying to figure out what to do with the rest of my life.

When I was eight, I fell in love with the Players' non-musical production of *Auntie Mame*, in which Father Bill became a last-minute understudy for the title character. After Dad died, I didn't know what to do with all the hurt, how to feel as much as I felt. Somewhere along the way, I realized I could feel anything I wanted on a stage. None of the activities at Woodmont had ever appealed to me. I couldn't see the point. But this was different.

So when I was sixteen, after seeing a rousing production of *The Curious Savage*, I scheduled my audition. Since then, I've starred in such gems as *Flowers for Algernon* and the one Father Bill wrote himself, *A Flock of Priests,* which

Father Bill called "theater of the absurd," and involved inappropriately snug spandex.

Tonight's performance is another Father Bill original called *A Very Paschal Mystery*, in which a series of Lenten bank robberies get solved, and the bank robbers themselves get unmasked and converted by an innocent bystander priest. I am the hapless bank teller who nearly gets shot, save for the sudden sincere prayer of Father Will, portrayed by Richie, who, at twenty-eight, is the only Player even close to my age. I think the play is hilarious, although Father Bill has promoted it as a dramatic thriller.

When I walk into the gym, Richie is pacing beneath a basketball hoop, pulling at the edges of his curly blond clown-wig hair. "Inner monologue," he whispers. I nod.

Father Bill, Dr. Roger, and Leaf are setting up the folding chairs in front of the stage. I think Father Bill is maybe pushing forty-five, but he has that Dick Clark thing going on, so he may actually be ninety-seven or something. He claims tai chi and raw-egg smoothies keep him young.

"Where's Linda with those sandwiches? I need some fuel." Dr. Roger rubs his belly, bunching up his FIFTY IS NIFTY T-shirt. He adjusts the brim of his fedora, which he wears even when doing checkups and fillings at his dental office. Richie swears that once, when a patient asked him to take it off, he wouldn't give her any Novocain.

"Don't worry. She'll be here." Leaf flips back one of her

two long mousy braids. Leaf, like Dr. Roger, is a nifty fifty, and this is her first Players show. Last fall, her husband left her after thirty years of marriage. Last fall also marks when she moved to Dayton, started tie-dyeing most of her clothes, and changed her name to Leaf because she "turned over a new one." Leaf e-mails the other Players "Cutest Puppies" slide shows accompanied by quotes with dubious attribution to the Dalai Lama. Leaf makes me nervous.

Perched on a chair downstage right is ninety-two-year-old Keenie, a tiny wrinkly fairy princess with short silver hair and a pixie nose. She waves. "Hiya, sweet thing."

I wave back.

"Thank Jesus God," Dr. Roger says, and I turn to see seventy-two-year-old Linda sauntering into the gym with a bag from Milano's. Linda owns heels in eight different shades of red—tonight's are fuchsia—and always smells vaguely of liquor and brisket.

Linda's blond hair, a hue she's told me is Sunflower Cascade, looks like hay. Her red lipstick is cracked, as usual, and her false teeth are perfectly aligned. She sets the Milano's bag down on the stage, and Dr. Roger leaves Leaf and Father Bill to finish the chairs. "I'm ready for my Italian special," Dr. Roger says.

"I'll just bet you are," Linda says, and laughs her hacking laugh.

"Please," Keenie says. "I'd like to keep my appetite."

True to form, the Players almost help me forget to miss

Dad, almost forget that someone has to figure out how to tell Mom I'm applying to mortuary school. I got my acceptance letter to UD a month ago, and Mom seemed thrilled to pieces that I was following in my brother's footsteps, that I'd be close to home, that UD is a Catholic school. I know she's not going to be happy about this new choice, and the dread of telling her already circles like a shark in my stomach. Unfortunately, how to do this is a mystery even Father Will can't solve for me. I'm going to have to do it myself.

By seven thirty, we're all ready to go, standing in a circle, holding hands, and praying to Saint Genesius and Saint Cecilia, respectively in charge of acting and singing. Father Bill beams at us. "You all break a leg. Especially you, Father Will."

Richie sets his lips in a serious line. "I will do my very best."

"We know you will, honey," Linda says, although I think she secretly likes being one of the bank robbers and shoving Richie to the ground at the end of Act One.

At exactly eight o'clock, the curtain goes up, and we're off. As I open the bank for the day, looking out the imaginary front window downstage, I find my family in the second row—Uncle Lou, Aunt Irene, Mom, B, and Linnie, who has removed the beret. And next to Linnie is Liz. She's wearing a high-collared, short-sleeved shirt that looks silky and exotic, even from a distance. Her hair is swirled up elegantly on top of her head, held in place by what looks like two sticks, and she still manages to look cooler than anyone in her vicinity. I can't believe she came, and I do my best to not think about it too much. It's stressful enough that my family is here.

During the robbery, Dr. Roger, wearing a ski mask and, of course, his fedora, yells, "Don't make any funny moves, and we'll all get through this." His shouting smells like his sandwich, passionate with ham and onion. And he gets so into the yelling that through the tiny mouth hole in his ski mask, a spray of spit arcs up and lands in my eye. Dr. Roger's oniony saliva actually stings and makes my eyes water, which makes it seem like I'm so scared, I'm crying.

Offstage, after the scene, Richie says, "Oh my God, that was *so* realistic."

I almost tell him what really happened, but instead I shrug, and he whispers a quick and meaningful, "Bravo, bravo."

Keenie, as usual, is the best one of us all, stealing the last scene from Richie as she chides the bank robbers to go back to church and treat their mothers nicely.

After the show, my family clusters together near their seats, except for B, who of course found a brand-new friend in the audience to chat with. And Liz and Mom are also talking again like old friends. Uncle Lou scans the gym and keeps yanking at the lapels of his red-checkered suit jacket. He looks more like Dad than ever. Uncle Lou once told me that people used to ask if he and Dad were twins, growing up. "No way," Uncle Lou would say, offended. "I'm older than that little shit." While Dad was still alive, Uncle Lou called him his little brother. Or "that little shit."

Aunt Irene stands about six inches taller than Uncle Lou, and always wears her salt-and-pepper hair in a bun. She looks a little like someone's parole officer, which I guess is how I might look if I were married to Uncle Lou. Now Aunt Irene sees me walking toward them, and waves. "Nice job, honey!"

Uncle Lou shakes his head. "Well, that was a real piece of work." Aunt Irene slaps his arm with her program, and Uncle Lou adds, "Oh, and happy birthday, kid."

"It's actually next week," Mom says. "Saturday, remember?"

Aunt Irene swats Uncle Lou again. "Yeah, remember you said you're taking her to lunch on Sunday? Jesus, Lou, get your head out of your ass."

"Why don't you get your head out of my ass?"

Aunt Irene pulls a pack of menthols out of her purse. "I'm going outside."

"Can I come with you, Aunt Irene?" Linnie asks. Aunt Irene doesn't respond, but Linnie follows anyway.

"Good riddance," Uncle Lou says, and rolls his sharp blue eyes. Dad used to say how some Dago ended up with blue eyes was beyond him. Uncle Lou would respond, "Hey, I'm just like Sinatra," and sing "My Way" until a vein popped out of the edge of his round bald scalp and

59

zigzagged like a lightning bolt down his forehead. Our very own geriatric Harry Potter.

Mom, who looks somehow different than she did earlier, squeezes my hand, and I realize what's different: her curly hair is now piled on top of her head, secured, interestingly enough, with two pencils. She and Liz look like twins.

I look from Liz to Mom. "What happened to your heads?"

"Liz did mine at intermission," Mom says. "Our hair texture is the same." They share a look and smile.

"What do you think?" Liz asks.

I am disturbed, but I have to admit that it looks good —on both of them. "It works."

Liz smiles. "And you were great."

"You don't have to lie. It was kind of ridiculous."

"Of course it's ridiculous, but it's fun," Liz says. "And I think it's really brave."

I decide I'd like to have Liz follow me around everywhere.

Once we round up Aunt Irene and Linnie and B, we all go for ice cream, and Liz comes with us. Of course Aunt Irene and Uncle Lou like her just as much as everyone else. After Liz drives away, when we're all saying good-bye in the parking lot of the Tasty Twist, Aunt Irene says, "That girl's a real spitfire."

I laugh. "Does that mean she's like a dragon?"

"I suppose that's one way to put it." Aunt Irene often looks at me like Mom does, like I'm speaking another language that sounds like English, but isn't quite discernable. And at moments like these, I wonder if I should just stop talking entirely.

For a second, I get a little jealous. I don't seem to make anyone light up the way Liz does. I've known all these people for years: shouldn't I have figured out how to do that by now? Watching Liz work her magic almost feels like a reminder that I'm somehow damaged goods. If Dad hadn't died, would I be more normal, friendly, interesting, a better conversationalist? Maybe I'd be more like Liz. My dragon friend.

Uncle Lou says, "Let's hit the road," and we all hug good-bye.

Looking out the window of the backseat on the drive home, I notice the shadows the streetlights cast on the dark lawns and sidewalks. I decide I like the idea of Liz as a dragon. One of my favorite storybooks was about good-luck dragons, how their arrival always means that something wonderful lies ahead. If that's true, then, as far as I'm concerned, Liz can spit as much fire as she wants. And if I stand near enough to it, maybe I'll glow a little, too.

four

Sunday night, B drives back to his house on the UD campus. He lives with five other engineering guys, and even though that sounds pretty rotten to me, I'm guessing he's glad to get away from our house and boring family things like my play. Or maybe just from his boring family members like me. We didn't get to talk, not really, all weekend. Yesterday he helped Mom dig her vegetable garden all day, then he helped Linnie with her math homework, and after that it was time for him to go.

On Monday morning, I push my scrambled eggs around my plate and wonder how I'm going to break my mortician news to Mom.

Mom points to my food. "Are you not feeling well?"

"Just not hungry."

"You should eat something."

"I know. Breakfast is the most important meal of everyone's life."

"Hey," Mom says, "it's not like I'm slipping you arsenic to start the day. I just want you nourished."

"I know. Sorry. Maybe I'm worried about our Spanish quiz."

"Honey, you're good at Spanish. You'll be fine."

On my way out the door to catch the bus, Mom calls, "Oh, and please tell Liz I said hi. You're welcome to bring her over any time."

"Okay I will," I say, even though I won't.

The weekend is over, and I'm wondering if it actually all happened, if Liz and I are really friends now. But she smiles when she sees me in homeroom.

Liz has lunch at our corner table on Monday and Tuesday and Wednesday, and it's the most fun I've had at lunch here, well, ever. Until Thursday, when Becky smiles and grabs my arm. "Guess what? I got accepted to UD, too. Maybe we can be roommates!"

"Yeah, maybe." I wonder when everyone will find out that I have other plans, and I'm hoping I'm not going to be there when it happens. Up until now it's been easy enough to say I'm going to UD, even if I had no idea what that meant. Even if I didn't care. Now, though, I'm not used to caring, and it makes me nervous. I fold my arms over my chest and slide a few inches away from Becky.

Patty makes a gagging sound and sticks her tongue out. "Don't you guys want to get out of town? Why would you go to school here? It's Dayton, for God's sake. The most boring place on earth. I can't wait to get out of here."

"Erin—I mean Mom—says Dayton is actually a healing energy center," Charlie says. "That's why they had the Peace Talks here and stuff. So maybe it's not such a bad place to be."

"I've heard that too. And aren't you going to school in Cleveland?" Liz asks Patty. "I heard on NPR that they officially christened it the armpit of America, which sounds so much better than Dayton."

"What do you know?" Patty asks. "Have you even been accepted anywhere yet?"

"Actually, NYU and Carnegie Mellon."

Patty hesitates to respond, like she's deciding if it's worth it to keep fighting Liz, since it turns out Liz might actually be the coolest person at the table. "Really?" Patty finally says. "Congratulations."

Liz raises one eyebrow and stares at Patty. "Thanks," she says slowly. What's even stranger is that then they start talking about New York, where Patty's always wanted to live and where Liz, of course, has visited many times. They talk through the rest of lunch, and it seems like Liz has worked her magic again, now describing her plans to travel the world and be a famous journalist. And I wonder if that's it for me. Now Liz and Patty will be best friends. Maybe they can hang out with Mom.

While I pretend to read my history book and not watch Patty and Liz talk about the East Village, I hear Charlie say, "Hey, what do you think about living in Dayton?"

I turn and realize he's talking to me. "Um, I don't know." I think about how much it seems to rain, how downtown rests under a perpetual coat of dingy, like it could use a fresh coat of paint. It's not shiny like how New York City looks on TV, that's for sure. But I also think about my favorite Sunday breakfast spot, the Golden Nugget, where Dad used to always take us after church. About summer picnics at John Bryan State Park or Wegerzyn Gardens and Dayton Playhouse shows—Dad loved those. Maybe he would have loved Players' shows too. "I don't know. It's familiar."

"Familiar's not a bad thing." Charlie smiles at me, which makes me remember what Liz said on Friday. There's a softness in his eyes, like he sees something beautiful in me. And I don't have the faintest idea what to do with that. He takes a drink out of the stainless-steel mug he uses for all beverages so as to reduce waste, and I find myself watching where the mug touches his lips.

I start to smile back, but suddenly worry I have something in my teeth, so I do this sort of half smile without opening my mouth that must make me look like a total idiot. *Stop being ridiculous, Donna. No one likes anyone. We're just talking about Dayton, for God's sake. Say something. Ask a question already.* "So where are you going?"

"Actually, I'm thinking UD. I just got accepted, and they have a new environmental studies program. With whole classes about making silverware out of potatoes." Charlie smirks. "I can carve you your own set if you want."

I force myself to have what feels like the most awkward conversation of my life with Charlie, and I don't get to talk with Liz at all, which doesn't seem to matter since she and Patty are so busy chatting. It's easier, I decide, not to talk, not to want anyone to talk with me.

At the end of lunch, Liz asks if I can come over to her house after school, and I'm so relieved she still wants to talk to me that I almost hug her. "I have a present for you," she says.

Liz's basement has a fireplace, a big shaggy rug, and a wooden bar in the corner with a sink and everything. It's hard to know where to look first. All over the walls are pictures of her parents in these exquisite costumes—silvers and golds and rich burgundies and indigos—on elaborate stages with sparkly sets, which are a far cry from the painted bedsheet backdrops the Players use. Written below each of the photographs is a tantalizing location—Amsterdam, Paris, Naples, Rio de Janeiro.

Next to the fireplace stands a wrought-iron statue with

a number of arms. Liz tells me it's Shiva, Hindu god of creation and destruction. She likes the symbolism of his fireplace proximity. I'd like to see him juggle bowling pins. The basement also has big sliding-glass doors that open onto a back patio with umbrella tables and a hot tub, which makes me a little envious.

I call home to make sure Mom doesn't worry about where I am, but no one answers. Instead the voice mail picks up, and it's Dad's voice, in his fake almost-British accent. "You've reached the Parisis—Brendan, Donna, Linnie, Martha, and Nicky. If you leave a message with our answering service, we'll be sure to ring you back. Ta, ta." No matter how many times I listen to it, hearing Dad's voice makes something hopeful lift in me, some kind of outrageous notion that he's still here. But then I lose equilibrium as the thought falls quickly away, like riding the Drop Tower at Kings Island. I leave a quick message and hang up, staring for a minute at Liz's hot tub to catch my breath.

We all used to get excited to change the message every few months and make Dad use a different accent and say something else. Since he died, it's stayed the same. That first year, I called all the time when I knew no one was home, just to hear Dad say my name. Once, when B asked Mom if she wanted to change it, she replied with an emphatic "No." One time last fall, when Aunt Irene and Uncle Lou were over for dinner, I overheard Uncle Lou bring it up with

Mom, and she said, "It's my voice mail, and I'll decide what to do with it." I wonder if she calls to hear his voice, too.

I join Liz on the shaggy rug and sit cross-legged, examining the package she hands to me. I squeeze it and crinkle the white tissue paper, feeling the bulky and pointy parts. I smile at Liz.

"Open it, already," she says.

I untie the thin red ribbon and pull apart the tissue paper concealing a twelve-inch plastic skeleton mounted on a silver rod and stand.

"Well, do you like it?"

I stop smiling long enough to say, "Perfect," and, "I think I'll call him Maurice."

Liz nods. "Yeah, he looks like a Maurice."

"I don't know what to say."

" 'Thank you'?"

"Oh, yeah, thank you."

"Happy funeral home," she says.

I run my fingertip over Maurice's smooth skull and tap my fingernail against it. *Click. Click.* "Hey, um, you and Patty seemed to be getting along today."

"Her bark is worse than her bite." Liz leans back on her hands and pulls at the carpet. "She's not so bad when she's not worried about what everyone else thinks." I'd never thought about Patty as anything other than the Evil Twin. I guess Patty worries too, like me.

Liz shrugs. "But I guess everyone can't be like us."

"What do you mean?"

"We know who we are."

I want to say, *We do? Then tell me, who am I?* But instead I pick up Maurice by his base and watch his arm and leg bones swing at the joints. "Yeah."

On Friday, Liz tells me she's going for a long weekend trip to Pittsburgh to visit CMU with her parents, since seniors have Monday off as a college prep day. "I'd ask you to come," she says, "but I know you've got birthday plans with your family."

"I could cancel them."

"I don't think your mom would like that."

"It's my birthday," I say. "But you're right."

After school, I say a quick hi to Mom and tell her I'm going to my room to take a nap and do some studying, which I hope she knows means, leave me alone. I really just want to start working on my application.

"Dinner at six. So be up by then. Are you feeling all right?"

"Yep," I say. "I'll see you for dinner."

In the basement, I read the catalog again and imagine myself using paintbrushes in restorative art. Maybe restoring bodies is like restoring frescoes from the Renaissance, uncovering some kind of beauty. Understanding Grief sounds interesting, and Cemetery Issues sounds good too.

I like cemeteries. When I was maybe eight, we all went walking in Woodland Cemetery so Dad could show us the Wright brothers' graves. Dad made himself into an airplane and took off down the path until Mom declared him too sacrilegious for words. Then he stood in front of Mom and said, "I'm ready for my penance now, Sister Martha," looking so actually penitent that Mom eventually giggled.

I liked reading everyone's names on the gravestones, wondering what those people were like when they were alive. And I liked the spot way up high in the cemetery where you could look out over the whole city.

In the center of Chapman's catalog, I find the application. I fold the perforation and carefully tear out two pages. I fill out my name and address and high school, feeling very accomplished. I turn it over and look at the last page, which lists three essay questions: *Why do you want to study mortuary science? What do you think makes a good funeral director? What makes you think you'll be a good funeral director?* I think question number three sounds a little aggressive, and I wonder if Patty helped write it.

I pull out the last new composition notebook I got for Christmas, the one with the picture of the ocean on the cover, which I'd been saving for something good. The one I've been using to write about funeral stuff, as Mr. Brighton suggested. Dad used to carry a little notebook with him. One summer, when I was eight or nine, we were sitting on a blanket on the lawn at Fraze Pavilion, waiting for a concert to start, and Dad pulled his notebook out of his back pocket and quickly scribbled something.

I asked him what it was, and he said, "I guess it's like a journal. Things I don't want to forget. Things I liked or didn't like."

B offered to help Dad set up a daily journal he could keep on the computer so he wouldn't lose it, and Dad said, "Hell, no. A person should know what his own handwriting looks like."

I don't think B ever took to the notebook writing, but I never forgot. The notebook Dad used was too little for me, but I think he'd approve of my ocean notebook and that I know very clearly what my own handwriting looks like —kind of blocky, without a lot of frills or loops.

I start on the first application question. It turns out I don't quite have an answer I can write yet, so I go to number two. For this one, all I can think of is: *Grandpa-like. Nice. Sturdy hiking boots. Doesn't talk too much.* I close my notebook and decide to take a nap.

After dinner, Linnie brings her dirty clothes down to the laundry room and leans against my desk, flicking one of Maurice's dangling arms. "This is a little creepy."

"It's a present from Liz."

"Still, creepy."

I wouldn't think my sister, with her green hair and eye makeup springing from a color palette I'd call "Bruised," would be bothered by a skeleton. "*You're* creepy."

I move Maurice a few inches away from Linnie. Now both bony arms swing and shake—skeletal jazz hands. Maurice must know it's almost my birthday. Jazz hands go with birthdays.

"Mom won't like it," Linnie says, reaching for Maurice again.

Maurice laughs in the way skeletons do—at me, at my sister's hair, at the black stapler, and the retractable pens sprouting like plastic weeds out of the white mug with the blue lettering: THE PLAY'S THE THING—we all got them from Father Bill for Christmas.

"Mom doesn't have to look at it."

"Whatever," Linnie says. "I'm going to watch TV."

I put on my pajamas and crawl into bed with my ocean notebook, still contemplating essay questions I can't answer.

Mom knocks on my door and walks in. "What time do you want to go?"

I know she's talking about Dad's grave. On the first birthday I had without Dad, I asked Mom if we could visit him. And every year on my birthday since he died, we've gone and planted flowers. Maybe planting flowers is a Cemetery Issue. I don't know. "Is nine okay?"

"Yes." Mom walks over to my bed and kisses me on the forehead. "Happy almost birthday." Maurice catches her eye, and she turns toward my desk. "What is that?"

"My skeleton." I decide not to tell her his name. Maurice prefers to go incognito.

Mom folds her arms, like she's about to give me a lecture. "Donna, that's a little dark, don't you think?"

"Liz gave it to me for my birthday."

"Oh." Mom seems stumped. Now that the skeleton came from Liz, maybe it seems more interesting than dark. "Okay."

When she leaves and I'm alone again, staring at my notebook and the Chapman application questions, knowing Maurice is watching me, I feel sad and a little angry. I guess some part of me thought figuring out what I wanted to do would make everything better, would make me happy and full somehow. Instead, I've now inherited more questions I can't answer yet.

Wilbur Wright, 45

Cause of Death: Typhoid fever

Surviving Immediate Family:
• Father: Milton
• Brothers: Reuchlin, Lorin, Orville
• Sister: Katharine

Open-casket viewing

Funeral Incidents:
• Hearse drawn by white horses
• The *Dayton Daily News* reported, "Thousands Follow Sad Cortege."

Saddest thing someone says: "Wilbur had plans no one will be able to carry into execution."—Orville Wright

Orville Wright, 76

Cause of Death: Heart attack

Surviving Immediate Family:
• None

Funeral Incidents:
• New jet fighter planes fly over Woodland Cemetery in tribute

five

"What's the matter with you?" Mom asks, shaking the extra dirt off of the silver spade.

"We're at the cemetery," I say. "People are often troubled at cemeteries."

"Donna Marie, we've been coming here for almost four years." She gives some final pats to the dirt around the red petunias we just planted in front of Dad's gravestone. "I'm not talking about the cemetery."

I touch one of the flowers, feel the satiny petals. Dad loved petunias; so do I. Silently, I say hello to him. As usual, I wish I could talk with him in person, tell him my big news, get his approval.

"So?" Mom asks. "Is it because you turned eighteen today?"

"Mom," I say.

"Something about school?" She pulls off her gardening gloves.

"No, and nothing is the matter with me."

"You're a terrible liar," she says, and reties the silk scarf that keeps her hair from frizzing out to eternity.

I just shake my head; she won't understand. She won't want me to become a mortician. She'll want me to go to regular college like everyone else and not ask any questions about it. Mom likes things to go according to plan, and this is decidedly unscheduled.

"Help me up," she says, holding out her hand. "Your brother's bringing something special for lunch."

I stand and pull her up. I watch the petunias quiver a little with the breeze, imagine that's Dad waving happy birthday to me.

"And"—Mom pauses until I turn to look at her—"you'd be surprised at what I understand."

At home, B has brought us an extra-large mushroom-and-onion pizza from Marion's, the really good kind with the sweet tomato sauce and cut into lots of little squares. My favorite.

After we finish the pizza, Mom says, "Now close your eyes."

When I hear her start singing and B start singing and Linnie very faintly joining in, I open my eyes and see a triple-decker chocolate cake with eighteen flames hovering over eighteen purple candles.

I blow out the candles, and through the smoke I look at the big chocolate cake Mom baked and iced, at the purple sprinkles she got just for me, and I decide maybe I would be surprised at what she understands. Maybe I shouldn't be afraid of telling her; maybe it would be okay. I remember that Uncle Lou and Aunt Irene are taking me and Mom to lunch tomorrow, and I decide it would be good to have them present as a buffer. Just in case. Uncle Lou, whether intending to or not, always creates a diversion.

The next afternoon, Uncle Lou plucks the lemon off the edge of his water glass and puts it on his bread plate. "I'm not a goddamn girl," he says, shaking his head. And then, to me, "So how many boyfriends do you have these days?"

"None," I say, and before Uncle Lou can ask any more questions that make me feel uncomfortable and awkward, as Uncle Lou is apt to do, I add, "So, I have something to tell you two."

Mom gets that look on her face like she's terrified I'll say I'm pregnant or something. Which is pretty funny considering I still haven't even kissed anyone. She puts down her roll but keeps hold of her knife, a clump of butter smeared on its tip.

"You're not knocked up, are you?" Uncle Lou asks, a little too loudly, and two middle-aged women in corduroy jumpers and cream-colored turtlenecks at a neighboring table turn to us, aghast. Maybe I look more promiscuous than I thought.

"No, everyone," I say. "Not pregnant."

"Thank God," Mom says, and makes the sign of the cross.

We are at Vandermeer's, which is Uncle Lou's Special Event restaurant, and I guess that means my birthday is a Special Event. Aunt Irene was supposed to join us, but Uncle Lou says she wasn't feeling well. I think that's Aunt Irene's way of saying she can't stand Vandermeer's and doesn't get what Uncle Lou sees in it. Today, Uncle Lou sports an orange Hawaiian shirt and Kelly green polyester pants, which he has identified as his "lucky trousers," something I have zero desire to interpret.

Possibly inspired by said lucky trousers, Uncle Lou winks at the turtlenecked women, who quickly look down at their dinner rolls.

Mom glares at Uncle Lou, who shrugs and leans back into the pink cushion on his faux-wood chair.

Taking in Vandermeer's décor—funeral home, circa 1972—I hope I'll have some decorating input at Brighton Brothers or wherever I work. Because seriously, the dim lights and the pastel floral drape patterns will have to go.

I don't understand why a funeral home can't be brighter —you know, more of a place that doesn't make you want to kill yourself while you're burying someone you love.

I fold my hands in my lap. I inhale and exhale. "I'm going to mortuary school."

"Is that with the birds?" Uncle Lou asks.

"Dead people," I say. "Birds are aviary."

"You're going to school with dead people?" Uncle Lou asks. "Why on earth would you do that?"

I want to say, *It just feels right*, but that doesn't seem like a good enough answer—not for him and certainly not for Chapman's application essay questions.

"Absolutely not." Mom's lips are set in an even line, and a crease divides her forehead. She turns to me. "Honey, you've already made your college plans." I can tell she's attempting not to raise her voice, and I know I'm about to raise mine.

Our waiter saves us all, for a moment. His name is Rocky, and he looks less like Rocky the fighter than Rocky the squirrel.

"You like Stallone?" Uncle Lou asks.

"I'm sorry?" Rocky says.

"Sly Stallone," Uncle Lou repeats, leaning in.

"Never heard of him," Rocky says.

"You're shitting me." Uncle Lou raises one thick white eyebrow.

"No, sir." Rocky takes a deep breath, and, to our great

surprise, is shitting no one. He seems to be trying very hard not to let Uncle Lou get to him. "Can I take your orders?"

We order lunch, and when Rocky exits, Mom says, "Lou, that was rude."

"Well, Jesus, Martha," Uncle Lou says, "what do kids watch these days?"

Mom ignores the question and turns to me. "You've already been accepted to a wonderful school, and that's where you'll be going."

"But I don't want to go to that wonderful school. I never wanted to go there."

"This is the first I've heard of it." Mom rips a piece off her roll. "Besides, it's too late to change your plans now."

"Says who?"

"Says your mother." Mom rips a piece of roll off the smaller piece she just tore off. I wonder if she might shred the whole thing. "Lou, how's Sylvia since her foot surgery?" Which is Mom's way of saying we're done talking about this.

"You can't ignore me," I say. "I'm right here."

"Right now," Mom says, "we're talking about your aunt's surgery. You can participate or not. Your choice."

I choose to not participate, which seems unfair, given that we're supposed to be celebrating my birthday.

At dessert, I ask for a virgin mudslide instead of pie, and everyone looks at me like I'm some brand of nuts. "That will be my dessert," I try to explain.

"You saw they have blueberry pie?" Mom says.

"Yes," I say, "but this will be fine." I smile at Rocky.

"You don't want some dessert with it?" Uncle Lou repeats.

I shake my head.

"She's a drinker, Rambo," Uncle Lou says to Rocky.

Rocky nods solemnly, writes something else on his note-pad, and walks away.

Uncle Lou leans across the table and squints at my hand, resting next to my water glass. "It's definitely hereditary. The way you sit with your index finger pointed out like that. Nicky did that all the time."

I look down at my hand, at my pointy index finger like Dad's, and I wish he was here right now. Without looking up, I say, "It's not too late to change my college plans."

Mom sighs and says, "Donna, I'm glad you found something you're excited about. Believe me. But it can't be this." Her voice sounds soft, and she smiles at me like she's sad. "You're already so—" She stops herself. "I just don't think mortuary school is the best place for you."

Under the table, I fold my hands together, pressing my fingers into the backs of my hands.

"UD is a good school and seems like such a happy place." Mom brushes crumbs off the tablecloth. "You'll make lots of friends and have good role models around."

"You don't think I'd find any friends or role models at mortuary school?"

"That's not what I'm saying."

I feel fluttery in my chest, and my neck is getting hot. I want to yell, but my voice comes out quiet and low. "What are you saying, then?"

"I just think Communications is a great major for you. You'll learn how to interact with all kinds of people. Live ones."

"Virgin mudslide for the young lady." Rocky steps up to the table and distributes two blueberry pie slices and one chocolate drink that I wish was full of alcohol.

I slurp the mudslide loudly on purpose through my straw. I glance at Rocky. "Sorry, my mom doesn't usually take me out in public. I haven't learned how to interact with live people yet."

"Watch it." Mom stabs her fork into her pie.

"Enjoy your dessert," Rocky says, backing slowly away from the table.

I watch purple juice bleed out of the pale piecrust, like Mom's wounded it. I know how the pie feels. "Dad would have thought this was a great idea."

Mom lets her fork drop, and it clanks against the plate. A few drops of juice splatter onto the white tablecloth. She grabs the edge of the table and doesn't look up.

I know I shouldn't say anything else. I know I've already crossed some line, and I can feel something like a lightning storm in the air. But I can't stop myself, and I'm angry. I've finally found a job I actually want to do, and Mom wants to stop me. "Dad would want me to do what I love."

Mom looks up at me, eyes like steel. "Well, your father isn't here. It's just me."

"I know," I say. "And it's just me, too."

We stare at each other, and I can almost hear thunder rumbling or someone whistling in a dusty Old West town.

Uncle Lou clears his throat. "So, how much does a mortuary school education go for these days?"

"Lou," Mom says, releasing her grip on the table, "Donna and I will finish this discussion later." She forces a smile. The storm appears to be over, for now. "What I want to know is if you and Irene made plans for that trip to South Carolina."

I'm grateful for the detour and impressed that it's also a useful one. Uncle Lou loves to talk about the beach, and can go on for at least twenty minutes marveling at beverages served in pineapples. Mom may understand Uncle Lou, but I'm pretty sure she'll never get me at all. And I'm not looking forward to discussing anything later.

That night, I avoid Mom and return to the basement and my application. I complete the rest of the fill-in-the-blank parts and reluctantly check "deceased" after I write out Dad's name. I look again at the essay questions, and I know that mortuary school just feels right, even if it's not a good enough answer.

Or maybe it is. I remember one of my favorite stories about Mom and Dad. At B's old computer, I sit down and start writing. *Sometimes something just feels right, like when my parents described how they first met at the Beavercreek Roller Rink in a six-skater pileup.*

In the morning, well after Mom has left for work, I reread my essays, print them out, and set them next to the application on the kitchen table. Also on the kitchen table, Mom has left a note. *We'll talk later. I do love you (whether you know it or not). Mom.* Which means she'll try to convince me to go to my brother's school and play nice with the other college kids. And until a week ago, that would have been fine.

Out the window above the counter, the sky looks like the Little Miami River—steely, dirty, cloudy. I make myself a peanut-butter-and-banana bagel for lunch and drink a tall glass of milk, staring at the application like it might crawl somewhere if I take my eyes off of it. Ridiculous.

Pretending the line on the floorboards in the front hall is a tightrope, I walk one foot in front of the other, back and forth until I feel a little dizzy. The clock ticks through the silence, and I whisper the word "hello," just to hear the sound of my voice. I say it again, louder and louder. "Hello. HELLO!" I walk fast over to the table and my application and shout, "Should I do this? Is anyone listening? Are you listening?" With my hands gripping the edge of the table, I close my eyes and listen for a rumbly voice I worry I'm starting to forget. I wait for him to say, "That's it. You're on the right track, sweetheart." I squint my eyes tighter, thinking that might improve my hearing. Nothing. But then I feel my hands getting warm.

When I open my eyes, a ray of sun extends over my hands and my application, like when Indiana Jones finds the location of the Ark of the Covenant in that underground chamber, just not as precise and, I hope, not ending with anyone's face melting off. Still, I guess sunshine is as good an answer as any.

I sign my application and drive the forty minutes to Chapman College of Mortuary Science. I take Route 4, which isn't as busy as the highway, and travel slowly, reviewing all the intelligent and charming questions I'll ask the admissions counselor. *What are the strengths of your program? From my research, I noticed that you're the only program in Ohio with decomposition experts from three countries—how have you seen students benefit from that wisdom?*

When I walk through the tall glass doors, an oversized oak desk stands before me. I have to get up close to see the lady behind it. She wears a peach cardigan and a white silk blouse, and her graying blond hair perches on her head a little bit like a dust mop.

"Where do I turn in my application?" I ask.

"Right here." She holds out her hand.

"Um." I pull the application to my chest. "I have a few questions."

"Okay." She grudgingly brings her hand back and folds it with the other one on the desk. "What do you want to know?"

Suddenly, I can't think of any of my impressive questions, and before I can stop myself, I ask, "What's your policy on death?"

"Excuse me?"

"Well," I say, feeling like a derailed train plummeting off a bridge, "if I die while I'm a student, do I get anything fun, like a free embalming or something?"

She unlaces and then relaces her fingers. She sighs. "No."

"Okay, what else can you tell me?"

She sighs again, breathes in like she's rewinding her inner message tape. "The program is a year," she says, which is, in fact, how the message starts on Chapman's voice mail. Maybe she recorded it. "After that, most students typically do a one-year internship before entering the workforce."

"Last bolt on the casket, eh?"

She doesn't laugh. "That it? Or do you have more pertinent questions?"

I'm not sure for a second if she said impertinent, but I think my time is done here. "Nope." I hand her the application. "Sign me up."

"Actually, there's an application process," she says, glancing at my paperwork, "Ms. Parisi. So I can't really do that."

I force a smile. Now who's being pertinent?

I take myself on a walk around the campus, keeping an eye out for Lars and Sarah and Betty from the catalog, but I don't see any of them. I do see a few wooden benches, some gingko trees with the stinky berries, old brick buildings, and people milling about with backpacks and books and teeth that aren't as white as I was led to believe.

One of the buildings has a gold plaque with two lines of writing: THE SUZANNE PALMISANO RESTORATIVE ARTS LABORATORY on top, and underneath, RESTORE IN PEACE. I walk up the path to the door and try the knob. It's unlocked, so I walk in. Down the hallway ahead of me, I see a long window with bright light washing through and over the patch of hallway floor below. I tiptoe farther in and peek through the window.

Below, I see what looks like an art studio—long tables and paintbrushes and carving tools. About twenty people in lab coats are working with what I think is clay, shaping it into things I have to squint to realize are parts of the human face—noses, ears, cheeks, even what I'm guessing is an eyelid, which one woman is gluing eyelashes onto. She holds it out to the man next to her, who nods as if to say, "Nice job."

Behind me, I hear footsteps, and turn to see a guy in a white T-shirt whose exposed arms and neck are covered in multicolored tattoos. He's got a white lab coat tossed over his shoulder. He tilts his head to the side and smiles at me. "Don't tap the glass or try to feed the animals. They bite."

"Or it looks like they could make teeth to bite me."

"Right on." He pulls the lab coat off his shoulder and slides it on. "I'm Jason."

"Donna." I try to figure out what to do with my hands, and end up putting them on my hips, which feels totally silly. I slide them behind my back and pull at the dangly straps on my backpack. "I'm thinking of becoming a student here."

"Rad. When you do, try to get to class on time, even if the instructors don't." He flashes another smile at me and heads down the hall and around a corner.

A few seconds later, I see him walk through a door in the room below, and all the people in lab coats turn to look at him and stop the work they're doing. They sit in tall chairs next to the long art tables and pull out notebooks. Jason holds up a clay model of a human head and starts to talk. I can see them all laughing. I have no idea what he's saying, but I smile too. I've never seen a teacher with that many tattoos, and it looks like everyone is, in fact, restoring in peace.

By the time I get home, Mom's car is in the driveway, and I pull in right next to her. She's walking up the sidewalk to the front door with grocery bags in both hands.

I remember unloading grocery bags with her when I was little. On the way home from the Kroger, Mom would keep the box of Dutch cocoa sugar cookies out so we'd have a treat. Once we got inside, she'd pull a kitchen rag off the sink and promptly wipe the cookie crumbs from my face. "There," she'd say. "That's presentable."

I remember her doing the same thing the day of Dad's funeral. Some cousin with stinky perfume had left a lipstick mark on my cheek, and Mom marched me to the funeral home water fountain, pulled out a Kleenex, and went at my face. I protested, dragging out the word "Mom" into two syllables, the skilled pronunciation perfected by all fourteen-year-old girls.

Mom paused, immobilized my protest with that mythical look that could petrify plants and animals, and then wiped off the rest of the lipstick.

Now she turns as she hears the car and waves to me, a little white flag kind of wave. I'm just not sure we're going to have a truce.

I follow her into the house and down the hall to the kitchen with the last of her grocery bags. "So," I say, "I turned it in. My application for mortuary school."

"I thought we were going to discuss this." In slow motion, she puts a gallon of one percent milk in the fridge and carefully closes the door.

"I never said I wanted to discuss this." I lean against the kitchen wall and hold my backpack against my stomach and chest.

Mom unloads cans and boxes on the counter and folds up the paper grocery bag. She doesn't look at me and holds on to counter like she's steadying herself, like she held on to the table yesterday. "When do you find out if you're accepted?"

"In a month, I think," I tell her, and then remember the nice lady in the peach sweater. "But maybe longer."

"If you're accepted," Mom says, handing me a box of garbage bags to go in the closet next to me, "we'll discuss it then. Because I want to. And I'm your mother. And because I want what's best for you."

I take the box from her, and the phone rings. "Can you get that?" Mom asks on her way down the steps to the laundry room, where Clorox and dryer sheets go.

"Hey, kiddo," Uncle Lou says. "What's the good word?"

"Turned in my application for school today."

"Oh," he says, "for the aviary."

"Right." I sit down at the kitchen table and thumb through Mom's pile of unused coupons, including ones for string cheese and Drano, which I think may have some sort of cause-and-effect relationship. "Mom just ran downstairs for a minute."

"Honey?" he says. "Go easy on your mom, will you? She's doing her best to raise you kids right and keep it all together."

For a moment, silence hangs between us, and I see Mom very clearly, holding my little sister's hand and greeting each relative and friend as they made their way to the white cushioned kneeler in front of Dad's coffin. And I see her later that night, after we'd all said good night and I came out to lie on the living room floor, tired of my bed, and she sat crying at the dining room table with an untouched cup of tea.

Now I hear Mom on the creaky middle step. I know she's had it rough, but I don't know what to do for her. I'm struggling to figure out what to do for myself. "Mom's back," I say in the phone to him. *Uncle Lou*, I mouth to her. She nods, taking out two cans of cream of mushroom soup and folding up another brown bag.

"Bye, Uncle Lou," I say.

"I love you," he says.

I hand Mom the phone and watch as she stretches the cord across the kitchen so she can put the bags away under the sink. It's rare for my mother, master multitasker, to do one thing at a time. Put away groceries, talk with her brother-in-law, thwart my happiness.

six

On Tuesday at lunch, Patty and Becky are working on a presidential history handout they forgot about that's due this afternoon, Charlie's still reading his herb garden book and making notes, and Jim has crafted a paper football he's shooting through various invented goalposts, like Becky's lip balm and lipstick tubes and the salt and pepper shakers. Liz and I are sharing french fries and a chef salad when she says, "Oh, I almost forgot. I have a proposal for you."

From her purple bag she pulls out the *Dayton City Paper* and shows me a circled blurb for a workshop called "Rituals," which is scheduled to start a few weeks from now.

"Wanna take this with me?" Liz asks. "It sounds amazing." Today Liz wears a red-and-white polka-dot scarf rolled up thin and around her head like a headband, with the long silky ends hanging down her back. And she has a different ring on every finger. The one pointing to the amazing rituals workshop has an inch-long silver lizard crawling up toward her fingernail.

"I'm pretty sure nothing in the *City Paper* is amazing," Patty says. Since she must not be paying such close attention to the presidents, I figure she's trusting Becky to do most of the work. Figures.

"Don't be so trapped by expectation," Liz says. "And besides, I wasn't talking to you." She looks at me. "What do you think?"

The blurb reads, *Learn about rituals of all of the major religions and spiritual paths. This extended evening workshop will introduce you to rituals for living and dying, rituals to attract love, protection rituals, and rituals to discover your true purpose in life.*

I nod, curious and flattered. No one has ever asked me to do something like this before, and I don't know how anyone says no to someone like Liz. "Okay, sure."

"I hope you have an amazing time," Patty says. "See, I'm not trapped."

"Whatever," Liz says. I guess she and Patty aren't best friends after all.

When everyone else takes their trays up to the line, Liz closes the paper and looks me in the eyes. "I'm so excited to learn about this stuff with you."

I want to say thank you, but I look down and start tearing little pieces off my napkin. "So do you think we'll get to study Pagan stuff at all? I have an aunt who's a Witch. Aunt Selena."

"Really? That's so cool. Can I meet her?" Liz's eyes are bright, and I think she may actually be salivating.

I wish I hadn't said anything. "No one in my family actually talks to her."

"Witches don't mix with the Catholic Italians? Seems like a good match to me."

"She stopped going to church, and Aunt Sylvia was sure Aunt Selena hit her with the evil eye. And everyone stopped talking to her. Except my dad would call her sometimes, even though Mom didn't like it. At all." Words are spilling out of my mouth, and I worry that Mom is right, that I don't know how to interact with living people in any kind of balanced way. It's either nothing or all this.

Liz's eyes open wide, and she leans in closer.

"Oh, yeah, and Uncle Lou told me once that Selena was psychic or something." With each word, I watch Liz get more interested as I get more uncomfortable. Then I remember something I hope might deter Liz, because it actually freaked me out a little. "They all say she's only psychic because she worships the devil."

Liz shrugs. "But listen, you're not them. You could talk to her."

I tie my straw wrapper into a knot. "I don't think so."

Liz frowns, but then shakes her head. "That's fine," she says. "Still, you know it's in your blood."

"I'm not sure it's genetic."

Liz makes that sharp direct eye contact again. "Donna," she says, "I think you have amazing personal power."

What I like best is that she means it. I know a faker when I see one, and she isn't faking. She really does think it. I just wish I could figure out how to locate that amazing personal power without sacrificing small animals to the Dark Lord.

On our way out of the cafeteria, I see Charlie waiting by my locker. Liz looks at him and winks at me. "Later, skater," she says, and walks away.

And there I am, with my throat feeling like it's about to close up.

"Hey, I think that class you and Liz are taking sounds incredible. You'll have to tell me how it is." I guess Charlie wasn't totally paying attention to his herb book either.

"Okay." I see that look again in Charlie's eyes, because he's staring right into mine. I remember hearing once that eyes are the only places other than the brain with brain cells in them, so you really can see inside of someone that way. I hope Charlie can't read my brain cells and know that I'm wondering what it would be like to kiss him. Or that I'm wondering what would happen if we went out on a date that went wrong. Like Charlie would ask me all kinds of interesting questions, but I couldn't think of anything to say, and so drown us both in awkward silence, which would lead Charlie to promptly toss me into the girlfriend recycling bin. Then how on earth would I survive sitting at the same lunch table with him and everyone else for the next two months? This road, I decide, can only end in disaster. I blink fast a few times, hoping that might throw Charlie off my trail.

"Are you all right?" he asks.

"Something stuck in my eye." I smile. "But it's gone now." I tell my brain cells to shut it, and force myself to think about more attractive things, like rain forests and Greenpeace. Just in case.

After dinner, while we're loading the dishwasher, I tell Mom there's a class down at the community center I want to take with Liz, and she says, "Sweetheart, that's wonderful." I think Mom is just relieved I'm taking an interest in activities with people my own age. I think she's also relieved I'm asking about a one-night workshop instead of a year-long degree program. "It's interesting," she says, "because I'm going to take a class at the community center too."

"Like on knitting or something?"

"Yoga."

"Really?" I realize my mouth is hanging open and that I may have responded as if Mom had just told me she'd decided to ride cross-country naked on horseback.

"You're not the only one who can try something new." She closes the dishwasher door with a little more force than usual.

"I didn't mean you couldn't do it. I was just surprised, is all."

"Yeah, I guess I am too." Mom puts on the kettle for her evening tea and seems to relax again. She smiles a little and looks unsure, something I rarely see. I've always wondered if Mom has a secret manual stored somewhere that tells her how everything should be done, from folding dish towels to making meat loaf. For Mom, there's always been a right way to do things; but at this moment, she seems more like a question mark than a period. "I just think it might be time to shake things up, you know?"

I think about my Chapman application, wonder where it is today. "Maybe that's what I want too."

Mom nods. "Maybe," she says softly.

And since Mom is all loose and into yoga, I think maybe now would be a good time to bring up my Witch aunt. I remember hearing Dad and Mom and Aunt Sylvia, one of Dad's sisters, talk about her once when they were figuring out who should come to my first Communion. I had been coloring a worksheet for school.

Aunt Sylvia said something about the word *Pagan* and made the sign of the cross about three times. "She casts spells on people."

"How do you know this?" Dad asked.

"I think she cursed me," Aunt Sylvia said. "Why else would Ralph leave me?"

"Ralph left you because he's a jamoke," Dad said. "I'd like her to come."

Mom said, "Nicky, I'm sorry. I'm just not comfortable with her being there."

Dad agreed, but he sounded a little sad.

But that was ten years ago, and I am eighteen now. I can ask my mom a question. I push in the kitchen table chairs and say as casually as I can muster, "Have you seen Aunt Selena in a while?"

"Why?" Her back is to me, but it sounds like she's got both eyebrows up.

"I was just wondering."

"No, I haven't seen her. Lou said that Irene saw her at the Dorothy Lane Market, but they didn't talk." She sets her favorite yellow mug on the table and puts an English breakfast tea bag in it. Her eyes are now narrowed toward me. "Just to be clear, your aunt is involved in things I don't approve of." Definitive Mom has returned.

"Okay." I take a drink of water, which I hope says, *I wouldn't dream of getting in touch with Aunt Selena*, even for Liz, but Mom doesn't look like she got that message.

The teakettle whistles, and Mom turns off the stove. She pours boiling water over the tea bag, the hot stream pinning it to the bottom of the mug. "Things you shouldn't be involved in."

"Got it."

On Good Friday evening, Mom and Linnie and I go to the Stations of the Cross at St. Camillus. Inside the dark church I smell incense and the polish they use on the wooden pews. Tonight's service doesn't require talking to anyone on the way in or out, and I like the excuse to be somber.

Father Dean walks from station to station, stopping in front of each statue of Jesus on his way to being crucified. At the station where Jesus carries his cross and Veronica steps out of the crowd to wipe the sweat and blood off his face, I think of Mom wiping Dad's face with a cool washcloth as he lay on the hospital bed she had set up for him in their room. Supposedly, Veronica's cloth somehow carried the imprint of Jesus' face after that. With a Kleenex from my pocket, I wipe the tears from my own cheek. I look down at it and search for the imprint of my face. All I see are dark spots in the tissue. One looks like a rabbit, but I can't be sure.

Jesus Christ, 33

Cause of Death: Suffocation and heart failure due to crucifixion

Surviving Immediate Family:
• Mother: Mary of Nazareth

Body covered with spices and oils

Clothing: Tunic

Entombment: Linen wrappings, cave covered by large stone

Special Guests in Attendance: Angel of the Lord

Funeral Sponsor: Rich Jewish leader, Joseph of Arimathea

Funeral Incidents:
• Body disappears from sealed tomb
• Jesus comes back from the dead

Dumbest thing someone says trying to be comforting, which in this case turns out to be true: "There is no need for you to be afraid. I know you are looking for Jesus, who was crucified. He is not here, for he is risen, as he said he would." —Angel of the Lord, post-descending from heaven and violent earthquake, sitting calmly on tombstone he rolled away, and scaring the crap out of Jesus' lady friends.

seven

Late Holy Saturday morning, the kitchen smells like vinegar and rain when I tell Mom I need to go out. She turns from the kitchen sink, where she's filling the teakettle with water. "But we're dyeing Easter eggs."

"I don't have to this year." I tighten the straps on my backpack and hope I sound convincing so I can make a quick escape.

Mom looks sad, but the frown changes course on her face and somehow flips into a raised eyebrow. "Where do you have to go that's so important?"

I do some speed-fishing in my brain for a good answer that isn't the truth, which is that I'm going to Brighton Brothers to tell them I turned in my application. "I have to look for some books. For that class at the community center."

It seems I caught a winner, because Mom smiles a little. She sighs. "Just try to be back soon so you can do at least one with me and Linnie, okay?"

"Okay."

At Brighton Brothers, when I walk in and say hello, no one answers. I call a little louder, and still nothing.

The doors to Viewing Room One are closed, but it doesn't seem like any visitors are here. I knock softly and slide open one side of the pocket doors, just enough of a crack to stick my head through.

In front of a black coffin that looks like it's right out of a Dracula movie stands a muscly man in a lab coat and hiking boots—Joe Brighton. He turns and grins at me.

"Hey, it's my pal, Donna P." He's wearing rubber gloves and is holding a triangular sponge. "My brother told me you stopped by."

"The other Mr. Brighton."

"The Evil Mr. Brighton." He stops smiling and nods with exaggerated slowness, but there's a little sparkle in his eyes.

"So I call you the Good Mr. Brighton?"

"How 'bout you call me JB instead?"

"Okay." JB is absolutely the tan body builder, mustache-free version of the dentist head, which I didn't know was possible until now. "I turned in my application at CCMS."

"Good for you." He sets his sponge down on a little cart next to the coffin, which I notice has silver spirals painted on the side. "Want your first unofficial class in restorative arts? I am, after all, the master." I remember the Restorative Arts Lab at Chapman and think of the tattooed teacher. I wonder if Jason and JB know each other.

I hesitate to answer him, although I'm straining my neck to see the coffin behind him, which I'm not totally convinced is vampire-free. "Sure."

"You picked a doozy of a day to stop by, so you're in luck." He rifles through what looks like the huge, multitiered makeup cases Father Bill bought for the Players last year, and pulls out a small tube. Turning back to the coffin, he says, "Shut the door behind you, would you? Despite what you might think, we don't usually like people wandering in."

I step into the room and slide the door shut. "Sorry."

"You're an exception, so it's okay. You're in training."

"Not yet. I haven't even been accepted." I notice folding chairs lined up on either side of the room, and up closer to JB and the coffin stand two shoulder-height flower arrangements bursting with black roses.

"You're in training as soon as you start to learn something. Wanna learn something?"

I step up next to JB. "Yes."

"Well, there you are."

And holy crap, here I am. In front of us is not what I

expected at all. Inside the coffin, which JB tells me is a toe-pincher, tapered at the end like they made in the old days, lies a woman with black curly hair piled high, tendrils dropping delicately over her white ears, contrasting with her shockingly white skin and a mouth gaping wide open.

"No, this isn't how we usually do it," JB says. Apparently this woman, Miranda Nethers, had some unusual requests for her viewing, the basics of which were getting made up to look like the undead. JB looks a lot like B does when he's figuring out a new mechanical gadget—thoroughly delighted.

JB calls his makeup case the Titan, short for the Titan 2000, apparently the fanciest, most complete mortuary makeup kit on the market, equipped to meet the needs of the most versatile artist. From one of the Titan's lower tiers, JB pulls out something that doesn't look like makeup, and I realize it's a tube of superglue. After applying two smooth lines of superglue on Miranda's top and bottom lips, JB seals her mouth. Suddenly I think of Patty and wonder if this trick could work on live people.

JB explains that he applied an initial coat of white foundation to help him get focused, although he knew he'd need another coat. He points out where he's already smudged it in a few places when he closed Miranda's mouth. "Makeup doesn't mix the same with a dead person's skin. There's no heat or oil to help it sink in like it does on a live person. So it's easy to mess up, but also easy to fix."

Which he does in no time, sweeping graceful strokes of a blend of white and beige cosmetic on her cheeks and chin and forehead. He paints her lips with a dark red that's almost brown, and I've got to hand it to him—she looks pretty undead to me. Finally he pulls out an atomizer and squeezes three puffs of powder over her face, then pulls off the plastic bib covering her neck and chest, revealing a black high-collared dress with lace at the throat.

"Scary."

"Really?" he asks, and then nods. "Thank you. I thought so too." He pulls a bottle of deep red nail polish from the Titan. "Now for the finishing touches."

As I watch JB delicately paint each of Miranda's fingernails, I notice how tense my whole body feels—not like I'm stressed out, but like I'm some kind of animal ready to pounce, all systems go. I can't remember the last time I paid this close attention to anything. And it feels amazing.

On Easter, as usual, Mom has the table set beautifully. A big platter of sliced ham with pineapple rings around it sits in the center. Steam drifts up from the dish of scalloped potatoes and the plate of bakery rolls. And Mom put almond slivers in the green beans, which I wish she did all the time since they taste so good that way. I'm sitting next to Linnie, then B, then Gwen, then Mom on the other side of me.

After we say grace and pass the food around the table,

B stands up, holding his wineglass. The sloshing Merlot looks just like the color JB used on Miranda's lips yesterday, and I almost say so, but luckily B starts talking first.

"We have an announcement to make." He smiles at Gwen, and I realize her eyes are sparkling and full. "Gwen and I are getting married."

"Oh, honey," Mom says, dropping her fork. "Congratulations. To both of you." She stands up and hugs B.

For a second I feel something drop in my stomach, and I don't know if I should be happy or sad. Then everyone's up hugging each other, and Gwen is squealing a lot. Surprisingly, Mom is too. Gwen wears the same sweet department-store perfume that Patty does, which makes the hug a little stifling, and I notice that with her heels on, she's still a few inches shorter than me.

When we sit back down, Mom says, "I'm so excited, I'm not sure I can eat."

"I know, right?" Gwen says, although usually she doesn't eat, at least not like the rest of us. For instance, right now her plate is full of green beans, a pineapple ring, and a tiny slice of ham. Gwen likes to avoid fats, and our Easter dinner clearly falls outside the Weight Watchers' guidelines.

From what B has told me, Gwen's not big on conventional cooking. I don't know that she actually cooks at all. Mostly she eats sprouts and dry foods or things like kelp and carrots. She often won't eat anything at our house. For instance, last Fourth of July, she asked Mom, "How much butter is in these cookies?"

"I'm sorry?" Mom said.

"The proportion," Gwen said. "You know, the percentage."

Without looking up, Mom peeled back the plastic wrap from a plate full of snickerdoodles. "I know what proportion means."

"Of course," Gwen said.

"And I have no idea." Mom held up a cookie. Exhibit A. "They're cookies. Cookies have butter in them. That's what makes them good."

Any normal person would have dropped it, but Gwen continued. "Actually, you could make them with yogurt."

Nobody asked you, Gwen, I thought.

"That's an interesting idea." This was Mom's way of saying hell would freeze over, thaw, and refreeze before she'd make snickerdoodles with yogurt instead of butter. Mom is a diplomat.

I'm not. "Yogurt's gross," I said. Then I made Gwen an abominably strong gin and tonic—a tactic I no longer use because of the repercussions. When Gwen drinks too much, at least as far as I've seen at family functions, she starts to dance. Or she likes to have sing-alongs. So that Fourth of July, I had to mine my musical depths.

"Let's have a sing-along," Gwen said.

"Yes, please," Mom said. "Donna, why don't you play

something?" And I found myself at the piano with Gwen breathing a gin-and-flat-noted version of "Send in the Clowns" behind me. The clowns never came. But who knows? Maybe they'll show up for the wedding.

Gwen says, "Mrs. Parisi, I hope you'll help me make plans. Mom and Dad aren't so into the wedding thing."

When she says this, I feel a wave of sympathy for her. I remember B telling me that Gwen is really different from her parents. She's about to graduate with a degree in exercise science, and both of them are overweight couch potatoes. And they don't actually seem to take an interest in anything she does. I wonder if she's even told them she's getting married. As much as I don't think Mom gets me, I've never doubted that she takes an interest in my life.

Mom reaches over and squeezes Gwen's hand. "Of course. Whatever you need. I'll be happy to."

I decide maybe Gwen could use a little extra niceness. "Me too. I can help."

B looks at me and smiles. "Thanks, Donder."

Linnie asks, "Do I have to wear a dumb dress?"

"I'm sure I can arrange that, even before the wedding. I've got closets full of them." Mom stares at Linnie. "Any other ideas of what you could say at this moment?"

Linnie slowly smashes one of the potato slices on her plate. "Congratulations."

I can't say I'm feeling a lot more enthusiastic, realizing

that helping Gwen may very well involve a whole array of things I'd call dumb, dresses notwithstanding.

"So," Mom says, leaning into the table, "when will the wedding be?"

"Just after Christmas," Gwen says. "It will be a New Year's extravaganza. So there will be lots of things for you to glitter, Donna!"

My earlier sympathy is waning.

"And helping someone else plan her wedding can always give you pointers for your own." Gwen grins and winks at me. I have the sudden urge to shrink myself to the size of the saltshaker, climb onto one of the pineapple rings, press a button, and shoot myself off into space. Since I can't do that, heat rises almost instantly to my neck and cheeks.

"She's right," Mom says. "Maybe you'll fall in love with someone at UD too."

And even though a little part of me tells me to take a bite of my roll and let the conversation flow to other places, the words come out of my mouth. "Or at CCMS."

Mom glares at me.

"Because I'll probably go there," I say a little louder.

"I've never heard of CCMS," B says.

"They teach mortuary science," I say.

"You want to be a mortician?" B says *mortician* in the same way I think he might say *pole dancer*.

109

"Yes. I do." I fold my arms across my chest, which I hope B knows is my way of saying, *See how interesting I am? If you'd been paying attention to me at all, you might have noticed earlier.*

"Metal," Linnie says, like she might, in fact, realize how interesting I am.

Gwen glances around the table, at B's open mouth, at Linnie smashing her scalloped potatoes, at Mom's frown. She turns to me. "So when do you start school?"

"She hasn't been accepted yet," Mom says, like she's forcefully shutting a door. "Okay, someone pass me the potatoes before I pass out." She takes the bowl from Gwen. "Now, Brendan, have you thought about groomsmen?"

Yesterday JB said I'm already in training, and it felt so good. Today it feels like training's about as close as Guam. I take a big drink of water and wish I could get through a meal with Mom without active combat.

Gwen gets excited about groomsmen and a follow-up question from Mom about cake, so the conversation leaps from funerals to Funfetti, about which I have nothing to say.

Miranda Nethers, 35

Cause of Death: Ovarian cancer

Surviving Immediate Family:
• Life partner: Lish McBride

Makeup: Alabaster white theatrical base, Dead Red lipstick, black eyeliner, also used as lip liner, Drop Red Gorgeous nail color

Clothing: Black chiffon Victorian gown

Casket: Vintage gothic toe-pincher coffin, burgundy velvet lining

Deceased's request as stated in last will and testament: "I want to be made up to look undead, like the fucking sexiest vampire chick you can imagine, for an open-casket viewing."

eight

I tell Liz about B and Gwen when she drops me off after school on Monday.

"A New Year's wedding will be fun. You can get all fancy." She puts her car in park in our driveway.

"I guess."

"Speaking of fancy, are you planning on going to prom, D?"

"Is that my new nickname?"

"I guess. Does it work?"

"Yeah." No one but my family had given me a nickname —that one being shared with a reindeer—so I feel like anything else is an improvement. "And no prom for me."

"Then me and you have a date to do something else fun."

"No one asked you either?" I pull my backpack up onto my lap.

"Well, no. I just don't want to go." Liz, I've discovered, seems to always have lots of choices about everything. I wonder what that's like.

Two weeks later, Mom goes to her first yoga class at the community center, and she comes home with flushed cheeks and bright eyes. Stray hair from her ponytail has curled around her face, and it occurs to me how pretty she is.

"So how was it?"

"Really wonderful," she says. "And our instructor is part Japanese and part Cherokee; he's really interesting." She looks at the kitchen table, covered with the books I have spread out for my last two finals tomorrow. "How's studying?"

"Okay. I need another hour or so, and then I'll head to bed."

Mom looks at me and shakes her head. "I can't believe my baby is graduating in just a few weeks. Both of my babies. It seems like you both just started."

B's and my graduations are a week apart, and it does seem like only yesterday that he started UD and I started Woodmont. That life turned upside down and it felt like I lost both Dad and B in the span of one week. That I started a new school and have never felt at home there.

Mom's eyes fill with tears, and I know she's remembering too. "Oh, life goes on, doesn't it?"

"Yes, it does," I say, feeling like I'm lying, but not wanting to upset Mom.

She wipes at her eyes and puts her game face back on. "Have you heard from Chapman yet?"

"Not yet." I feel my stomach getting tight, and I steady myself for another fight.

Instead, Mom says, "At yoga tonight, we had to take deep breaths. Maybe that would help you too. Just fill up your belly first, though. I never knew I wasn't breathing deeply before, but I wasn't."

"Okay." I watch my mother show me how to take a deep breath, which seems utterly out of place in the kitchen, where she concocts casseroles and does cross-stitch.

When she goes to take a shower, I do my best to concentrate on my books, although I'm definitely wondering if Mom was secretly replaced by an alien robot, the deep-breathing, New Age kind.

Although I guess I can't judge. I am going to a rituals class with Liz tomorrow, so maybe I'm a New Age robot too.

When Liz picks me up the next night, and I see Patty in the front seat of the Jeep, I feel ill.

"Hey there," Liz says slowly. "Patty decided she wanted to take the class too."

"Great," I force myself to say, and hope I don't sound as devastated as I feel. What was going to be my really fun thing with Liz has now become something else.

"Hop in," Patty says, like she was the one who had the idea in the first place.

"Okay," I say.

Liz turns to the backseat and smiles at me, and it looks like she'd like to say more, like she's got an explanation, and that at least makes me feel a little better.

Once we get to the center, there are about ten of us plus the instructor, who I half expected to be wearing a long black robe and to be very pale. I did not expect a ruddy-cheeked woman in a red hooded sweatshirt and jeans, but there she is, introducing herself as Kirsten, the rituals class teacher.

The community center room we're in has a bunch of old couches and soft chairs, which it seems Kirsten has arranged into a circle of sorts. Liz and Patty and I sit on one of the couches, and Patty makes sure she sits between Liz and me.

Patty checks out Kirsten, smirks, and crosses her legs.

I hear Liz say, "You know, Patty, you didn't have to come. We could call your mom to come pick you up."

"No, I want to be here." Patty stops smirking. "I think it'll be really interesting."

Kirsten talks for a while about all kinds of things, how rituals can be as simple as a prayer before bedtime or before meals. "Often, effective rituals are balanced," she says. "As in, if you want something new to come, sometimes you have to let go of something else. For instance, in many Christian rituals, there's an opportunity to say you're sorry for your sins before you petition the deity for anything else. Or in many earth religions, you acknowledge and thank the gods and goddesses and spirits around you and release any negativity before you welcome in new energy."

Then Kirsten explains how rituals can take us from one place to another, like rituals welcoming new babies into a community or coming-of-age rituals for young men and women in Native American or other traditions. Or rituals to help the dead journey to what's beyond, and to help the living move to a peaceful life without them.

My ears perk up at that. I wonder if Dad has journeyed to what's beyond, and I worry that maybe he hasn't, since I haven't moved to anything I'd call a peaceful life without him.

Liz glances over and gives me a tiny smile. Her eyes are soft.

At Dad's funeral we sang that song "On Eagle's Wings." *And He will raise you up on eagle's wings, bear you on the breath of dawn, make you to shine like the sun, and hold you in the palm of His hand.* I cried as I sang, and I cried as I listened to the sound of other voices when I couldn't sing anymore. Maybe God did take Dad that way—it sounds so beautiful and tangible. Eagle's wings and dawn's breath and glowing warm and safe in a big divine hand. But going to church doesn't feel like that to me, in a building that's often stuffy and with so many things to do right and wrong and to feel bad about either way. More of a divine fist than an open divine hand. It just sort of makes me feel numb and bored, kind of like how Patty looks right now.

Her eyes seem glazed over, and I notice she's tapping her boot on the floor, her knee bouncing up and down. That Patty may be bored right now baffles me since all of this seems so fascinating. And I'm assuming it pisses Liz off, because she clamps her hand down on Patty's knee and mouths the word *Stop.*

Patty stops and rolls her eyes.

Kirsten says that in ancient Egypt, they took great care getting dead bodies ready for the afterlife, and all of a sudden I imagine Mr. Bob Brighton decked out like King Tut. Which is not actually a great look for him. I push that out of my mind and wonder if that's what I'd be doing as a mortician. If that's one way of loving the whole person —you know, getting them ready for the afterlife.

I remember Dad in his coffin and noticing the makeup. Did JB do that to get Dad ready? And what does that say about the afterlife? You need lipstick to get by? What with the lipstick and the eagle's wings, I worry there's a real possibility that the afterlife could be an awful lot like a musical Father Bill might write for the Players.

By now Kirsten is quoting someone named Joseph

Campbell and talking about following our bliss—how cultures used to have coming-of-age rituals in place to help young people do just that, but now we have people of all ages wandering around not sure what to do with themselves or their lives.

And as she talks about how each person may in fact have something he or she is deeply supposed to do, the only thing I can think about is death. I wonder if my bliss is death, which sounds ridiculous. But also true. Because right then being a mortician doesn't feel like an *if*. It's more like a *when*. I feel the certainty slip over me like a new fancy dress that I'm not quite sure how to wear. Does it fit? Do I look stupid? Will anyone even notice I'm wearing something different?

For a moment, I look to my right, and both Patty and Liz are paying attention. I guess Patty's not bored anymore. And I'm so interested in what Kirsten says that I forget to be self-conscious or even mad that Patty came with us.

At break, when Patty goes to use the ladies' room, Liz grabs my arm. "I'm sorry! She called, and she was so bummed. Her prom date has mono or something, so he can't go this weekend. I couldn't get the whole story because she wouldn't stop crying. I didn't know what to do."

"It's okay." I know it's childish, but I'm totally relieved that Liz didn't ask Patty to come with us. I can feel better about Patty as a charity case.

When class starts again, Kirsten says, "Now I want to

hear from you. I'd like us to go around the circle and each share a ritual we do, or at least one we know about."

No one said anything about class participation, and I feel myself start to sweat and hope my deodorant from this morning takes me and my armpits through the night. Then Kirsten adds, "You can also pass," and I let out an almost audible sigh of relief.

Sharing works its way around the circle, with everything from saying a prayer to the four directions each evening, to lighting candles in church.

Liz says that every time she takes a shower, she sings.

"A very powerful water ritual." Kirsten nods. "And claiming your own voice."

I can see Liz eating this up, and I'm glad Kirsten said those words to her.

Even Patty says that every morning as she puts on her makeup, she looks herself in the eyes and tells herself how beautiful she is and that she better keep working to maintain it.

"Interesting, Patty, thanks," Kirsten says, and I like her even more for her diplomacy. Then Kirsten holds out her hand to me.

I think for a moment of the quiet place in my chest where I go whenever I need to escape the world. "Pass," I say.

On the way home, Liz decides we're going to do a springtime love attraction ritual on Saturday night, while everyone else is at prom. Since no one has asked me to go, and since Liz has declined what I've now discovered to be about five invitations, I think that's a great idea. Patty, however, bursts into tears. "I can't miss my senior prom." She sniffles.

"You could go by yourself," Liz offers.

"That's even worse," Patty wails.

Come Saturday night, Liz, Patty, and I are situated in Liz's basement, where Liz has lit what seems like hundreds of candles and is burning an incense stick in one of the Shiva statue's multiple hands. The smoke alarm went off once already, and Liz's mom asked us to open the screen door to let some air in, so it's a little chilly.

We each sit on big cushions Liz took off the couch. I have goose bumps, which Liz has said will enhance the ritual, that I'll feel "more alive." Right now I'm just cold, and wondering how much longer we're going to "sit in silence to prepare ourselves."

I look at Liz, whose eyes are closed, and Patty, who is checking out her fingernails. I whisper, "Should we paint our faces?"

"No," Liz says, opening one eye. "This is serious."

"Face paint can be serious," I say.

Liz looks at me with an expression I've seen Mom use —maybe we all have one of those "settle down" faces at our disposal. Liz takes a deep breath and says, "We will begin." From under her cushion she pulls out three pieces of homemade paper and three purple pens and divides them among us. "Now we list all that we want in a partner."

After several questions from Patty about what *partner* means and if it's the same as *boyfriend*, Liz uses sage to smudge the room and us and our paper. After one shot glass each of chocolate liqueur, we make our lists.

Good dancer, smart, nice hands like Dad's. Does that belong? Then an image of Charlie, environmental champion, pops into my head. *Interested in the world; kind.*

After we burn our lists to release them, and set off the smoke alarm once more, Liz's mom says we're done with the gift of fire. So we end the night eating Cheerios in Liz's blaze-free kitchen, and Patty invites us to a senior picnic she's attending tomorrow.

"I can't. I have a Players meeting tomorrow." I'm assuming the chocolate liqueur made me do it; otherwise I have no clue why I'd say that in front of Patty.

Liz adds some Cheerios to her bowl. "Your theater troupe?"

Patty laughs. "Are you still doing that weird thing?"

"Donna knows it's weird. That makes a difference. Besides, everyone knows you can learn from unusual and interesting people." Liz slurps milk from her spoon.

I wish that Liz could be around all the time to be my interpreter. She always makes everything sound so much

121

better than it is. "Although, I'm not sure what I'm supposed to learn from Leaf," I confess.

When I describe Leaf, Patty says, "She sounds like a freak. Why else would her husband leave her?" I nod in agreement and feel bad at the same time, like I've betrayed someone. But what if Patty's right? Freaks get left. Freaks might not even ever get found. Right then I have a sinking feeling that that's what I am, and fear pours cold and damp over my skin—what if Patty knows? What if everyone knows? I swallow the thought and the fear deep down into a back corner of my gut, hiding it as best as I can.

Patty lifts her bowl and drinks the last of her milk. "Sit up straight," she says, staring at my shoulders and setting her bowl down. "Tall girls shouldn't slouch."

"And short girls shouldn't tell people what to do," Liz says, taking Patty's bowl to the sink. Still, I push my shoulders back just a little.

On Sunday afternoon, when Father Bill is supposed to hand out a new script, all I can think of is what Patty said about freaks last night. And what Kirsten said in class. If you want something new to come, you have to let go of something else. Like this. Before the meeting, I tell Father Bill that I have an announcement to make. I'm intending to quit.

But then Father Bill says we need some cast bonding and that he's planned a June Lock-In for us, full of theater

games and improv, and after that, Keenie hands me a graduation card saying DREAM BIG. LIVE LARGE with $150 from
all of the Players.

When Father Bill asks if I still have something to say, I
shake my head. A ray of sun from the window glares off
his bald head. "Okay then, calendars out!"

I close my eyes. All I can imagine is sitting around in
a circle on the gym stage, holding hands, and chanting,
"Light as a feather and stiff as a board," and trying to
levitate Leaf.

nine

The day before graduation, I'm home alone when I see the mailman pull up outside. Walking out to the mailbox in a T-shirt and shorts, I'm noticing spring shifting to summer. The sun feels just a little warmer on my neck and arms and legs, and the driveway feels nice and toasty—but not burning hot, like it will get—on my bare feet.

The mailbox still has the "Parisi" that Dad painted in red, and it reminds me of the fake handwriting he would use to leave us letters from Santa Claus. Just a little different, a little fancier than his regular writing.

Inside are bills for Mom and a piece of junk mail addressed to Mr. Domenic Parisi, the kind that Mom always replies to, informing them that her husband has died and requesting that they please stop sending things to the house. Sometimes they stop; most times they don't. And when they don't, Mom gets mad and I get sad, wishing Dad would just come back already and pick up his mail. So I fold up this piece to stuff it in the bottom of the kitchen trash can.

Underneath another bill for Mom, I discover an envelope addressed to me from Chapman College of Mortuary Science. For a second I stop breathing. Recognizing that's not a reasonable practice to continue, I start breathing again, leave Mom's mail on the table, and take the letter downstairs to my bedroom. I set it on my bed and look at it. From the window, not a single ray of sunlight is beaming in. It's just me and a rectangular envelope with my fate inside it. I slide my finger under the flap and open it. As I read the letter, I feel a smile bloom across my face.

I grab the phone and call Liz and tell her that it's official. I've been accepted to Chapman College of Mortuary Science. I pace back and forth in my room; it's hard to stay still right now.

"Congratulations! Woo-hoo," Liz yells, and I have to hold the phone away from my ear for a second. "I knew it. Wow, that's fantastic."

"Now I've just got to convince Mom that it's fantastic. Maybe I should have you tell her."

"She'll come around, D. No worries."

"Thanks," I say, although I'm not so sure about that.

"And I've got some news too."

Liz has decided to go to CMU, so in the fall she's going to Pittsburgh. And there's something else: their journalism program offers special early internships, and Liz landed one writing travel articles for the young traveler for *Global Adventure Magazine*. Starting next week, she and her parents will be in Ireland for a month.

"Liz, that's great," I say, but I've stopped pacing.

"Well, we're both going out with a bang," Liz says. "I hear there are all kinds of Witches in Ireland—maybe I'll meet some. And maybe the universe is going to provide me with an Irish boyfriend." She giggles.

If Mom doesn't lock me in the basement, I'm going to the mortuary, and Liz is going to the Emerald Isle. Suddenly my news doesn't sound so exciting.

"Hey, are you all right?"

"I'll just miss you is all." We had planned to do all kinds of things. Go out to Yellow Springs and hike in the park, go to the Strawberry Festival, learn how to make astrology charts for ourselves. Okay, Liz had really come up with all of these ideas, but I was excited to do them with her. And I'm not sure I'll do anything without her.

"I'll miss you too. And listen, I'm not gone all summer. We'll still have time to do fun things when I get back."

That night, I wait for Mom on the front porch. When she comes through the door, I hand her my Chapman envelope.

She pulls out the letter and reads it. "Sweetheart," she starts with a voice that is more sour than sweet, "this is not the best place for you."

"I think it is." I stand in front of my mother, and I'm ready to fight.

"Well maybe you're only eighteen years old," she says sharply, "and you don't know any better."

"Like you know anything." I know it sounds childish, but I can't think of anything else to say. Or I don't know how to say anything else, anything really important. All I can do is repeat, "I think it is."

I see her start to respond, but instead she closes her mouth, like she's doing it with sheer will. And she closes her eyes and takes a deep, long breath—so long that I feel like I might have stopped breathing in the meantime. If this is her new battle tactic, it's working, because I'm confused and totally off guard.

When she opens her eyes, she smiles. "Donna, I love you." Her face looks peaceful, and her voice sounds tranquil.

I stare at her.

"You're just going to have to tell them no, that you've been accepted elsewhere."

"I'm not going to do that." I can't defend myself in terms of having already mastered all that a Communications degree could offer, but I know UD is not the place for me. I know what I want and what I'm going to do, no matter what. "You can't stop me, you know. I'm eighteen years old."

"And how are you going to pay for mortuary school?" Mom has the expression of the villain who's found the upper hand. *Aha, I've got you now.*

I hadn't thought about this. I always assumed Mom would help me pay for college. I guess I could ask Father Dean to let me return to the St. Camillus basement dungeon to stuff as many bulletins as I can get my hands on. I wonder how many bulletins equal the first tuition payment. But then I remember Mr. Brighton's offer—I have my own card to play. I fold my arms across my chest. "I'm getting a job. At Brighton Brothers. This summer. And I can get student loans."

Mom sets her purse down on the floor and sighs. "You're right. I can't stop you." She reaches out and touches my face. "But you've got to know that I don't approve of this. And there are some things we need to talk about."

I step back from Mom and her hand.

For a moment, her hand is stretched toward me, trying to reach me but not touching. Then her arm falls to her side. "I'm worried about you."

"Well, I guess that's your problem." I step over her purse and into the house.

Graduation is a blur of orange robes and family members flooding out of the Woodmont auditorium. Afterward, on the front lawn of the school, Gwen takes a picture of me, Mom, B, and Linnie. I offer a halfhearted smile, and out of the corner of my eye, I see Becky's aunt take a picture of Becky and her mom and dad. Mr. Bell looks so proud, smiling at Becky like she must be the most amazing creature he could imagine. Mom has her arm around me, and I'm suddenly aware that no one's on my other side, gazing at me with that kind of admiration. Then three-year-old Leah tugs on Mr. Bell's pant leg. "Me too, Daddy!"

Easy as pie, he hoists Leah up onto his shoulders, and she squeals as Becky's aunt snaps another shot. I feel an ache in my chest and a yearning to be that small, to be lifted up again onto Dad's strong shoulders, to breathe in some air that would feel cleaner and purer, to get a bigger view of it all.

Then, Becky's pulling me into a group picture with everyone from our lunch table. Liz stands on one side of me, and Becky's on the other. Patty and Charlie and Jim line up behind us. Patty smiles so wide I think her stupid face might break. "This is the best time of our lives," she says, shaking her head.

I shake my head too, and look toward the cameras. *God, I hope not.*

Becky has tears on her face, and I feel like I should be as moved as she is. But more than anything, I can't wait to go home.

"Don't worry," Charlie whispers. I feel his breath warm in my ear. "It's almost over."

I turn back to him and smile as flashes go off in front of us.

This time, I walk right into Brighton Brothers and back to Mr. Brighton's office, like I know what I'm doing.

When I show him my letter, he smiles and says, "I guess this means you're serious. And interested in that summer job?" He seems almost as excited as I am.

I'm also relieved that I'll have something to do while Liz is away. "Why, yes I am."

"Okay, then," he says. "For starters, how about a tour?"

"That sounds good."

"Might as well dive right in. Let's start in the prep room."

I follow him down to the basement, where a big glass door leads into a room conveniently labeled PREP ROOM. It dates back to the fifties, Mr. Brighton tells me. It's a rectangular room with one small window up high in the back. There are three long skinny tables—two stainless steel and one fancy porcelain, which Mr. Brighton says cost him an arm and a leg.

On the fancy porcelain table lies the body of a blond-haired boy, who looks younger than me and wears a white button-down shirt and khaki pants.

"Very sad," Mr. Brighton says. "A suicide." He tells

me the boy's name is Henry Kunkel, and that the immediate family will come for a private viewing this evening.
Mr. Brighton has already embalmed Henry, and JB's going
to get him ready for the family's visit. The family won't
hold any other visitation hours, even though Mr. Brighton
encouraged them to. "It's still death, and his friends and
family still need to grieve. But it's their choice, and we have
to honor that."

I know how lonely I've felt, and looking at Henry, I realize that loneliness and despair can have depths even I can't
imagine. I realize there's a lot I have to learn.

On the back of the door, four long white coats hang
on hooks. Mr. Brighton explains that both he and JB do
embalming—JB mostly does the makeup, and they have
relatives who help sometimes with the wakes and services.
Mr. Brighton's son wasn't interested in the business; he
actually became a kindergarten teacher and now has a
three-year-old daughter. "You'll get to meet Delia," he says.
"She's the most beautiful thing I've ever seen." I knew he
had that grandpa vibe going on, and I know from his smile
that he loves that Delia.

On a long counter against one wall are boxes of shower
caps and gloves and gallon containers of pink juice that I'm
guessing I wouldn't want to drink.

On our way out, Mr. Brighton touches the porcelain
table where Henry rests. He closes his eyes and nods his
head, and I think of how sometimes at St. Camillus they

do veneration of the cross and people go up like they do in a Communion line and silently touch or kiss the crucifix. In church, I'm pretty sure veneration means thanking Jesus for dying for us, but Mr. Brighton's gesture seems to me at this moment more of a way to say thank you for living and doing the best you could. I lower my head too, and do my best to venerate Henry.

Once we're outside, I notice goose bumps all over my arms, and rub them with my hands—the temperature has definitely shifted.

"We've got to keep it cold in there," Mr. Brighton says. "Otherwise, it wouldn't smell so pretty." He chuckles—I'm assuming because the room actually smelled like Clorox and Silly Putty, neither of which I've seen in scented candles.

Upstairs, we go through a parlor area outside of Viewing Room Two. Folding chairs are lined against the walls for extra seating, and inside there are some love seats and chairs, all very formal looking. In the viewing room itself, I can see dents in the carpet where the casket usually is. I remember this spot.

"Dad was here."

"My dad was in this room too." Mr. Brighton pats my shoulder. "No way around it in this place. And there have been so many since then, that it gets easier. This room can't just belong to one person. It belongs to all of us."

I hold my hand on my stomach and take a deep breath like Mom showed me. Mr. Brighton is right. No way to get around it; not if I'm going to work here. It has to belong to everyone. And, I tell myself, I'm going to work here. I go to my quiet place and ask Dad not to take it personally. I hope he understands.

On the second floor, a spacious living room branches off into three hallways. Mr. Brighton points to the first two hallways and says, "This is where we live. Me and Mrs. B. and Joe. And this," he says, walking me down the third hallway, "is something for you to think about once you start school. Often, mortuary students live where they work. You don't have to, but I think it's a good idea. You get the feel for it."

He opens a door to a warm-looking room with butter yellow walls, a bed, a desk and a big armchair, and a sink next to another door, which opens to a little bathroom with a shower and toilet.

"We haven't had a student in years, but we use this as a guest room sometimes. So it's in pretty good shape. Your own room and bathroom. You'd share our kitchen. And let me tell you, Mrs. Brighton makes a great potpie. I'm hungry just thinking about it."

His voice seems far away as I step into the room and turn my head slowly to take it all in. The room feels fresh and open and has two big windows on one wall. I imagine Maurice the skeleton on the desk. And on the bed, which is twice as big as mine, I can almost see the oversized purple star-shaped pillow Dad gave me for Christmas when I was ten. I have the simultaneous feelings of being terrified and wanting to go jump on the mattress.

I step back out of the room and nod at Mr. Brighton. "Okay."

"Anyway," he says, "it's something for you to think about."

Before I go, Mr. Brighton and I agree that I'll start work in two weeks. He wanted me to take a month so I could have some vacation, since I just graduated. But I know that Liz is leaving this week and that I've got tuition bills coming soon, so I convince him I won't need that long.

On Thursday morning, Liz comes over to say good-bye. Her flight leaves in the evening. Her hair is pulled back on the sides, and she's wearing a short beige jacket over a sleeveless teal dress. She looks so grown-up. I feel young and small.

From her purple bag she pulls out a book called *Everything Witchcraft*. "I'm going to read up on things for us to do when I get back."

Then she pulls out an orange votive candle and hands it to me. "I anointed it for you. All I had was olive oil, but olive leaves have something to do with friendship, right?"

"It kind of smells like pasta." I smile a small smile. "I like pasta."

"You can use it for rituals or whatever you want. I'll miss you," she says, hugging me. "And I'll send you postcards."

"Lots of postcards." I didn't feel like crying at graduation, but I could right now.

That night, when I'm in bed in the dark basement, I hear someone coming down the steps and see Linnie's silhouette in the hallway light. She says softly, "So, Liz left today?"

"Yeah."

"And she'll be gone for a whole month?"

"Yes. Thanks for reminding me."

"I'm sorry. I know you'll miss her." Her voice is kind and gentle, at least for Linnie, and not what I was expecting.

"Thanks."

"You're welcome."

As I hear her walk up the steps and close the door, I roll onto my side and stare through the dark, making out the shape of the window and the blinds and the curtain. I hear the nighttime bugs clicking and chirping outside the window. What would it be like to sleep in the yellow room, no Linnie or Mom upstairs? Just me. I'm not sure I could do it even if I want to. Usually, the quiet lulls me, but right now I feel afraid, like everything's changing so fast I can't keep up.

Henry Kunkel, 15

Cause of Death: Blood loss

Surviving Immediate Family:
• Mother: Justine
• Father: Richard
• Grandmother: Taylor

Makeup: Ivory and tan cream cosmetic blend over scars on wrists, pale tan cream cosmetic on face

Clothing: White IZOD dress shirt, khaki pants, and navy blue fabric belt

Casket: Pine with cotton lining

Private family viewing. No visitation hours.

Comment made during funeral planning: "We just need to be done with this and move on." —Richard Kunkel

ten

On Friday night, Becky calls me while I'm watching a made-for-TV movie with Linnie. I take my phone out to the front porch to talk, and Becky says, "Jim's soccer friends are having a graduation party tomorrow, out in Beavercreek. Want to come with us?"

"On your date?" It's still getting cool in the evenings, so I pull the orange afghan from the wicker couch over my legs.

"Jim's cousin Tim will be there. He's cute, and he's in college. He asked if I had any cute single friends, and I thought of you."

I realize that if this guy's related to Jim, he's also related to Patty, an immediate red flag. And I realize that Patty may also be involved in this event. "Thanks, Becky, but I'm not sure. B graduates tomorrow."

"And that's going to take all day?"

I know no one will mind if I go out. B's graduation is in the morning, and we're going to lunch afterward. And of course Mom already said she's worried that I won't do anything while Liz is gone. I guess watching bad TV with my little sister on a Friday night doesn't help my argument against that. Mom is still going to yoga class—a couple of nights a week now—and actually suggested tonight that we stretch together and then have "our talk." I can't think of anything worse, except for going to a stupid party and feeling awkward. I look for an easy out. "Um, so will Patty be going with us too?" If Patty's coming, then B's about to have a late-evening graduation dinner that I can't miss.

"She's going out with some new guy, so she can't make it. Bummer, I know."

So now, faced with Becky's Patty-free invitation, I try to figure out what Liz would do. Liz, who just got on a plane to fly over the ocean at a moment's notice.

"I know you don't usually go out," Becky says, "but come on—we just graduated. And I want you to be there."

I know what Liz would do. "Okay."

"Okay, really? Awesome! And I think you'll really like Tim."

Well, Becky can be excited enough for both of us. And we'll see if cousin Tim is what I asked the universe for.

On the way to the party, I touch the long crinkly gypsy skirt Mom let me borrow. I don't think I've ever seen her wear it. She pulled it out of the cedar closet off of my room in the basement and said that the skirt was from her wild youth, about which I'd prefer to remain blissfully in the dark.

In the car, Becky wants to talk about us rooming together at UD. Apparently there's some kind of form she wants to mail in, so I decide I can't keep my secret any longer. And of course now, in Jim's car, I'm not just telling Becky, but also Jim and Jim's cousin Tim, who is nineteen and about to be a sophomore at UD, and who is, in fact, exceptionally cute. He's got very light brown hair, almost blond, that hangs to his shoulders, and hazel eyes that he uses a lot for direct contact, which makes me nervous.

I hold on to the door handle—maybe I'm thinking of jumping out, rolling and bumping over gravel and concrete to make my escape. "I hate to drop this on you, Becky, but I'm not going to UD."

"You're not?'

"No, I applied somewhere else and got in."

"Are you going to tell us where?" Jim says.

"Chapman."

"I haven't heard of that."

Oh, come out with it, Donna, I say to myself. Then out loud: "It's a college of mortuary science."

"Like funeral stuff?" Tim asks, and of course looks me right in the eyes. "Tight."

"You're going to be a funeral person?" Jim asks.

"Like with dead people?" Becky asks.

"Usually funerals go with dead people," Tim says. "Sometimes I paint dead people. It's cool." That was a response I wasn't expecting, and since Mom's made her opinion of mortuary school painfully clear, it's especially nice to hear. In addition to cute, Tim just got much more interesting.

"Tim's an art major," Jim says, which sounds a lot like the way he described Charlie's parents as hippies, a sort of *I know you'd never believe it, but here's living proof that these species do exist.* Like introducing a dog-headed lady at the circus.

"Everything is art," Tim says, a far-off look suddenly clouding those hazel eyes. "Death is art. Life is art. Pain is art."

"Drinking is art," Jim says. "I hope they have beer."

"I hope I can find a roommate I like for college." Becky sighs.

"Hope is art," Tim says.

I almost giggle, but realize Tim is serious, so I nod seriously with him.

* * *

An hour and a half later, Becky and Jim have disappeared, and I'm sitting next to Tim in the corner of an old basement couch, shared with two soccer players with girls on their laps. The basement smells like beer-soaked carpet. I can't be sure, but I'm guessing that someone's parents are not going to be pleased when they get back into town.

Tim has asked me about mortuary school and what I think about the use of color in photographs, and I realize as I tell him, how much I actually like black-and-white pictures. He's told me all about his drawing and sculpting classes, and the most exquisite flower he'd ever seen in the Mojave Desert; *and* he has told me I'm the smartest and most fascinating girl at the party.

Also, I'm drinking a Leprechaun, a very sweet concoction of orange juice and something called Blue Maui, which looks a lot like Linnie's recent hair experiment. And I'm wondering if this drink is about to turn me into a leprechaun, because in addition to smart and fascinating, I'm feeling pretty magical. "I think I'm a little drunk."

"It's okay," Tim says. "You only graduate from high school once."

"I hope so."

Tim slips his arm around me. "It's kind of crowded," he says, glancing at the soccer players and their lap-lady friends. "You don't mind?"

His arm feels warm and nice, like the rest of my new leprechaun self. I hope I'm not turning green. "No, I don't mind."

"You're more beautiful than you know," Tim says.

I fiddle with the silver turtle ring on my index finger.

Half an hour later, Tim rounds me up another Leprechaun and himself some more beer from the keg and then settles back next to me on the couch. He clinks our plastic cups and says, "Cheers."

We both take a drink, and Tim says, "You've got some blue stuff on your lip."

I reach up to wipe it away, but he grabs my hand, and before I know it, he's kissing me very softly. I feel the hairs on the back of my neck rise.

"I think I got it," he says, and smiles as he pulls back.

I touch my lips. "I think you did."

Close to midnight, we pile into Becky's car for the twenty-five minute trek home. Becky is Leprechaun-free, so she's driving now, and Jim's in the front with her.

In the backseat, Tim lies down with his head in my lap, his hand cupped right above my knee, under my long skirt. I'm feeling awfully warm, so I pull my jacket off and cover Tim with it, like Mom covers me with a blanket when I fall asleep on the couch. "Have a nice nap," I say.

"Thanks," he says, and pats my leg.

I close my eyes and rest my hand on the back of his neck where his hair softens and curls.

Becky puts on a CD with lots of guitar and some ethereal kind of synthesizer effect that seems to fit just perfectly with my new leprechaun identity. Jim says, "I love this one."

I close my eyes and listen. I feel the motor rumble through me as we move faster on the highway.

And I also feel Tim reach farther up my skirt. His fingers play around on my thighs. This is new. This is, wow. He plays over my underwear and then under it. I think I should stop him, but his fingertips are soft and gentle, and I think of guitar strings and that Spanish folk music Mom plays sometimes—love songs. I am an instrument.

"I think Donna's asleep," Becky whispers to Jim.

"Tim too," Jim says. "If you weren't driving..."

Becky giggles.

Tim strums faster, and I'm floating somewhere. I clutch at the hair on the back of his neck so I don't float away altogether.

Then he slips a finger inside of me—I'm surprised how easily it glides in—and his thumb makes circles. Now he finger paints. I feel wet, and I imagine shimmery paint where his hand slips and slides. I am a canvas.

"My parents are out with Tim's parents," Jim says. "They'll be home late. You should come in when you drop us off."

"Should I?" Becky says.

Tim brushes and strokes and dips his brush in the paint

well, in and out. Oh my God, what's happening to my body?

"I think so," Jim says. "I think that would be a great idea."

Tim presses his thumb, makes a firm smudge, and all of a sudden I feel like I'm swallowing something delicious on the whole outside of myself, like I'm turned inside out. With my eyes still closed, I see a kaleidoscope of red and blue and purple light. I suck in air and gasp just a little. My eyes snap open.

Tim stops pressing and stroking, rests his hand on the inside of my thigh.

Jim turns around. "Hey there, sleepyhead," he says, smiling at me like a dad. "We're almost at your house."

"Okay," I say softly, and close my eyes again. Tim squeezes my leg. I squeeze the back of his neck. I melt into the car seat.

On Sunday morning, I can't believe Liz is gone and I have no one to talk with about what happened. After church, we go to the Golden Nugget for breakfast, and Mom says, "How was the party?"

"It was fine." I can't stop thinking about Tim and what happened in the car, and I wonder if he's thinking about it too. And I take a big bite of peanut butter pancakes, hoping that Mom's yoga training doesn't involve reading minds.

That night, Becky calls me and says Tim called Jim

and asked for my phone number. She's very excited. "He's totally into you."

I wish I were already working at Brighton Brothers, because I check my phone several times every hour on Monday and Tuesday. I wish for Liz again. And no one calls but Becky asking if Tim called. I tell her he hasn't.

On Tuesday night, sitting on the front porch and listening to crickets, I start to worry that I might have done something wrong. I'm not actually sure what I've done, which is another reason I wish Liz was around for consultation. I know it wasn't sex, exactly, but I'm pretty sure this falls under that heavy-petting category we were warned against in St. Camillus sex ed.

But what I also know is that I never felt anything like that before, that it felt good, and that I'm warm now just thinking about it.

On Wednesday, Mom says she's going out with some people from her yoga class, so not to be worried if she's home late. "Will you be all right?"

"Mom." I use my end-of-the-conversation voice with her and think it sounds quite convincing.

"Fine," she says, and I notice her unusually shiny lips.

"Are you wearing lipstick to yoga?"

"A woman needs to be prepared at all times."

"For what?" Now I'm curious.

"Life," Mom says, and this time *she* ends the conversation, kisses my cheek, wipes away the lipstick mark she has probably left, and heads out.

An hour later I'm eating popcorn in my bedroom when my phone rings. I forget to breathe again for a minute when I realize it's Tim, who asks if I can go out on Saturday with him to a party on campus.

I start to say yes, but then I remember the Players Lock-In. "I can't." I also can't imagine how to tell him about the Players, although he may just say, *Theater is art*. Still. In search of fresh air, I wander out to the garage and through the side door outside. Pink-and-orange brushstrokes stripe across the darkening sky, and the sun has almost disappeared for the day. "I have something with my family. Could we hang out on Sunday?" I ask, hoping I don't sound as anxious to see him as I feel.

"Why don't you call me on Sunday and we'll make some plans."

"Okay."

"You know," he says, his voice like syrup, "I've been thinking about you. And our ride home from the party."

"Have you?"

"I had a really good time."

"Me too."

When I get off the phone, the pink and orange have faded into a blue-gray. Inside, I close the garage door and notice size eleven work shoes in the same spot they've been for four years, next to the shovels and Mom's gardening gloves. They sit side by side, laces undone and empty. What would Dad think of Tim? What would Dad think of me?

I go into the bathroom and splash my face with cold water. I feel the drops run down my forehead and cheeks.

On Saturday night, Father Bill twists shut the two locks on the gym door, slides in the bolt above them, turns around and grins at us. "Well," he says, "six o'clock Eastern Standard. We're locked in right on time." Like Pontius Pilate, he mimics washing his hands.

Father Bill says we're going to need positive attitudes all around, but I find it hard to locate mine. Our very first activity is to act like trees.

Something knots and double knots in my stomach. I've graduated from high school. I'm not going to a normal college like everyone else. And right now I could be on my first real date with a college guy. Instead I'm with Father Bill, who is asking us to find our centers, our bubbling hot lava cores, and to let our elms or magnolias grow from there.

Five hours, six cups of punch, and eight improv games later, Father Bill has suggested we get some sleep, get an early start in the morning. Everyone stretches out in sleeping bags, girls on one side of the gym and boys on the other, both areas designated with markered signs and masking tape. I am drifting in and out of sleep to the hum of the water fountain motor when I feel a nudge and hear "Psst."

I look up and see a shadowy Linda, dimly lit by the red exit lights at both ends of the gym. She's waving a bottle above me. I squint. "Is that alcohol?" I ask.

"You betcha. Jackie D," she whispers, and swings the bottle. On our side of the gym, Keenie's air mattress is vacant, and Leaf's sleeping bag sprawls empty, too.

On the boys' side, Dr. Roger, Richie, and Father Bill lie still, sacked out in their sleeping bags. I slip on my sneakers and follow Linda on tiptoes through the side gym door, propped open with a brick. At the bottom of a short flight of steps, Keenie and Leaf are sitting on two big rocks at the edge of the parking lot. Above them, the headless Saint Camillus stands on his big marble dice.

The June night air feels cool on my neck, and a full moon washes the concrete lot into a bumpy ocean. Leaf smiles at me. "Isn't it fun to be up so late?" she asks.

"I guess." I'm sure Tim is still awake, telling some other girl how beautiful she is.

"Just us girls." Keenie grins at me and pulls her cardigan around her.

Linda hands me the bottle and sits on the bottom step, next to the rocks where Leaf and Keenie sit. I hesitate. This feels like high school, but not high school at all. I consider going back to bed.

"Drink up and be somebody," Linda says.

Going back to the gym with "the boys" seems less appealing, so I take a small swig and hold out the bottle to her.

As I sit on the concrete and lean against the gym wall and a line of ivy, Richie peeks his head out of the door above us. "I hope you gals weren't going to leave me out."

"Of course not." Linda pats the step next to her.

Richie climbs down the steps and sits, taking the bottle from Linda. He drinks and splashes some whiskey on his mustache. A drop dangles from the right edge of it. "Gosh that makes me loose," Richie says. "I think I'm a little drunk."

"Let's tell secrets," Keenie suggests.

"I have one," Leaf says. "I never wanted to be a nurse."

"Saint Camillus is the patron saint of nurses and gamblers," Richie adds.

"I didn't know that." Leaf pats Richie's knee. "Well, I'm not a nurse anymore anyway. After *he* left, I went moping into the hospital in Altoona every day. Until this other nurse I couldn't stand at work—you know what she said to me?"

Linda shakes her head. "I sure don't."

"'No one's forcing you to be here,'" Leaf says. "That's what she said."

"What does that mean?" I ask.

"It means that I'm in charge. No one's forcing me to

do anything. If I want to be somewhere different, I've got to take myself there." The purr of a car engine whooshes by, over the hill. "Anyway," Leaf says, "I'm happy where I am right now."

"But you're alone." I hug my knees to my chest. I know what it's like to be left.

She looks from Linda to Keenie to Richie to me. "No I'm not." She stands up and brings me the bottle.

I hold the bottle by its neck, wrapping my fingers around the cool glass. The moonlight makes the whiskey glow like a topaz. "Thanks," I say.

She nods and smiles. I notice her smooth complexion and how graceful she looks leaning back against the rock, content and warm in the moonshine.

Saint Camillus de Lellis, 64

Cause of Death: Natural

Surviving Immediate Family: None

Physical Characteristics: Reported to be 6'6", suffered throughout life from a leg wound and long-term abscesses on his feet.

Entombment: Remains located in the altar of the Church of Mary Magdalene, Rome.

Deathbed Words to Carmelite General: "I beseech you on my knees to pray for me, for I have been a great sinner, a gambler, and a man of bad life."

"We want to assist the sick with the same love that a mother has for her only sick child." —Saint Camillus de Lellis (while he was alive)

Post-death Incidents: Canonized 132 years after death

Formed the Brothers of the Happy Death to support plague victims.

Was said to possess the gifts of healing and prophecy.

eleven

When I get home on Sunday, I'm exhausted, but the thought of Tim makes my heart start beating fast and I don't feel so sleepy anymore.

Mom is sitting in lotus position on the living room floor, listening to some kind of flute music. She smiles and opens her eyes when she hears me come in. "So, are you officially bonded?"

I nod and smile, remembering all of us dancing around in the parking lot in the middle of the night.

"Linnie's out, so it's just you and me for dinner tonight. She has a new *friend*. His name is Snooter."

I sink onto the couch. "What, is he a chimpanzee or something?"

Mom almost snorts when she laughs. "More aardvark, actually."

"I can see that."

"You should think about getting yourself an aardvark, Donna."

I cross my arms. "Maybe I already have one. Did you ever consider that?"

"Don't get defensive. I didn't mean to insult you."

"Maybe you did."

"How would I know if you had a boyfriend? With Liz out of town, I don't know if you're even talking to anyone."

"Do you think I'm a total loser? I don't need a stupid Communications degree to talk to people. I do just fine." I jump up. "Maybe I just don't want to communicate with *you*."

I walk off to the basement and slam the door at the top of the steps.

In my room, I tell myself to calm down, and lie on my bed for a minute. I close my eyes. I imagine Tim's lips against mine and his hand soft between my legs. When I call him, he doesn't answer, so I leave a message.

At dinner, the silence feels as thick as the mashed potatoes I scoop onto my plate. I press into the center of the scoop with the back of my spoon.

As I fill my mashed-potato cavern with thick brown gravy, I say, "I'm starting work tomorrow. At Brighton Brothers."

Mom stands up and turns on the TV, which I know she hates during dinner.

We both turn our heads away from each other and toward the television as the weatherman reports another sunny day tomorrow.

On Monday morning, for my first day of work, I wear all black—skirt, blouse, shoes with little heels on them. When he sees me, Mr. Brighton smirks. "By the way, you are allowed to wear other colors. Nothing too flashy, but there's not a uniform."

"Oh," I say.

"Don't worry, Donna, you look just fine. Come with me." As we head down the hallway, Mr. Brighton tells me that JB is off for his summer hiking in Colorado and should be back later this month. "He says he needs the mountains or he couldn't keep doing this." Mr. Brighton shrugs. "Whatever it takes for each of us."

At the end of the hallway, Mr. Brighton has set up an office space for me, right by the back door, where he says deliveries are made. A pile of binders sits on a long desk, and next to them, a few supply catalogs and a little cactus plant with an orange bow on it. "Some reading material," he says. "And a welcome gift from Mrs. B." He sits down in a folding chair next to the desk.

I smile and delicately touch one of the spiky spines on the short fat plant. "Tell her thanks."

"You can tell me yourself." I turn and see a short lady with shoulder-length silver hair and wide hips. I also notice that she must wear at least a D-cup in bra size, which suddenly makes me feel a little prepubescent with my A's. I make sure to look at her face and say, "Thank you, Mrs. Brighton."

"You're welcome, and please, Greta or Mrs. B. We're so glad to have you. Bob hasn't been able to stop talking about it."

"Okay, Mrs. B. I'm glad to be here."

"You've got a full day, so I'll let you two get down to business. But make sure to come upstairs for lunch. I've got chicken salad." Mrs. B. squeezes my hand and pats my cheek and walks off.

"Thanks, honey," Mr. Brighton calls after her. "She puts raisins and walnuts in it. It's out of this world." He also tells me there's a wake this afternoon and that I can help to greet people and point them in the right direction.

I'm glad he has faith in me, and I'm nervous, too. I sit down in the cushioned chair behind the desk and find it reclines back a little.

The wake is for Mitzi Baumgartner, who died at the age of ninety-three, watching her favorite soap opera and holding a whiskey sour in her hand. "This is the easy kind," Mr. Brighton says. "It's a good one for you to start with. Mitzi lived a full, long life. It's much harder for the family when someone dies too soon, like they didn't get to finish everything."

I flinch.

"It was like that for you?"

I nod.

"Some people say everything happens for a reason; people die because God wants them to die or bring them home."

I remember hearing that. And hating it.

"You want to know what I think?" Mr. Brighton pushes the binders out of the way and leans his elbow on the desk. "That's a load of horseshit. People die when they die and not because God wants to take someone's dad away from them. There's not a reason. It just happens." He sighs. "But I don't say that to families."

"Why not?"

"Most people don't want to hear that."

"I would've wanted to hear that."

"Well, most people also don't want to work here."

I glance down at the coffin catalog I'm excited to page through. "I see your point."

"Anyway, usually best not to say anything, to be polite and kind and respectful, and let people be how they are. Family and friends arrive at two."

At 1:50, I'm standing in the front lobby, feeling nervous and unsure that I can keep down my chicken salad, even though it was, in fact, out of this world. But something happens when the first group of people comes in. I feel my

156

feet firmly on the ground, and I nod at the three elderly women who come through the door. I hear my voice gentle and calm, directing them down the hallway to the second door on the right. It turns out I do just fine being polite and kind and respectful, all afternoon long.

On my way out that evening, Mr. Brighton shakes my hand. "Baptism by fire. You did good." I remember how lost I felt when Dad died, and I saw how lost some of Mitzi's children and grandchildren looked. Greeting them with kindness and showing them which way to go, even just down the hall, made me feel useful and needed. I realize that I did do good; that, strange as it seems, I sense that I belong here.

At home, I have a postcard waiting for me on the kitchen table. On the front are the greenest hills I could imagine. On the back, Liz has written, *I know people write it all the time, but I really wish you were here. Can't wait to see you—I'll be home the first week in July.*

When I take my phone out of the black purse I borrowed from Mom, I have a message from Tim, who wants to go to a movie on Friday night.

Mitzi Baumgartner, 93

Cause of Death: Brain aneurism

Surviving Immediate Family:
• Sons: Phillip and Karl

Makeup: Champagne Ice cream cosmetic, You're a Peach lipstick and nail polish

Clothing: Mitzi's favorite gingham line-dancing dress

Casket: Stainless steel, pastel green silk lining

Special Guests in Attendance: The Old North Dayton Senior Swingers Line Dancing Squad, and Mitzi's Tuesday night poker posse

Funeral Incidents:
• Karl and Phillip bring trays of shot glasses full of Old Granddad around to all the visitors and lead a rousing round of "For She's a Jolly Good Fellow."
• Four empty bottles of whiskey end up in the Brighton Brothers recycling bin.

twelve

Come Friday night, since Mom has decided to sit on the front porch to read, I can't avoid telling her I'm going on a date. At first she's all giddy and says she can go read inside, but when she finds out Tim's in college, she insists on meeting him.

When Tim arrives, and the three of us sit on the front porch together, I feel like I might pass out. The grounded feeling I discovered all week long at Brighton Brothers seems to have crumbled away in some kind of inner seismic disruption.

Mom says, "So what are you two going to see?"

"There's a French film playing at the Neon."

"Oh, the one about the swimmer and the geologist. I saw it. The cinematography was breathtaking, and the dialogue was used so exquisitely—sparse but very powerful. Sit up close so you don't miss any of the subtitles." Mom never told me she went to see a movie, and the thought of her sitting through one not in English fits better in some alternate universe where ice cream is hot and gerbils are in charge of political parties. I didn't think Mom had been to the movies since last winter, when she and Linnie and I went to a cheesy romantic comedy with dialogue that unfortunately was neither sparse nor powerful.

"Tight. That's what I heard too." Tim nods. He's wearing jeans and a white T-shirt and some sort of embroidered vest. He looks very calm.

"Then what?" Mom asks.

"What do you mean?" Tim asks.

"Are you doing anything after the movie?"

"We'll play it like we play it, I guess." Tim grins.

Mom smiles too, but it's more of a tight-lipped, I-might-suffocate-you-with-that-throw-pillow kind of smile. "What does that mean?"

"It means we don't know yet," I say.

"Yeah," Tim says, laughing a little. "The night is young. And so are we."

"And young people need their rest," Mom says. "Bring her home right after the movie."

"Mom, I'm in the room."

"Bring yourself right home after the movie. And have fun."

* * *

In line for tickets at the Neon, I apologize about our conversation with Mom.

"No biggie," he says. "Moms will be moms." Then he kisses me on the cheek, close to my ear, and whispers, "And we don't have to listen to them."

In the theater, after Tim's picked us seats toward the back, about ten giggly older women in red hats and feather boas sit down behind us. All of a sudden it feels like a whole row of moms-gone-wild have come to chaperone us. I find myself sitting up straighter, although Tim doesn't seem to notice.

The movie consists of extended shots of rocks and swimming pools and people with very serious faces staring at rocks and swimming pools and each other. Watching the movie consists of my constantly moving Tim's hand out of the center of my lap and worrying that the red-hat ladies are watching. I'm trying to enjoy the warm feeling of Tim's hand on mine when he gives up reaching for anything else, but I feel distracted.

I'm guessing I have a serious face right now, too, attempting to figure out how Mom got through this awful movie unscathed.

Sitting in our driveway with the car windows rolled down, Tim inhales through his nose and closes his eyes. He smiles.

"What?"

"The air feels warm. Dry. Like the Mojave." He turns and looks at me. "It's quiet there, and romantic. Kind of like it is right now."

I watch Tim lean toward me, and I close my eyes as he kisses me. I kiss him back, and our lips feel soft against each other's. I wonder if he can tell that my mouth feels as dry as the Mojave, and try not to worry about it. I also wonder which window Mom is standing at. I'm sure she heard Tim's car pull up. He reaches under my T-shirt.

I grab his hand, put mine on top of it. "My mom is right inside."

"So?"

"So, she could come out." I wonder why messing around was so much easier in a car with two other people. Although, I guess it was three. I almost forgot the leprechaun. At this moment, I don't feel magical, relaxed, or particularly beautiful. I feel aggravated and excited and nervous.

Under my shirt, Tim inches his hand up farther, and I let him. With his other hand, he squeezes my thigh, very gently. "So do you want me to stop?" He whispers into my ear and licks it. "Should I stop?"

"Yes."

I think he's surprised, and actually I am too. My tingling body does not want him to stop, but my mind does, and as per usual, I can't access my heart for a reliable opinion. I look down at my feet and the coffee-stained Styrofoam cup peeking out from under the seat, and I think of Charlie and his stainless-steel mug. From the cup and the empty plastic soda bottles next to me, I see that Tim does not follow the one-container rule.

Now outside of my T-shirt, both of Tim's hands rest on his jeans. I notice they look strong and smooth. And tan, like Dad's. I think of the handmade paper in Liz's basement. Maybe the universe did deliver him to me. I reach over and touch one of his hands. "Next time, maybe we can go somewhere else."

"Sure," he says, but he's looking past me out the window at something in the darkness.

When I got out of the car, Tim said he'd call me on Saturday, but now it's Sunday, and I still haven't heard from him. I'm not sure if I should call him, but I want to.

Linnie spends all day out with Snooter, and when they come home, I'm sitting on the porch paging through Mom's gardening magazine and daydreaming about Tim and his lips. Mom hears Snooter's car and comes to the door holding one of her new yoga books. This is the first time I've been around when Linnie brings Snooter into the house, and from the looks of what's approaching, this is going to be an exciting encounter.

Linnie's long hair hangs in green-and-black stripes—a little painful on the eyes right next to Snooter's bright red spikes. It's like Christmas and Death had babies. The screen door bangs behind them.

"You can't make me fix it. We did each other's." Linnie stands with her arms at her sides, feet planted firmly in her combat boots.

Mom holds the yoga book to her chest and looks closely at Linnie's head. I can tell she's doing one of her breathing exercises. She steps back, nods, and looks at Snooter. "The green looks good. Vivid. Emerald tones."

"Excellent," Snooter says. "Thanks. I appreciate the feedback."

Linnie looks like she's not sure if she should smile or not, and I understand because I don't know either. There are lots of reactions I could have predicted from Mom, but complimenting the shade of hair was not one of them.

Snooter turns to me. "Hey, you must be the big D."

"Or Donna is fine."

"Right on." Snooter's eyelids are droopy, like he's a little sleepy, but a happy kind of sleepy, like some sort of Seven Dwarfs blend. "You've got some cool chicks in your fam, Lin."

"While you have this hair," Mom says to Linnie, "I'd like you to wear a hat to church. We can go out and you can choose one." Mom's voice is very calm.

Linnie squints at Mom and then nods, with a little hint of a smile. "Okay."

When Linnie and Snooter go inside, Mom looks at me, and both of us crack up at the same time.

"That is a look," Mom whispers, giggling. "How did I do? I'm working on peaceful responses."

I'm surprised Mom wants to know what I think, but I like it. And I can tell she is working on something. "Then I'd say you did fine."

"Thanks." She wipes her eyes and sits down across from me. "So, have you heard from Tim?"

I shake my head.

"You can do better anyway."

"You think he's not going to call." My voice is sharp. I am not, apparently, working on peaceful responses. "He's going to call."

"I didn't say he wasn't."

"You didn't have to say it." I don't know if I'm mad at Tim for not calling, or Mom for deciding that's okay, or me for caring at all. For caring that he might think I'm some kind of prude, that I might have ruined my shot to have a cute college boyfriend or any boyfriend at all.

Mom inhales and exhales and pats my leg. Then she stands up and goes inside.

A few hours later, right before dinner, Tim does call, and it turns out he's right outside. "Let's go," he says. "We need ice cream."

I go out to the kitchen, where Mom's baking potatoes and steaming broccoli. "Tim's here," I say. "I'm going to skip dinner."

Before she can answer, I run out the front door.

Sitting in the front seat of Tim's car, I feel like I just sprang myself from jail, and I giggle.

"What's so funny?" Tim says.

"Everything," I shout.

Tim laughs with me and drives us to Young's Dairy, out in Yellow Springs, where it smells like farm. Once, Dad took Linnie and me here to pet the goats. Linnie was terrified and wouldn't go near the mama goat. I was terrified too, but I did it anyway. As I touched the goat's coarse coat and felt her shaking, I realized she could commiserate. I felt so proud of myself when Dad smiled at me and said, "That's my girl."

This time goats aren't on the agenda. Tim and I sit at the benches outside Young's, eating double-scoop cones of the best homemade ice cream in the Dayton area.

One scoop in, Tim gets a call on his cell phone. "I've got to take this."

"Okay," I say, but he's already started to walk away.

Sitting alone on the bench, I tune in to the sounds around me—goats bleating, leaves rustling in the breeze, a woman's laugh that sounds a lot like a cackle, and a very familiar voice. "You come here often?"

I turn and see Charlie holding his own cone and sporting a significant chocolate mustache. I smile at him and all of the sudden wonder if there's something on my face, and how I look. I sit up and straighten my skirt. "Sometimes. You?"

"I'm here with my mom and dad. We're heading up the road to buy corn from some guy they met, and I convinced them we needed ice cream before corn."

"Two great tastes that go great together."

Charlie laughs. He reaches over and touches the scalloped sleeve of my shirt. "I like this."

Where his fingers brush my shoulder, my skin feels like it's about two hundred degrees. "Thanks."

"Sure." He licks his ice cream, and I'm glad I'm already sitting down, because I'm feeling a little unstable in the knee joints.

Then behind Charlie, I see Tim heading toward us.

"I've got to go," I say.

"Hello, sudden."

"I'm, um, here on a date," I blurt, and wish I hadn't. I make myself stand up.

"Oh." His eyes change, but I can't pinpoint how. "Well, have fun."

I smile a little and walk fast to Tim. Tim didn't seem to care that I was talking with Charlie, because he doesn't say anything but "Ready to go?"

I also try not to care that I was talking with Charlie as Tim and I head back into downtown Yellow Springs, with its cute little bookstores and Full of Beans Coffee House and shops with big iron dragons and purple cloths draped in window boxes.

Right past 3-D Comics, Tim takes me into this combination thrift/consignment/antique store. We split up and wander around through packed displays of scarves and knickknacks and books and old pictures. While I'm gawking at a whole set of wineglasses of the saints—each glass with a picture of a saint and a little history—I feel someone stand close behind me and a hand go over my eyes.

"I hit the mother lode," Tim says. "Keep your eyes closed, and turn around." When I do, he takes my hands and puts something that feels squarish into them. "Okay, take a look."

I look down and see an ornate cherrywood box with a little cross on top and the letters RIP engraved in gold.

"Open it," he says.

Inside the box is a stack of black-and-white photographs of people, maybe from the early 1900s, all dressed up, and dead, in their coffins.

"What is this?"

Tim explains that he learned in his photography class that people used to take pictures of their dead family members, like a last shot for the photo album. He shows me the backs of the pictures, and the faint handwritten names of each person. They all share the same last name. "Black-and-white photos—your favorite, right? Do you like them?"

I gingerly touch the old pictures, looking at the close-up

shot of some woman in pearls who was probably some-one's grandma. "They are totally creepy," I say. "And I love them."

"Good," Tim says. "I'm getting them for you."

Later that night, I fix myself a plate of cold chicken from the fridge and walk down the stairs to the basement smil-ing, still feeling giggly from my spontaneous date, and try-ing not to worry that I'm thinking about Tim and Charlie both.

I find Mom sitting at my desk, holding my box from Tim in one hand and the pictures in the other. She's frowning. "Donna?"

I explain the pictures to her just how Tim explained to me, but that doesn't make her any happier. "Honey," she says, "we need to talk. Now."

I look down at the chicken, which doesn't seem so appe-tizing anymore. "There's nothing wrong with me." I point to the gift from Tim. "Those are beautiful. They're art."

"I'm not saying there's anything wrong with you." She looks at the pictures, puts them back into the box, and shakes her head. "You've gotten so far out, I don't know where you are anymore. I don't know how I let this happen."

"Let what happen?"

She sets the box on the desk and looks up into my eyes. "Since your Dad died, it's like you've disappeared."

My legs feel shaky underneath me, like they might just decide to stop holding me up. "I don't know what you're talking about."

"Honey, it's time for you to let your life be normal and happy. To be part of our family." Mom stands and walks to me. She puts her hands on my shoulders and holds them tight. "I need you here with us. In the land of the living."

I try to wriggle out of her grasp, but I can't. I feel helpless, holding a plate of chicken and listening to the pain in Mom's voice, watching her eyes, desperate and full, right in front of me.

"It's not too late for you to go to UD."

"Yes," I say, feeling my hands tremble, like I could drop the plate at any second, "it is." I close my eyes, willing myself to disappear, like Mom thinks I already have.

I feel her hands let go of my shoulders. I feel where her fingers were pressed into my skin.

When I open my eyes, she's still standing there, staring at me. "I don't know what to do, Donna. What do I do?"

I stare back at her. "Leave me alone," I say, and then louder, "Leave me alone," until I'm yelling it and until she does and I'm standing by myself with a plate of chicken I can't even think about eating and a box full of dead people I don't know.

On Monday and Tuesday and Wednesday, it's a relief to escape to Brighton Brothers for work. Home feels like a library, but significantly more hostile and with a lot fewer books. Mom and I say nothing to each other, and when I'm at home, I stay in my room as much as I can.

On Wednesday night, when Tim's name pops up in the window of my phone, I answer quickly, eager and hopeful for another adventure with him, away from here.

"You'll never believe where I am," he says.

"The Mojave Desert?" I hope he thinks I'm as funny as I do.

"Yeah, how'd you guess?" Tim sounds more surprised than playful.

"You talk about it all the time," I start to explain. "Wait a minute, are you really in the Mojave Desert?"

"Totally."

"Are you coming back?"

"Yeah." Tim sounds far away, and I guess, literally, he is.

"Do you know when?" I hope he doesn't notice that my voice is shaking.

"When it's time. And who knows? Donna, the desert is a fickle mistress."

I have no idea what that means, and I'm pretty sure that Tim doesn't either. Actual pieces of information I discover are as follows: He must again find the most beautiful flower; the desert is hotter than he remembers, and so is his old friend Tina, who hopped into the car at the last minute. Tim tells me I should seize the moment while he's gone. I wonder if that's because he's found someone else he wants to seize.

I feel confused and abandoned. I take out the orange candle Liz gave me and set it on a dish on my desk. When I light it, I smell the olive oil and realize my fingers have oil on them too. I rub the oil into my hands and watch the flame dance and jump like it's reaching for something it can't quite grasp.

The next day, Mr. Brighton asks if I'd like to sit in during an arrangement conference. I agree, if he thinks it's okay. He tells me that the same rules apply as when greeting the family and friends during the wake: Be polite, kind, respectful. And let him do the talking.

Two sisters, Mrs. Jane LaRue and Mrs. Carla Banniker, will come in for the conference, to set up the wake and services for their father, Jake Dixon, who was eighty-seven. His body is being embalmed in Florida and then sent up here, where he lived most of his life. Mr. Brighton knows the sisters; he did the services for their mother two years ago. They came in with Jake for the arrangements then. After that, Jake moved south.

Later that morning, Mr. Brighton and I walk Mrs. LaRue and Mrs. Banniker into his office. I guess they are in their sixties. Mrs. Banniker is plump and short like Mrs. B, and Mrs. LaRue is short and rail-thin, but from the basic shapes of their faces and the sound of their voices, it's clear they're sisters.

Mr. Brighton introduces me as his assistant, Ms. Parisi. I nod and smile, just a little, as we sit down at a round table in the corner of the office.

"Oh, God, Janie," Mrs. Banniker says, staring at me. "She looks just like those pictures of Mom when she was young." She starts to cry. "Both of them now. It's just us."

"I know, honey," Mrs. LaRue says, and smiles at me. "Our mother was a beautiful woman. This is a compliment."

I want to ask if Jake ever left their mother to go to the Mojave Desert on the spur of the moment, but I figure that doesn't fall under the category of polite. So instead I say, "Thank you."

"Bob, do you still have Mom's paperwork? Because we'd like the same arrangements, if that's possible. They were two peas in a pod."

Mr. Brighton nods and pulls out a folder from his binder.

Mrs. Banniker starts to cry again, and says, "I'm sorry," between sobs. "He was our daddy."

Mr. Brighton slides a box of tissues toward her.

"You don't have to apologize," I say. In her plump adult face, I see the shadows of a young girl, and I put my hand on her arm. "It just hurts." I'm surprised at how easily the words come and that they're just right, that I know exactly how to touch her arm and not say anything else.

Mrs. Banniker's breathing gets easier. She wipes her eyes and blows her nose.

At the door on the way out, Mrs. Banniker shakes Mr. Brighton's hand and then mine. "Thank you both. So much."

Through the front window, Mr. Brighton and I watch them drive away. "You've got a knack, assistant."

I let myself smile just a little, sensing that I brought at least a little comfort to Jake Dixon's daughters. I've finally found something that fits me, something I'm good at. It's strange but true. I know my way around a funeral. I'm a natural.

Friday is the Fourth of July, and I'm off work. Late that afternoon, I tell Mom it's been a long week at the funeral home and maybe I'll meet her later at the barbecue B is having at his new apartment, which will eventually be B and Gwen's apartment. I lie and say I might bring Tim after we go to another party that night. Mom says, "Donna, please be careful."

I want to tell her that I am actually several states and a whole desert away from danger, but instead I nod.

Mom stares at me as if she'd like to say other things, but I force myself not to look at her, and I will her not to say anything. My willpower takes a minute to work, but finally Mom picks up the bowl of potato salad she's made and walks away.

As I cozy up in front of the TV, my phone rings, and it's Liz. I've never been so excited to hear from anyone in my life.

She just got home after an eight-hour plane trip and sounds like she's ready to run a marathon. "I've got a plan for us—a Celtic Adventure," she says. "I just need a couple of weeks to get ready."

"And maybe unpack?" I laugh, and so does she.

She won't tell me any more details about our adventure. I want to tell her about Mom, but what would I say? My Mom thinks I'm some kind of crazy person and doesn't understand the one thing I've found that brings me satisfaction? I don't want to say that out loud, and I'm not sure I could without crying my eyes out. So I unleash other floodgates and tell her about Tim, about working at Brighton Brothers. About Tim skipping town.

"Wow, D, a college guy? When he gets back, I need to meet him."

For a second I get nervous about that thought. While Liz was gone, I started to feel like I might be a little beautiful myself. But what if Tim likes Liz better? It's not hard to imagine, because it's not hard to imagine Liz up and driving to the Mojave. "Yeah, I'm sure we can set something up."

The next day, Liz picks me up and we go to the new Italian restaurant in the Oregon District. Liz orders us a tomato, basil, and mozzarella salad, with the olive oil drizzled on top and the kind of wet mozzarella they have at the Italian grocery. The food tastes better than any food I've eaten in the last month, and my iced tea seems sweeter and colder than anything I've drunk.

I just feel giddy to have my friend back, and also a little nervous because she seems to have gotten even cooler while she was away. She wears her hair in a low ponytail, and she has on a white tank top and a short jeans skirt. Of course Liz makes something so simple look elegant, but it's her new bracelet I can't stop looking at. All the way down her forearm, a silver snake coils, its head jutting out just over her wrist.

"I bought her at a country fair," Liz says, and pets the snake. "Her name is Sassy." Liz holds out the *S* sounds and giggles.

"She's beautiful." I look down at the tiny silver turtle on my index finger and think that snake could make short work of this critter.

"Well, I'm glad you like her," Liz says, "because I got something at the fair for you too."

From her purple bag she pulls out a big square brown box, tied with a white string. Inside the box is a huge silver turtle necklace, and this turtle is about three times the size of the snake head on Liz's wrist. "I thought it would go with your ring," she says. "It can be your power amulet. The lady who made her says she has Mother Earth medicine."

I pull the turtle out, and it almost fills the palm of my hand. She looks powerful, and I remember the sea turtle from the aquarium. "She needs a name, too."

"Terra," Liz says. "Not like Tara, but T-E-R-R-A, like the earth."

"Terra," I repeat, and slip the chain over my head. Terra rests right between my breasts and looks up at me with big silver eyes. "What medicine does your snake have?"

"Transformation. I can keep changing into whatever I want."

Of course Liz just keeps shedding her skin and becoming something more beautiful each time. I look down at Terra. And me? I just stay close to the dirt and keep moving along. Slowly, slowly, slowly.

Jake Dixon, 87

Cause of Death: Stroke

Surviving Immediate Family:
• Daughters: Jane LaRue and Carla Banniker

Clothing: Jake's tuxedo from his wedding, being shipped with the body from Tampa

Casket: Oak with blue satin lining and yellow crocheted pillowcase made by Jake's late wife

Funeral Plans:
• Open-casket viewing followed by cremation
• Prayer service led by interdenominational minister
• Jane and Carla to keep remains in ivory ceramic urn identical to their mother's; Carla will take Mom, and Jane will take Dad; in a year's time, they will trade.

thirteen

Two weeks later, it's time for our Celtic Adventure. In the dark woods, I follow Liz, white T-shirt flashing against shadowy clusters of oak and maple trees. "So this is where the magic happens," I say in a seedy car-salesman kind of way.

I'm trying to make myself feel better and less freaked out about being in the forest close to midnight on a Saturday. And I remind myself how good it is to have Liz back home.

"No," Liz says. "Yes, of course, magic is everywhere. But no. Come on." She keeps walking.

As my tennis shoes crackle over pine needles and twigs, a cool breeze tickles my ears. I wish I'd worn a sweatshirt. It was hot and muggy all day in Dayton, but now just forty minutes away, out in John Bryan State Park, the tree cover and the streams make for some cooler weather. My skin tingles, and my ears attune to each insect click and each flap of restless bird wings. Everything around me pulses, alive.

Liz stops in a clearing circled by tall fir trees, moonlight casting long pine shadows. She takes off her long sundress, just like that, and underneath, she isn't wearing anything but mules and socks with lightning bolts on them.

"Dude," I say. "Um, you're naked."

She kicks off the mules and pulls off her socks. "Sky-clad," she says, as though I should know exactly what that means; as though I should keep up. In that way that makes it hard to disagree. But now she's naked, so it's more complicated.

Liz stretches out her arms, palms up, closes her eyes, and tilts back her head. Her hair falls in beautiful curls, shiny like liquid pennies in the moonlight, all the way down her back. Her body is thin and white. She breathes deeply.

I realize I've stopped breathing. "I think I'm ready to go."

Without moving, she says, "Shut up and take off your jeans."

"But I'm cold already."

Liz lowers her head and arms. She points at me with her index finger. I try not to notice, but her nipples are also pointing at me. "Don't you want to live? Don't you want to know yourself? You're not having any life experiences."

For Liz, that's not the case. On her trip, she wrote an article called "Ireland for the Young Adventurer." She visited castles and pubs and the coast and little towns and farms. Young adventurer, that's her.

As for me, the only guy I've ever dated has escaped to the Mojave Desert, and I'm getting ready to head into another week at Brighton Brothers' Funeral Home, a mere ten minute drive from the house where I live, where I've lived all eighteen years of my life—attempting to convince myself that I don't need to leave Dayton to have a life, that mortuary college makes sense for me. That it's practical to go to Chapman and start working at Brighton Brothers. The thought makes me feel safe. And boring. Liz is right: safe isn't life experience, I think, looking at my naked friend in the moonlight.

"Fine." I slowly take off my long-sleeved shirt and jeans. But I leave on my bra and panties and socks. I don't even know myself that well. "Sorry. PG-13 is as much as I can live right now."

"Good enough," she says.

I'm wearing Terra; I figured tonight would be a good night for a power amulet. She's cool against my skin. I take my hair out of its ponytail and wish it went past my shoulders, like Liz's. At least I'm not as white as Liz; my skin is still darker even where the sun—or moon—doesn't usually shine. I ask, "So what's next?" My heart starts to beat faster. This is different than lighting candles in Liz's basement with her mom upstairs. I'm pretty sure I don't want to do a ritual.

Liz clears her throat. "I have a confession."

"What is it?" I cross my arms over my chest, tuck my hands into my armpits for warmth.

"I don't actually know..." she says, glancing at me like a guilty four-year-old, "what I'm doing."

"Holy shit." I'm irritated and relieved at the same time.

"I mean, I know I want to experience a Wiccan ritual." She walks to one of the fir trees at the edge of the clearing, runs her fingertips over the bark.

"Don't you need Witches for that?"

She presses her palm into the trunk of the tree. "Yes," she says, "you do."

Now I know what's coming. A breeze snakes over my shoulders and makes me shiver. "Liz."

"I'm just saying that one of us here knows a Witch."

I shift my weight from foot to foot. "You didn't meet any Witches in Ireland."

"Nope. But I tried. I met a juggler and someone who swallows fire. Just no Witches."

"Didn't you read that book? You must be practically an expert now."

"I know a little."

"Good," I say. "Like what?"

Liz leans her back against the tree. That has to be scratchy. "Well, everything you do comes back to you in threes, and, um, you're not supposed to manipulate anyone."

"Right." I drop my arms, exposing my almost naked self to Liz. "So what are you doing right now?"

"Kind of manipulating you, I guess."

"I am happy for you to learn anything, but not for you to take me into the woods and get me naked for no good reason."

"But I do have a good reason. And she's just a phone call away." Liz steps away from the tree. "Besides, aren't you having fun?" She spins with her arms stretched out, giggling.

"Honestly?"

She stops spinning and nods. "Yes."

"No." I cross my arms and press them against my chest. "This is officially no fun."

Now in the clearing, she looks a little sad, and Liz without steam depresses me. Despite the red alerts from my brain, a wave of compassion pushes me to speak. "Maybe we could use a little guidance."

"Do you mean it?"

"She's not Celtic, you know," I offer. But I've already opened Pandora's Box, and I'm going to have to call my aunt, whom I haven't seen in four years.

"Oh, wow," Liz says. "I could, I mean, *we* could learn a lot from her."

I pull on my jeans and do up the belt. I'm not that much bigger than Liz, but I'm tired of comparing our naked legs. And July or not, I'm cold. "I'm not sure she'll even want to talk to me."

"It's not like you two ever had a fight." Liz stretches her arms out again. "And Witches are supposed to be open, right?"

"I don't know."

"You'll really call her?"

"On Monday. I promise."

"Whoopee!" Liz yells, and wraps her arms around me for a hug.

"Whoopee." I tentatively pat her bare back with my hands. "Now, please, put on your dress."

On Monday morning at seven thirty, Mom pours boiling water into her favorite floral teapot. She's in her long blue housecoat, and she has morning-Mom hair—half frizzed out, half pillow smashed.

"Good morning," she says, and these words, like any we've exchanged in the last month, rest like land mines between us. So if one of us steps just slightly forward or back, we could set off a horrible explosion. "Are you hungry?"

"Not even close." I sit down at the kitchen table and rub my eyes. I haven't wanted to ask all weekend, and I still don't, but I remember Liz's whoopee face. And things feel so rotten with Mom, I doubt they could get any worse. "I need Aunt Selena's phone number."

Mom sets the kettle on the stove. She puts the tea bag tin back in the cupboard.

"Did you hear me?"

"What for?"

"Well, usually I like people to hear me when I talk to them."

"You know what I mean. Why do you want her number?"

"I have a question for her."

"You can ask me." She takes down the bright red mug Linnie made in ceramics. "I probably know your dad's family better than she does."

"It's not about Dad's family." I go to the fridge and push the English muffins out of the way to get the orange juice. Bent over behind the door, I say, "It's Witch stuff."

"Oh." Mom leans against the counter and looks at me. I notice her eyes are puffy and tired. "I'm sorry, honey, but no. I just don't feel comfortable."

I pour myself a glass of juice. "Are you worried she's going to try and convert me?"

"Don't be flip, Donna Marie," she says. "You know I think Selena is involved in dangerous things."

"Mom, Witchcraft doesn't have anything to do with the devil," I say. "I learned it in my rituals class."

"So now you're an expert," Mom says. "And I don't want to talk about it anymore."

"Is that the peaceful response?"

"Maybe it's too early for the peaceful response." Mom pushes a piece of cinnamon bread into the toaster.

I push the conversation, probably also into some kind of toaster. "Yoga's not very Catholic either."

"Yoga has nothing to do with this."

"Everything has something to do with everything else." I realize this is true as I say it out loud.

Mom's blue eyes are icy. "I said I don't want to talk about this anymore."

And now I don't want to talk about it anymore either. "Thanks for nothing," I say. "I've got to get ready for work."

I stomp downstairs. I'm awake now, and angry. And I was wrong. Things could get worse, and in fact they just did. In my room I decide I don't need Mom's permission to call my own aunt, to call Dad's sister. As soon as I hear Mom get in the shower, I take a pen and paper and go to the big box in the closet where I know she keeps Dad's things.

When I open it, I smell him, and it almost takes my breath away. A bottle of his Woodsman cologne stands in the corner of the box, and the whole thing smells like Dad on Sundays. Underneath his favorite tie and a plastic bag with his wedding ring, I see his little black notebook, and beneath that, his address book. I take the address book and find Selena's name, in his writing, and copy the number down. Then I slip the lid back on the box and the box back in the closet. I hold the number next to my chest and close my eyes. "I know you understand," I whisper.

* * *

When I get to work, JB is back from the mountains and has a three-foot stack of back-filing and sorting ready for me.

"Great," I say.

He glances apologetically at the pile of paper. "I'm not so much the business in this business. In case you couldn't tell."

"I really don't mind. I could use some filing today."

"Thanks, kid," he says. "I'll come check in later. And I'll be down in the prep room if you need me. Little Sal Laterno was in a bar fight that didn't end so well for him or his face. So I've got my work cut out for me."

I am actually delighted to have the pile of papers and an excuse to avoid calling Aunt Selena. I touch the pocket of my khaki skirt, and the paper where I've copied down her number crinkles under the fabric, still there. Of course, now that I have the number, I find that I'm starting to feel nervous, and I wonder if it really is a good idea to get in touch with my aunt.

A few hours later, I think of calling Liz and telling her that I couldn't get the number. Or that Aunt Selena turned herself into something, like a hamster, and can't be reached. As I prepare for a deceptive phone call, I see a long box full of flowers come in through the back door—I'm assuming for the Laterno viewing tonight—and the box is followed by the hands holding it up, attached to a tall, sandy-haired guy with long earlobes. Matt Capinski.

He makes eye contact with me and tilts his head to the side. "What are you doing here?"

I straighten the now-one-foot stack of papers in front of me and hold on to the sides. "I work here."

"Why?" The way Matt's looking at me, it seems like he'd be perfectly content to stand there and harass me all day.

I try to stay calm, and look around for potential weapons on my desk in case I have to defend myself. All I've got is a ballpoint pen, a small cactus, and lots of ways to give him some really nasty paper cuts. "It's like an internship. I'm starting mortuary school in the fall."

"You work here?" he asks, in the same way one might say, *You really wanted that mayonnaise on your ice cream?*

Then I realize I've got another weapon. Flower power. "Well, what are you doing here, with gladiolas?"

"My mom runs Forever Flowers." He kind of mumbles this. "But I'm leaving for Michigan U next month to study something normal."

"Nothing's more normal than death." I shrug. "For instance, you'll die one day."

Matt doesn't seem so comfortable standing in front of me anymore. He sets down the box and pulls out a receipt. "Sign this."

When Matt leaves, I look at the purply-blue gladiolas and hope they don't look too much like the bruises on Sal's face. Then I look at my phone and think how to best phrase the lie to Liz. Just then my phone rings.

"Hey," Liz says. "Did you call her?"

I pull the paper out of my pocket. "No."

"You're still going to, right?"

"My mom thinks she's dangerous."

"Of course she does." Liz laughs. "She's probably saying a novena for you right now."

"Probably."

"Do you think she's dangerous?"

"No," I say, and realize I'm lying. Something inside me hesitates and is afraid, but I can't say that to Liz. "Actually, I was just about to call her. We've been busy this morning." I guess I'm on a one-lie limit. Shit.

"Nice," Liz says. "Let me know when you do."

After I hang up, I trace the phone number with a pen. I sit up straight and smooth out my skirt. I imagine it can only be my amazing personal power that compels me to pick up the phone and dial.

"Hello?" A soft, rich voice.

"Hi, Aunt Selena? This is Donna. Your niece."

"Donna? Well, hi. What a—oh, I'm so glad you called."

She sounds genuinely glad, and I relax a little. "I actually have a favor to ask."

Salvatore "Little Sal" Laterno III, 27

Cause of Death: Excessive blood loss and brain hemorrhage

Surviving Immediate Family:
• Grandfather: Salvatore "Big Papa" I
• Father: Salvatore II
• Sister: Marlene

Makeup: Nose reconstructed out of clay molding, feature builder injected to puff out and reshape crushed jaw, olive cream cosmetic

Clothing: Red silk shirt, gold cross given to Sal by Great-grandma Laterno

Casket: Walnut, white velvet lining

Special Guests in Attendance:
• Salvatore "Big Papa" Laterno's "assistants," in dark suits and sunglasses, stationed at all entrances to Brighton Brothers, three hours prior to the viewing to "make sure everything runs smoothly."

fourteen

That weekend, I get to Carillon Park early and walk past the pioneer house and the Wright brothers building, which houses a replica of the world's first airplane, and up to a patch of grass right under the Carillon, which has fifty-some bells in it. Across the way, the Little Miami River runs gray and shallow, like it could use some rain.

Liz is waiting for me, with a big yellow blanket spread out right under the bell tower, where the evening sun still feels warm. She hands me a brown grocery bag full of cheese, crackers, some sparkling Italian lemon water, and paper cups. She's wearing a black cocktail dress that looks a little too dressy for the park, and I think she's trying to impress someone. "You're a good date," I say. "She'll love you."

"Except that I can't stay." She explains that her mom and dad have to host a last-minute fund-raising dinner at their house, and they need her to be there. "I'm so sorry, Donna. Please tell her I'm sorry, too." She hugs me quick. "You still have to be excited, right?"

My stomach feels empty. "Of course." I promise Liz I'll call her tomorrow, and sit down on the blanket.

Five minutes later, I see her coming across the grass and up the hill. Long, straight brown hair and big coffee-colored eyes. Knee-length red sweater with a tie-belt and flared dark blue jeans. She looks to the other corner of the tower first, then turns to me. She smiles and holds her hand to her heart.

I remember when I was six, and Aunt Selena walked into Nonna's wake. I was standing with Mom, and noticed that the hushed conversations all hushed just a little more. Everyone backed away from Aunt Selena while she walked up toward Nonna, and I remember telling Mom, "That's not very nice. Someone should talk to her." So I smoothed out my fluffy yellow dress, walked over to Aunt Selena, and said, "I'll go up with you."

When she crouched down next to me, her long blue dress bunched up on the floor around her, and some of it touched my foot. I remember thinking it must be magic fabric. And I remember everyone staring at us. "Thank you," she said to me in a soft, smiling voice. "You must be Donna."

"You're right," I whispered. "Did you know 'cause you're a Witch?"

"No, silly," she said, and touched my cheek. "I know because you look just like my brother. I know other things 'cause I'm a Witch," she said, and winked at me. "Maybe we'll talk about them someday."

Then we held hands and went to see Nonna, who looked like a statue with her hair done up how Aunt Sylvia would do it fancy for her in rollers, like poofs of white icing.

Aunt Selena closed her eyes and said, "*Ciao*, Mama," and I said "*Ciao*, Nonna."

Then I felt Dad put strong hands on my shoulders. He and Aunt Selena stared at each other, and Aunt Selena started to cry, and then they hugged tight, right over me. Then Dad pulled away from Aunt Selena and pulled me away too, even though I struggled to stay right next to her. So I stood again by Mom and watched Aunt Selena walk out by herself.

Now at the park, I stand up, just as tall as she is. She walks over and hugs me tight, and her perfume smells familiar, musky, and warm.

"Oh, you do have his eyes." Aunt Selena takes both of my hands like she did at Dad's funeral, when I saw her last. Her eyes turn wistful and watery. "You know he's still with you."

I feel naked, like in the woods. I don't say anything.

She nods. "The spirits are all around you."

"What?" I look over my shoulders and laugh nervously. "Like backup singers?"

She rubs her fingers over the oval purple stone on her long necklace, and grins. "Kind of."

I look over my shoulder. "Who's there?"

Aunt Selena asks, "Who do you think?"

I feel my pulse quicken in my chest, and I wish Aunt Selena wasn't staring so intently at me. "I don't know. Dad?" For a second, I smell his aftershave, and I close my eyes. My heartbeat slows, and I think of Nonna slipping me dollar bills at the end of every visit. "Nonna, maybe."

"Yes," Aunt Selena says, "and someone else I don't know. Another grandmother?"

I think of Grammy, Mom's mom, who made Barbie clothes for Linnie and me. "Dead people all around me." Trying to smile, I sit down on the blanket.

"I think that's how it's going to be for you." Aunt Selena's grin widens.

This doesn't seem like good news. I grip a patch of grass next to me. "What's so great about that?"

"It's your destiny," Aunt Selena says, joining me on the blanket.

Great, it's my destiny to be haunted by creepy backup-singer corpses. I have a quick flash of Dad and Nonna in sequined outfits singing "Ooo" into a microphone. Too scary. Too much. I don't want to know this. Aunt Selena seems to be enjoying herself, and I feel like I just realized I'm taking a shower on the front lawn during a block party. I cross my legs and then my arms. I muster up a definitive voice of my own. "Don't we have some snacks to eat?"

"Yes, we do. And wasn't your friend Liz going to be here?"

"She had to cancel. She's really sorry." I pour her a cup of the lemon water.

"I have to say I'm not disappointed. I get you all to myself." She smiles and takes the cup from me.

I slice some of the white cheddar and put it on a napkin between us, with some crackers. I ask Aunt Selena about her work, and she tells me about the Web pages she's created and the candle shop she's opening in Yellow Springs.

For the next half hour, I keep asking questions so I don't have to say anything about myself. I end up eating almost the entire double-sized dark chocolate bar with chili peppers that Aunt Selena brought. When there's nothing else for me to eat or ask, I look at my watch and the sun going down. "Sorry, but I need to go."

"Okay." Aunt Selena glances at me, and something sad clutters her eyes. She blinks it away.

I look up at the bell tower and feel small. A slight chill drifts up from the river, and I rub my arms.

"You should come see me sometime. I want to know what's happening in your life." Aunt Selena writes down her address on a napkin. 919 Willow Street. "I'd love to spend more time with you. When you don't have to get home so fast."

Her hand is warm, and her eyes are kind. She sees me. And she'd like me to visit her. I wonder if my crew of dead relatives is also invited.

On Monday, I'm at Brighton Brothers, vacuuming the viewing rooms and looking over my shoulder every thirty seconds. After Aunt Selena mentioned all the dead people, I was uneasy all weekend. Dead bodies are one thing. Animated dead bodies or filmy spirit beings are something else entirely. Will some ghost appear to me while I'm brushing my teeth? Trying to avoid Mom on the way to the kitchen? While the first two seem perhaps less likely, it doesn't seem far from the realm of possibility that I'd run into an apparition while dusting a coffin. Sleep last night came in neurotic spurts. I'm exhausted today, and I feel raw.

When I bring Mr. Brighton the mail, he's staring at the picture of the elder Mr. Brightons—his dad and grandfather —on his desk. "Sometimes I wonder if I'm doing them proud." His eyes are wistful, like Aunt Selena's were when she thought of Dad.

I suddenly remember my first day of kindergarten: Dad handing me a silver pencil case at breakfast, saying, "Do me proud, kid." And I wanted to, more than anything.

Now I feel like Mr. Brighton, looking at pictures and wishing they'd talk back and let me know how I'm doing. Since I'm guessing Mr. Brighton hasn't been getting a lot of feedback from his pictures either, I say, "I think you are."

"Thanks, Donna." He shakes his head like he's hoping the wistfulness will come out of his ears or something, and he smiles at me.

After work, I'm restless and tired of anxiety. I call Liz and tell her Aunt Selena would be happy to meet with her some other time. With my head full of pictures of the ghosts who might be trailing me, I don't want to drive home. And going home makes me feel like I'm stuck anyway, in the same place I've always been. I decide I need a walk in the woods with my headphones on, maybe this time while the sun's still shining its last few rays of the day.

I drive out to Yellow Springs, toward where Liz and I did our almost-ritual, right by the store where Tim bought me my picture box. As I maneuver through town, I pass Willow Street. Of course. This is where she lives. I keep driving a few blocks, but then I turn around. I can't resist. And a tiny voice that seems more from my heart than my head says, *Maybe you'd like to see her again.*

I follow the slight curve onto Willow and park when I see a 900 address. The sidewalk jags up here and there, and all the houses stand like a motley group of old friends—beautiful, weathered, quaint. They aren't big, more like cottages. I decide they must have exquisite gardens. This is where I'd love to live.

On a long black mailbox, I see a 919 and next to it, a crescent moon painted in silver. On the small porch, big wooden wind chimes dangle from a coconut. They make a soft hollow sound, like slow drops of water into an empty sink. I walk up the few front steps and knock on the door.

In the stained-glass door window I see Aunt Selena's face. She smiles through a bright blue panel and opens the door. "What a wonderful surprise," she says. "Twice in one week." She hugs me. "Come in, come in."

Her house smells of something warm and sweet. "I'm making brownies," she says. "Your timing is impeccable."

"I swear I didn't know." I laugh.

"Are you sure you don't have some kind of second sight?"

I shake my head. "I'm not sure about anything."

She leads me to a living room with a big blue couch and a rainbow of pillows. "Please, make yourself at home."

"Thanks." I sit, and the soft cushions pull me in.

"Would you like something to drink? Tea? Milk?"

I shrug. "Either one."

She leaves me to look at the sky blue walls, a mural of a giant tree painted on one of them. A million different trinkets and pictures sparkle and draw my eye. A red Chinese lantern casts soft light in the corner. I am entranced.

Aunt Selena returns with two short lime-green teacups, no handles, stacked in one hand, and holding a matching teapot in the other. She sets down the cups and pours a little into each. She hands me a cup, and the tea smells like roses. "It's been steeping a little while—shouldn't be too hot." She holds her cup to mine and toasts, "To family."

We drink, and I'm confused. "Aren't you angry at them? No one talks to you."

"You're talking to me."

"That's true."

"All they know about magic is the dark kind with demons. What I do and who I am doesn't have anything to do with that. Which I think you know."

I nod and find that I mean it. She's not bad or dangerous. In fact, she seems fun and alive in ways I long to be.

"Your dad was different. He didn't judge me, and he still talked to me, even though no one else knew it. Did you know he helped put me through college after he finished?"

I shake my head. I realize there's a lot Aunt Selena must know that I don't.

"They made fun of us—we were the bookworms." She taps the side of her cup with her fingernail and looks past me, her eyes getting shiny. "I figured out a long time ago that most of my family is more comfortable giving their power over to some faraway god than claiming control of their own lives. And I can't make them change."

"You're right, but—"

199

"But what?" A few tears roll down her cheeks, but she's smiling and her voice is calm. She wipes the tears with the back of her hand, and the charm bracelet on her wrist jingles softly. "I can keep dragging around every last disappointing moment from the past, or I can just live right now, when my niece, the spitting image of my sweet brother, has come to see me and share tea and brownies. Which would you pick?"

"Brownies."

"Exactly. You are where you are. Where you are is your destiny."

I sigh and sip my tea. "What if I don't know what my destiny is?"

"Honey, you can't see it," she says. "Too many ghosts around you."

I set down my glass. "Yeah, about that. It's been kind of freaking me out."

"I don't mean those ghosts. Those people are your ancestors. They're looking out for you, always. Your dad loved you and was so proud of you." She drains her cup and sets it down next to mine. "I mean things you're not letting go of. Old worries. Insecurities, maybe. Stale fear. Those ghosts. They can keep a person blind. Paralyzed." Aunt Selena refills my cup. "May I ask you a question?"

"Should I take a drink first?"

She laughs.

"It's okay," I say. "Ask away."

Aunt Selena leans forward. "What are you so afraid of?"

The tea warms my mouth and throat. I'm tempted to say *I don't know*—that's my first instinct, but that's a lie. I do know. Whether they're right behind me or floating up on a heavenly cloud somewhere, I'm not afraid of Dad or Nonna or anyone watching over me. Why should I be? They loved me, and I bet they still do.

I'm afraid they're shaking their heads and saying, *What a waste. We knew she could do better.* What I'm really afraid of is being boring, inconsequential. Not taking chances. I blurt, "That I won't ever do...that I won't ever be something—someone—amazing." I look down.

"Then you've only got one choice," Aunt Selena says as a buzzer goes off in another room. "And I've got to get some brownies out of the oven." She stands and walks toward the smell of chocolate.

"Wait," I say. "My choice? My one choice?"

Without turning around, but loud and clear, Aunt Selena calls to me, "Be someone amazing."

Over fresh brownies, I tell Aunt Selena I'm working at Brighton Brothers and going to mortuary school, and she smiles so big and for so long that I think her face must hurt. "That's it."

"What's it?"

"Who you are. You don't need to look so hard for your destiny. Don't miss what's right in front of you"

When I leave Aunt Selena's, I'm calmer, almost so calm

that I could fall asleep. I decide to get a coffee drink at Full of Beans for the twenty-five-minute drive home, and I'm surprised to see Mom sitting at a corner table with some guy. They are leaning close together, and I could swear the guy is holding Mom's hand. I'm not sure because I'm a little distracted by the fact that he looks like some kind of Egyptian god. Long shiny black hair hangs loose on his shoulders, and his skin is the color of creamy coffee.

In stark contrast, Mom looks paler than usual, like some beautiful alabaster princess about to be sacrificed to a god. "Donna, hi." She pulls her hand back and puts it in her lap. "This is my yoga teacher."

"Hi."

He bows his head to me. "Hello," he says in a voice as smooth as his skin looks.

"His studio's out here, so I came for class tonight."

I am having a little trouble breathing, so I say, "Okay. I'll see you at home," and quickly turn back around and out the door. In the car, I realize I never got coffee, but my heart is beating so fast, I feel like I've gotten an injection of pure caffeine. I'm not sure what just happened. I'm not sure if I want to know.

I'm sitting at the kitchen table, where Linnie has left a note: *Out with Snooter. Be back 11:30.* I'm reading Sunday's newspaper, and by reading I mean staring at the words and watching them all bleed together in black blobs on the gray paper. When Mom walks in, I notice that she's wearing a white sundress that shows off her shape and a little cleavage, too, and I realize she was wearing it with the yoga teacher. Her face is flushed, and she doesn't look directly at me as she hooks her big straw summer purse over the back of one of the kitchen chairs. "Need some dinner?"

"No thanks." I pull a red grape from the fruit bowl and pop it into my mouth, hold it in my cheek.

"So what were you doing out in Yellow Springs?"

I bite down on the grape, and it bursts in my mouth. I feel my neck getting hot. I think of yoga guy holding Mom's hand, like he was *with* her, like he was Dad or something, and I tighten my grip on the newspaper. "I could ask you the same thing."

"Be careful, Donna."

"You mean like I should be careful about spending time with Aunt Selena? Because it might be too late. I was out there visiting her, at her house." I fake a gasp.

"I didn't give you her number."

"I found it myself. In Dad's address book."

"You went through his things." Mom's face turns a deeper shade of red. "You had no right."

"He wouldn't mind. I'm still his daughter, and Aunt Selena's his sister."

"And I'm your mother."

"You should have seen it," I say. "She had all these upside-down crucifixes, and we did a blood sacrifice and everything."

"That's not funny." She holds on to the back of the kitchen chair, and I see her knuckles turn white.

"It is funny, actually, because it has absolutely nothing to do with who she is. You know, Mom, she's really great."

"I'm sure she is."

I break off a small bunch of grapes and find that my hand is shaking. "You should give her a chance."

"You should watch yourself," she says. "I'm just looking out for you."

"Well, you're doing a shitty job of it."

Mom doesn't say anything, but looks like I've just slapped her. I want to take it back, but I don't. I can't.

Into the silence in the kitchen, over the sound of Mrs. Grant playing piano next door, over the sound of the crickets, Mom says, "Well, maybe you should take care of yourself."

Quietly, feeling like I'm floating outside of myself, I say, "Okay, I will." I stand up and walk out of the kitchen and down the hallway toward the basement.

"You want to know?" Mom calls after me.

I stop, stand still in the hallway, and find myself looking at the painting of the ocean that Dad bought for Mom when I was born. He would always tell me that the idea of a daughter was as big as the ocean to him, and that he would give me my own ocean one day if he could. When I was eight, I told him I wanted it to be called the Hidden Sea. I thought it was funny because it sounded like hide-and-seek. He laughed and said, "Does that mean I'll never be able to find it for you?" I looked at him very seriously and said, "Just look for the best hiding spots. That's where it will be."

Now I feel like I could drown in that ocean in front of me, and Mom says, "You want to know what I was doing in Yellow Springs?"

I say nothing and wish I could dive right into that picture, into the blue green waves.

Somewhere down the hallway, from behind me, Mom says, "Trying to be happy. You should give it a shot."

Francesca Parisi, 75

Cause of Death: Fell down front steps/stroke

Surviving Immediate Family:
• Sons: Domenic, Louis
• Daughters: Sylvia, Selena

Makeup: Brick Red lipstick, clear nail polish

Clothing: Francesca's extra-good Sunday dress, with blue flowers

Casket: Maple with pink silk lining

Special Guests in Attendance:
• Carmen "Chooch" Ciccaroni, creator of Carmen's Fancy Fish Sticks, sold nationally

Funeral Incidents:
• Selena Parisi ignored by all but Domenic Parisi
• Six wailing women who pass out—two aunts, three cousins, one friend of family

Dumbest thing someone says trying to be comforting: "Well, she hated to clean, and now she doesn't have to do that anymore." —Toni Lombardo, cousin, to her sister Terri, in an effort to get Terri conscious and up off the floor.

fifteen

The next morning, I tell Mr. Brighton I've decided to move into the yellow room, if it's still okay—to get settled before school starts. All smiles, he agrees very quickly. I call B and ask if he can help me move on Friday, when Mom has an in-service day at St. Camillus. B says sure and that Gwen can probably help too.

When I get home from work, Mom follows me down to my bedroom. "We should talk."

"I think we've talked enough."

"Your brother tells me you're moving out."

"He should keep his mouth shut." Of course he called her. "I'll be gone on Friday, and then I can take care of myself." I sit down on my bed and look up at her. I hook the heels of my shoes on the bed frame. "That's what you wanted."

"Yes, I want you to take care of yourself. I want all of my kids to be self-sufficient." Mom's face is pinched, like when she has a bad headache. "I didn't mean for you to leave."

I shrug. "This is what I want." I'm not sure I believe this, but I hope I sound firm, confident, self-sufficient.

"Damn," Mom says. "Damn it."

I don't like when Mom swears, which she only does when she's really upset. And I don't like that she looks like she's about to cry. I don't like any of this.

"I want to help you move," she says.

"You don't have to. B probably also told you he's helping me."

"Can't we do it on Saturday? I'll be at work Friday."

"I know."

Mom's cheeks are red, and her mouth is tight. She blinks and breathes. She opens her mouth but then closes it, like she doesn't know what to say. "You know I want what's best for you. I want you to be happy."

A good daughter would make her mother feel better in this moment. Say thank you and all is forgiven. But I can't get the image of Mom in that coffee shop out of my head. I feel shitty, and I don't want anyone else to feel any better right at this moment, even Mom. Especially Mom.

*   *   *

On Friday morning, as I pack my suitcase and fill a handful of empty boxes Mom has in the basement, I quickly realize how little actually belongs to me. I can't take Mom's picture table with me or our dining room table or the ugly orange front porch wicker couch I love to sit on.

When I close the suitcase, I remember the time I almost lost it, the year before Dad died, two weeks before he started chemo. When we got to the Naples airport in Florida, none of our luggage was there. Somehow it had landed in Seattle, so we just had to go to the hotel and wait. None of us wanted to be on vacation. It was raining, and we were all miserable. And on the way into the hotel, we got splattered by dirty street water. In our room, Mom and Dad fought, and Dad yelled on the phone at someone from the airline. Mom went out and cried on the balcony, and Dad stormed out of the room.

B and Linnie and I sat for what seemed like forever, and my insides felt hollow until the phone rang. B answered nervously and then smiled. "She's on the balcony," he said, and then, "She's crying, I think," and then, "Okay." He set the phone down on the dresser, still smiling. "It's Dad," he said to Linnie and me.

I smiled at Linnie. "See," I said. "Everything's fine."

B went out and got Mom, who talked with Dad until she was grinning too.

When she hung up, Mom said, "Okay. Showers for everyone." By the time all of us kids were clean, and Mom had gotten into the shower, Dad came walking in with a big Wavecrest shopping bag.

"What's that?" Linnie asked.

Dad grinned at us standing in our scratchy white hotel towels. "Evening wear," he said. He reached into the bag and pulled out a hot-pink, terry cloth, Linnie-sized muu-muu and handed it to Linnie. "For you, mademoiselle," he said.

"Really?" she asked, like that was just what she'd wanted her whole life.

"Hold up your arms," he said, and pulled the muumuu right over her head. The hot pink did become her.

He reached in again and pulled out an electric blue muumuu covered with exceptionally happy dolphins. He handed it to me.

I rubbed the terry cloth, much softer than the hotel bath towel, between my fingers. "Thanks, Dad," I said.

"You're most welcome."

When Dad reached into the bag again and pulled out a chocolate brown muumuu with white seagulls, and handed it to B, my brother just said, "No way."

"Brendan," Dad said. "Everyone's doing it." He reached into the bag, pulled out a Dad-sized, almost neon, lime green muumuu, and waved it like a bullfighter at my brother. "Even me."

"No way," B said again. "I don't wear dresses."

"Suit yourself," Dad said, tossing B's muumuu onto

the double bed by the wall. "I'm going to check on your mother." He disappeared into the bathroom with the bag and shut the door. Mom shrieked and then giggled.

I went into the closet and slipped on my dolphin muumuu. I could still hear Mom giggling from the bathroom when I emerged from the closet, so I took Linnie's hand and promptly led her out to the balcony. "Come on," I said to B.

"I'm not going anywhere," B said, pouting and glaring at the chocolate fabric lumped on the bed.

"Suit yourself," I said, and pulled Linnie along.

"What are they doing?" Linnie asked.

"Don't worry about it," I said.

Two minutes later, B joined us on the balcony, wearing his muumuu. "Don't say a word," he said, and sat down on the lounge chair, tucking the muumuu between his legs.

And I didn't. I just enjoyed standing at the railing, letting the sea breeze blow around and under my muumuu, feeling like I could just fly right out and over the ocean.

Eventually, Dad and Mom emerged from the bathroom, she in her yellow muumuu with red tulips and Dad in his lime green number. Mom knocked on the balcony door and motioned for us to come in.

Inside, Dad held up the room service menu. "Tonight," he said in his best dramatic voice, "we're dining in. And by the way, B"—he nodded to my brother—"you look fantastic."

"Yeah, yeah," B said.

"Are we really getting room service?" Linnie asked.

A reasonable question since we never got room service. Whenever we asked, Dad would always say, "Room service is a scam. Overpriced and never very good."

But that night he said, "You can order whatever you want."

"Like we do for my birthday?" Linnie asked.

"Yes," Dad said. "It's a new holiday." He winked at her. "Muumuu Fiesta."

"I love Muumuu Fiesta," Linnie said. "We should get off school for that."

B ordered a hamburger and two plates of cheese fries. Linnie ordered onion rings and four scoops of chocolate ice cream. I ordered fettuccini and fresh-squeezed orange juice. Mom ordered a filet, and Dad ordered lobster. After Dad placed the call, Mom said, "That's going to be expensive, Nicky."

"Now's not the time to worry about that," he said, and kissed her on the lips. "Remember, it's a holiday."

"You're right." She took a deep breath and nodded.

After the room service came, we ate like we were starving, and Dad turned on the radio and found an oldies station. And we all danced, even B, who did the twist with Mom, yellow and chocolate muumuus swishing back and forth to the beat.

Later, I lay down next to Linnie, to the soft sound of her breathing and the warmth of that breath on my shoulder, and B conked out within two seconds of his head hitting the pillow on the rollaway bed.

My eyes adjusted to the dark room, with just a hint of light from the cracked-open bathroom door so Linnie wouldn't get scared.

That night, Dad and I were both on the side of the bed closest to the nightstand, and I watched him frowning just a little with his eyes shut. I knew he wasn't asleep, because he wasn't snoring. And probably, knowing I was watching him, he opened his eyes and looked at me. It almost hurt to look at him right then, because big shadows of fear and sadness cluttered his eyes. Still, I smiled at him, and he smiled back. "I love you," he mouthed to me.

"You too," I mouthed back.

And then he turned away from me and spooned up against my mother. Half an hour later, when I heard him finally start to snore, I let myself fall asleep, too.

It's Friday morning, and that night seems far away, like it belongs to some other girl and some other family. And my grown-up brother and his fiancée arrive to help me move. We pack our cars, with lots of room to spare, and get it all over to Brighton Brothers in one trip.

With hands on her hips, Gwen scans the yellow room. "This is a great space."

B kisses her on the cheek. "Hey, sweetness, can you give us a minute?"

"Sure." She hugs me, a quick awkward one from the side. "Call me if you need anything."

I can't imagine ever calling Gwen for any reason. She'll be calling me soon enough to go dress shopping. "You call her sweetness? Ick."

"Keep it to yourself, Donder." B sits on my bed. "Actually pretty comfortable."

"Yeah, it's not bad." I reach down and hold on to Terra. Her turtle shell feels good under my palm.

"You should make up with Mom."

I sit at the desk and open the three drawers. All empty. "You should mind your own business."

"She's just looking out for you. She's just Mom." He shrugs and laughs.

"Everything's so easy for you, isn't it?" I slam the top drawer shut, a little more loudly than I wanted to. "Did you even feel anything walking into this place?"

"You think I don't remember it? You think it's easy for me?" B stands up. "Shit, Donder. Not everyone wants to mope around for the rest of their lives." He heads for the door and then turns around. "Dad wasn't a moper. And I won't be one either. And for the record, in case you give a shit, Mom's not the only one who's been worried about you."

I hold my hand to my stomach, which suddenly feels like it's been punched, quick and hard.

When I don't hear his footsteps anymore, I shut the door

and lean against it. I look at Maurice standing on my desk next to the RIP box of coffin pictures from Tim, who may have been swallowed up by a sand dune. The pain in my gut aches, and I almost choke as tears pour out of my eyes, and my body shakes with the sobbing.

When I wake up, the sun is shining on my bed, and I smell something sweet and doughy. My head hurts, and I reach up and feel puffy spots around my eyes. From down the hall, I hear giggling that sounds like none of the Brightons I know.

I brush my hair, wash my face, and put on shorts and a T-shirt. I could use a distraction. And some waffles.

In the kitchen, Mrs. B says, "Good morning. We're babysitting today. This is Delia. Hope she didn't wake you up."

"Time to wake up!" Delia shouts. She's got long black hair, as curly as Liz's, and looks like a baby doll, a mischievous, oversized baby doll. I can see immediately why the Brightons are in love with her. Looking at her little face and big wide eyes, I can't help but smile. "Hi, Delia. I'm Donna. We both start with D's."

"Deeeeeeeee!" she yells, and can't stop laughing.

All morning I play with Delia, which is good because she gets Mr. and Mrs. Brighton tuckered out pretty fast. At noon, I excuse myself and say I'm going to do some reading. In the yellow room, I see that Tim has called, and I call him back.

"You'll never guess where I am," I say.

"Where are you?" Clearly, Tim is not as good at this game as I am.

When I tell him I've moved into Brighton Brothers, he says, "Rad. I'm almost at the Utah-Colorado border." He's at a rest stop because Tina and Bud ate bad burritos and are yacking behind the Texaco station. "So I was just thinking about you."

I wonder if it's the vomiting or the diesel fuel that brought me to mind, but I can't help but be glad he's thinking about me at all.

"I should be home in a few weeks," he says. "Then we can hang. Cool?"

"Cool," I say. It's not like I'll be doing anything else.

The next day, I wake up and feel like I'm supposed to be somewhere. Church. I bolt out of bed and wash my face. As I'm brushing my teeth and looking in the mirror, I realize that Mom's not actually here to make me go, and I'm not sure who to ask to see if I have to. Since I'm the only one currently around, I ask myself.

Looking at my reflection, I answer "No," which feels powerful and strange.

Then my new powerful and strange self decides my next course of action is to crawl back under the covers. As I drift back to sleep, I decide to say a little prayer. *Thank you for my new bed and a yellow room just for me.*

Two weeks later, on the Monday night before I start school, I'm paging through my textbooks, and my phone rings. It's Mom. "May I come over? I have some things for you." She tiptoes with her words, tentative.

"Yes," I say, and my voice sounds tiny, too.

Forty-five minutes later, Mom gets to Brighton Brothers. We stand in the front hallway looking at each other, and she glances down toward the viewing room where Dad was.

"Let's go upstairs," I say.

I take her up to the yellow room and notice she's carrying a brown paper bag. From the bag she first pulls a dark purple envelope. "This came for you."

She sets the bag down on my desk and looks around the room. "I like it."

While she inspects my bathroom, I open the purple envelope. Inside is a card with a quote on the front from someone named Rumi: *Let the beauty we love be what we do. There are a hundred ways to kneel and kiss the ground.* Inside is a note from Aunt Selena: *Blessings to you and your destiny. Remember you're already living it. Just be you. And come visit again. I'd love to see you.*

I slip the card into the envelope and set it on my nightstand, hoping Mom won't ask about it.

We don't talk about Aunt Selena or about the yoga teacher or even church, and I don't mention that Tim has called me twice from the road, both times when his travel companions were somehow ill. But I do tell Mom about watching JB put makeup on corpses like he's a salon professional, and how Liz and I went for a picnic. And Mom tells me she thinks Linnie's in love, even if she'd never say it, and that Snooter is the nicest boy with a ring in his nose that she's ever met.

"You don't know anyone else with a ring in their nose."

"That's true," she says. "But still."

We both laugh, and for a second it feels like relief, like everything could be okay. I want to enjoy the laughter, but I know that sooner or later, there are things we'll need to talk about, even if both of us would rather not.

Mom takes a large round Tupperware container out of the bag on my desk. "I thought I should bring you some back-to-school muffins. They're strawberry-walnut."

"So am I," I say.

Mom looks at me and smiles, as one does at the insane. "Okay, honey."

She sets the container on my desk and pulls a large Ziploc bag out of her purse. In it, she has paper napkins, plastic knives, and several restaurant packets of Sweet Dream butter.

Mom turns to me. "Your Dad would be so proud of you," she says.

My eyes fill, just like that. "Thanks, Mom," I say. "I needed that."

She pulls her purse straps farther up onto her shoulder, tugs at a piece of hair at the nape of her neck. "You know," she starts, and looks like she might be sick. Or hurt.

"What?" I take a step toward her.

She shakes off whatever malaise had appeared... mostly. "I'm proud of you too." For a second, we look at each other, her blue eyes into my brown.

Now I nod at her.

Before I say anything, Mom hugs me and pats my face.

I follow her down the steps and through the lobby of Brighton Brothers. She turns and hugs me hard and tight and kisses me on the cheek. I have the feeling that I'm falling into a deep cavern without a bottom. She walks fast, and I watch her fiddle with her car keys on the way out the door.

Up in my room, I sit on the bed and stare at my desk, at all of the provisions Mom left there. Back-to-school muffins.

Back to school. I go to the sink and fill my water glass.

When I go to the container, I notice there's an envelope taped on the top of it. Inside is a check from Mom. In the bottom left corner she's written *For Donna's Tuition*. The falling feeling returns, and I hold on to the edge of the desk and take a breath.

I set out one of the paper napkins and smooth the

creases. I rig it with a packet of butter, a knife, and a muffin. I don't have to go to Mrs. B's kitchen or search the meager supplies I have in my chest of drawers. Everything I need sits right there on that table. Mom left it all there for me.

sixteen

Even though I've been working at a funeral home all summer, and even though I live there now, my first day at Chapman feels big. I take the card from Aunt Selena with me in my backpack. Sitting in the auditorium with the new class, I remind myself that this is my destiny. After a brief orientation meeting, it's time for Embalming I, my first class of the day. Outside the student center, the sun shines steady from a cloudless sky; it feels like some tropical island, without the beach part. All Chapman's got is a goldfish pond.

There are fifty of us, so we'll be split into two groups for classes. I go with twenty-five of my classmates to the science building and settle into a chair in the middle of the room. The air-conditioning must be below forty degrees, because it's freezing. My body feels confused, and I wish I'd brought a sweater to go over my short-sleeved shirt.

Our instructor, Ned Troutman, runs the biggest funeral home in Cincinnati, and the centerpiece of his tan face is a long pointed nose. He wears jeans and black cowboy boots, and it's easier to imagine him rounding up cattle on a sunny ranch than draining pale bodies in a sterile prep room. He tells us that *embalming* comes from the Greek "en" for *into* and "balsamon," for *dried sap or resins*. Unlike the Egyptian method of drying out bodies, embalming meant introducing preservative resins into the body.

I can't help think, Dead body, I'd like you to meet preservative resins. Preservative resins, dead body. Can I get either of you a cocktail? I almost make myself laugh out loud, but I bite my tongue, choosing not to be the problem student on my first day. Suddenly I have a memory of being at a Christmas concert at St. Camillus when I was seven, and the lady singing the Ave Maria was so high-pitched and off-key that it was painful. B was on the end of the pew, and then Linnie, Mom, Dad, and me. I heard Dad make a noise, and saw that he was shaking. With a closer look, I realized he was shaking because he was laughing so hard. Mom shot him the evil eye, and me too, so I wouldn't get any ideas.

Of course, then, I couldn't help it; so I started laughing too. Still laughing, Dad glanced at me and held up a finger to his lips. He put his arm around me, and we both lowered our heads and shook and laughed in silence together as the

Ave Maria went on. The woman sitting next to me—in a white sweatshirt with a three-D crocheted Christmas tree jutting out the front of her stomach—seemed so enraptured that she didn't notice.

When it was over, Dad and I clapped with everyone else, tears running down our faces. When the woman next to me turned, sincere tears shining on her cheeks, and said, "I know—it gets me every time," Dad and I had to leave to get drinks of water and laugh out loud in the back of the church.

Thinking of Dad makes me somber pretty quickly, so I remain a good student for Mr. Troutman and learn about sticking tubes in arteries and how embalming is good because it allows family and friends to view the body without the disturbing effects of decomposition. Mr. Troutman ends the class by saying our role is a sacred one. "We do what others can't," he says, "so that others can grieve in the way they need to."

When he says this, I find myself sitting up straighter. I like the idea of having a sacred role. I've never had one before.

The next Saturday, Liz invites everyone from our Woodmont lunch table over to her house. She's making lunch for us and wants to say good-bye before she leaves for Pittsburgh the next day to start CMU. I think it will be nice to see Charlie, but I don't have any desire to see anyone else.

Liz has decided on a Middle Eastern menu, and I get there early to help. As I set out pita bread and hummus and falafel and some kind of yogurty dip with cucumbers, under a big umbrella table on the back patio, I ask her why she's doing this.

"It's sort of like a ritual," she says. "I want to say good-bye and thank you to this part of my life, so I can make room for the next one."

Once everyone arrives, I feel like I'm floating outside myself, watching. Charlie looks taller and more muscular. He comes over and gives me a big hug. "It's good to see you," he says, with a low voice, just loud enough for me to hear. I like Charlie's arms around me, and his smell, something musky. When I step away from him I have goose bumps all over both arms. I feel like I must be blushing and hope no one notices.

Charlie says he's picked the environmental law track in his program at UD, that he wants to work toward the biggest change he possibly can. As he explains the program and his goals, he sounds so articulate and clear. I'm impressed.

"You rock," Liz says to him, and I nod, which I hope he knows is my way of saying I agree.

Jim and Becky look the same, and Patty looks like she's been lying out in the sun every day.

"I hate to tell you this," Jim says to me, "but you've got a really big turtle around your neck."

224

Becky punches Jim in the arm. "I think she knows that."

Jim rubs his arm. "I was being funny."

Becky shrugs a little. "Oh."

Liz invites us all to sit down, and pours us each some Lebanese tea, which is sweet and has pine nuts floating in it.

"So, I hear you're dating cousin Tim." Patty sips some of her tea, and I have a flash of her as a hyper-tan, scaly old woman living alone in some big house, drinking a daiquiri and shouting at her pool boy because he's the only one around.

"Kind of," I say.

"What does that mean?" Charlie says, and I see something bright in his eyes.

"Well, he's out of town right now."

"But he'll be back!" Becky smiles at me like a mom. "And Jim and I introduced them. How cool is that?"

"I also hear," Patty says, "that you're living in that creepy funeral home. With dead people right below you. Doesn't that freak you out?"

I think about it for a minute and realize I've actually been sleeping really well at Brighton Brothers. "No."

Patty looks dubious, but I just shrug.

"Well anyway, *I'd* be freaked out," she says, and turns to Liz. "So, are you all packed?" Patty leaves for Cleveland on Monday, and she and Liz decide to compare decorating notes after lunch.

When we finish eating, Becky pulls a little stack of laminated pictures out of her purse. "I made one for each of us, and it has all of our contact info on the back, so we can keep in touch." The picture is of us at graduation, in our less-than-flattering orange robes. Everyone is looking at the camera smiling, but Charlie and I are turned slightly toward each other, which makes my face get hot. I set the card on the table picture-side down, and take a long drink of iced tea. On the back of the picture, Becky's put all of our e-mail addresses and phone numbers.

I'm not sure what to do with this. Liz's is the only number I really want, and I have it already. It's not like I'm going to be calling Patty to see if she's found someone new to torture in Cleveland.

"Thanks so much," Liz says. "That's really thoughtful."

Becky smiles and blushes. She shrugs. "It wasn't hard to do."

Liz brings out some sweet pastries for desert. She sets them on the table and stays standing. She holds up her glass. "I want to say thank you to each of you for making a place for me in your school and teaching me something important."

Looking at Liz, I feel like she's on some kind of other plane of existence than the rest of us. She seems so self-assured and easy in her skin, and we're all paying rapt attention to her.

"Becky, you have taught me about kindness." She looks

Becky in the eyes, and then turns to Jim. "Jim, you've taught me about laughter. Patty, you've taught me about confidence. Charlie, you've given me a bigger worldview. And Donna, you've taught me about transformation." She looks at me, and I realize I've scrunched up my forehead. "It's true, D." She nods at me. "Thank you all. Cheers."

We hold up our glasses and clink them together. Becky has tears in her eyes, and if I'm not mistaken, Patty does too. Jim may actually be blushing. And Charlie looks serene. And handsome. "Thanks, Liz," he says. "That's really special."

I nod, and I'm confused. I'd never thought about these people as teachers, but what she said about them makes sense. Still, transformation is snake power, and Liz has that all on her own, without me. I can't imagine what she's learned from me about that.

After everyone but me has left, I want to ask Liz what she meant, but I feel like I should know already, so I don't. Also, Liz looks like she might cry. She says, "Don't forget about me."

"Are you kidding?" I hug her and pull back, but she doesn't look like she's kidding. "It's not possible," I say. "I'm already counting the days until you come back to visit."

Driving away, I think it's much more likely that Liz will get swept up into her fabulous life at college in a different town and not think very often at all about her friend back

227

in Dayton, Ohio. Through my open windows, the air feels thick, like it does when summer's almost over and the fruit gets too ripe and falls off the trees.

Two weeks later, Mom calls to see if I'm free on Friday. She's making dinner.

"Special occasion?" I say, joking. Every night of my life, without fail, Mom has made dinner.

"No," Mom says, but she sounds like she's lying. I can't help but think of that night in Yellow Springs and Mom holding hands with Yoga Man, and I do my best to push the image out of my mind. Maybe he was just comforting her, a strictly teacher-student kind of counseling moment. Purely platonic. I know Dad was Mom's only one; there's no place for someone else. I heard her say so.

In the afternoon, I'm rocking on the hammock out behind Brighton Brothers, and the sun feels like a warm blanket. My body wants to take a nap, and my mind fights between concentrating on my Embalming I book and worrying about Mom. Just as my body is about to claim the victory, Tim calls. "So I'm back. What are you doing?"

"Napping. Studying. Wondering what my mom's up to." I'm surprised at how nonchalant I sound, but I'm too preoccupied to feel nervous about talking to him.

Tim says, "Maybe I can distract you."

I agree to go over to his house on campus, and that night we head up to his room on the second floor. It's a little dusty and smoky from some incense he's got burning by the window, and the only light comes from a little adjustable desk lamp. On the floor, a huge mattress sprawls, covered by dark green sheets and some kind of woven blanket. I don't see a chair anywhere, not even at the desk, which leaves the mattress as the only place to sit. So when Tim squats down on it, so do I.

His face is dark and tan from his trip, and, well, sexy. Sitting this close to him, in his room, I feel my heartbeat accelerate in my neck.

Like he knows, he reaches over and touches the spot where my pulse is pumping, rests his hand there. "I like your hair up."

My ponytail brushes against the back of my neck.

"I missed you," he says.

"Really?" It seems like life has turned upside down since the last time I saw him, like life has filled up football fields of space between us since that night at the soccer party. And even though my heart beats fast, I realize I feel different. I realize that I don't care quite as much whether he likes me or not, that I'm not all that nervous, and I laugh just a little.

"Something funny?"

"Life," I say. I decide I can wax philosophical too. "You. Me. Life."

He looks at me like he realizes I'm different too. "Lay back," he says, and I do.

229

He lies next to me and runs his hand down the front of me, all the way to the edge of my denim skirt at my knees. Then he runs it back up and leaves his hand right between my breasts. I realize I'm not wearing my Terra necklace, and I feel vulnerable.

Then he climbs on top of me, and as he lowers his body onto mine, I feel him hard, through my skirt, through my underwear. He kisses me, and I wrap my arms around his back and clutch at his T-shirt.

As he kisses me and rubs his body against mine, I feel myself getting wet between my legs. He sits up and slides back. He reaches up under my skirt with both hands and grabs the sides of my underwear. I feel his fingernails scratch lightly against the sides of my legs, as he pulls my underwear all the way down and off. He tosses them, and they land in a little navy blue pile next to his backpack. Standing up, he unzips his shorts and pulls them down and off. When he pulls off his boxer shorts, red cotton, I see his penis hard and pointing at me. I can't help but stare. This is a body part I'm not used to seeing, and I feel myself getting even wetter. And all of a sudden, I'm nervous again. I wonder if he has condoms like Liz told me I should use.

Tim kneels down and climbs on top of me again. He rubs himself against my skirt while he kisses my neck, and I close my eyes and let out a soft moan. I feel like some kind of animal and hope I don't sound stupid. Tim starts to push up my skirt, and suddenly a cacophony of voices goes off in my head. The first one is mine: *Really, Donna, with this guy?* Then Mom saying that sex goes with marriage, and Father Dean telling our eighth grade class that our bodies are our temples. And last but not least, the bearded God shaking his head and saying, *I told you the rules.* None of these voices are particularly sexy, and all of them are exceptionally distracting.

All I can do at this moment is say the word they're all saying now—the word that's echoing in my head. "Stop."

"Stop?"

"Yes, please." My voice sounds small and weak to me.

Tim lifts up off of me and rolls onto his side. "Are you okay?"

"I just can't right now."

"That's cool," he says, and I wonder if anything's not cool with Tim. "Hey, I'll be right back." He pulls on his boxers and leaves me alone.

I grab my underwear and shove it in my purse. I don't actually trust that Tim has cleaned his room any time recently. I redo my ponytail and stand up. A few minutes later, Tim returns, a look of bliss on his face. "Took care of business," he says. "It's all good."

I'm not sure of the appropriate response to that, so instead I say, "I think I'm gonna head home."

Driving home in the Lark, I feel like an idiot, like I missed something. Like I avoided doing something wrong and like I also avoided doing something I might really enjoy. I know all of the religious rules, but they don't seem relevant to me. I'm pretty sure that even if I did sleep with Tim, some kind of laundry chute wouldn't automatically open up under the bed and suck me down to hell. Although that could make a great amusement park ride—the Premarital Sex Plunge or the Virginity Vacuum.

Mostly, I wonder if it matters that I don't know how I even feel about Tim other than turned on. Can sex be just for fun? Maybe, but part of me wants it to matter, wants it to be with someone who matters. An image of Charlie hugging me at Liz's party rises in my mind, and I can almost feel his arms around me.

I wish Liz were here so I could go pick her up right now. I know I could call her, but the thought of her being so far away just makes me feel more lonely.

One hand on the steering wheel, I reach to open the window, but realize it's down already. I stretch my hand out into the air, and through my fingers, the breeze feels too hot for nighttime.

Thursday evening, after I get home from school, JB tells me that the group for the Abigail Chen visitation hours is pretty small, so I don't need to change and come back down.

I'm at my desk eating my leftover Caesar salad from lunch when Mom calls again. In addition to participating in her mysterious dinner tomorrow night, she also wants me to look at wedding cakes with her and Gwen and B at Bella's Bakery in the afternoon. Gwen requested my presence.

I agree, although I already feel weird about tomorrow. Wedding cakes only add a more sugary level of foreboding. I wish I could cancel and hang out with Tim, but then I think of his stupid mattress with the Anti-Sex Choir and decide that's not any better. When I hang up, I'm unsettled, and the salad flutters around in my stomach with little romaine lettuce wings.

A few minutes later, Mr. Brighton knocks on my door and tells me he's picking up the body of Rory Mahoney tomorrow and wonders if I'd like to observe Mr. Mahoney's embalming in the afternoon.

I try not to sound too eager when I say, "I'd love to. I mean, that would be very interesting."

Mr. Brighton grins a little at me. "My dad always told me that it's good to be passionate about your work. That means you'll do it well."

Abigail Chen, 42

Cause of Death: Heroin overdose

Surviving Immediate Family:
• Twin sister: Libby

Makeup: Ocher/Ivory covering cream blend

Clothing: Long-sleeved navy cashmere sweater to cover track marks, one half heart locket (sister Libby wears other half)

Casket: Oak, lavender cotton lining

Strangest thing someone says in the hallway: "Do you guys have any snacks?" —Teenage cousin, while texting on his cell phone

seventeen

Examining the three-tiered Simple Elegance wedding cake at Bella's Bakery, I can't help but think how the champagne icing looks like the nude cosmetic JB will probably have me order in bulk from the Coffin Cosmetics catalogue.

"I don't actually like that one," Gwen says to B. "What if we served fruit cups? That seems more simple and elegant to me."

I look to Mom, knowing instantly she won't like that. Indeed, a frown pushes her red-lipsticked lips downward. I used to use her lipstick for my Halloween makeup, but it never worked so well for me. In red lipstick I become some sort of cross between a burlesque dancer and a circus clown, but Mom and her pale skin make the red glamorous.

And recently she's been wearing a lot more of it. Now she crosses her arms. "Gwen, you have to have cake at your wedding."

I'm unsettled because something about Mom looks different, and it's not just the lipstick. Maybe it's her iron will to make sure Gwen doesn't make any fruit cup wedding decisions. She points to the Simple Elegance. "It's traditional."

I shrug. "So is a bris, but she's not having one of those."

"Is losing foreskin comparable to eating cake?" B asks, leaning against one of the glass pastry cases.

Gwen giggles.

"You know what?" Mom takes a deep breath, closes her eyes, opens them, and smiles without showing teeth. More than some other subjects, when it comes to weddings, Mom has some very specific ideas. So I'm ready for the reprimand, the lecture on the merits of cake-centric weddings, like the perfect wedding she and Dad had, and the tactlessness of mentioning circumcision in a bakery. Instead she says, "I think you should have whatever you want. Fruit cups, Oreos, whatever."

I squint at Mom and cross my arms. I know she's been practicing the peaceful response, but this seems over the top. "And you really wouldn't care?"

"No," she says, and to my surprise, she almost seems to mean it.

"Excellent." B eyes the espresso bar behind the register. "I'm going to get coffee. Anyone want some?"

"I could use some herbal tea," Gwen says with even more perkiness than usual. I can tell she's jumping at the opportunity for escape.

I ignore them and take a step closer to Mom. "Okay, I need to ask: Did you get abducted by aliens?"

"No." Mom grins like she has a secret, and that makes me nervous.

"Then why are you being so weird?"

B looks at me, then at Mom. He rolls his eyes. "Guess the two of us will get beverages for ourselves," he says a little loudly. "We'll be over there."

Mom wanders away from me in the other direction, toward a tower of cream puffs surrounded by miniature chocolate ghosts. Behind the ghosts are chocolate gravestones and chocolate *Happy Halloweens*. It's still September, so Halloween decorations seem a little premature.

Gazing dreamily at the ghosts, Mom rubs her fingers over the blue beads on her bracelet; one I've never seen before. I step next to her and point at her wrist. "What is that?"

"Do you like it?"

"Where'd you get it?"

"I've been meaning to tell you about my"—she clears her throat—"new friend."

"Your new friend."

She nods.

"Are you going to tell me anything else?"

"It's a man." The image of the long-haired Egyptian god-man from Full of Beans pops into my head.

This is it, I think. It's not like I didn't know this was coming. "Mom, is he your boyfriend?"

"I wouldn't exactly say that," she says, and I think she's actually sounding coy.

Holding extra-large paper cups, B and Gwen join us. "I got a cappuccino." With milk foam smudged above his lip, B grins.

"Mom got a boyfriend."

"I know, and I think it's great." He smiles bigger and foamier.

"Shut up and wipe your face," I say.

"Well, it is."

Gwen looks a little like everyone is speaking German and she doesn't quite understand what's happening. Or maybe like she does speak German but is doing her best to pretend she doesn't. She takes the napkin from under her cup and wipes away B's milk mustache.

"We'll see what's great once I actually know about it." I notice that one of the chocolate ghosts is missing a white icing eye. I know how he must feel. "Apparently everyone but me got the memo."

"And you wonder why." B shakes his head and uses a

flavor of voice I'd call condescending with a hint of disdain. "Look how you're handling this."

"I'm handling it just fine." I turn to Mom. "Is this the coffee-shop guy?"

Mom nods.

What's his name?"

"Roger."

My head feels like it might explode. My mother—who has long loved spending Saturday evenings with warm milk and the History Channel—out gallivanting around with some yoga guy named Roger. My mother the widow who said she'd only had one love. My dad. "That guy did not look like a Roger. Are you sure that's his name?"

Mom looks at me like I'm a little slow. "Yes. I'm sure."

B looks at me in a similar way. "Why are you so upset? Unless I'm mistaken, this is good news."

"I'm not upset." I notice that my hands are shaking, and put them in the pockets of my raincoat. In theory, I know B is right: I should be excited for my mom. I make myself smile. "So, Roger. What's he like?"

I know I sound like a robot, but this seems to work for Mom. She grins her secret grin again. "Maybe you'll find out tonight."

"We're having dinner at our house tonight."

"Well, he's coming."

"To our family dinner?" Now I sound like a person again, an angry one.

"I can invite someone to dinner. In case you forgot, I'm a part of this family." Mom narrows her eyes, and her face flushes. "I produced this family."

"Is Roger a part of this family?" Suddenly I'm feeling kind of claustrophobic. "I'm sorry, Mom," I say more quietly, "I have to get back to work."

She reaches out and touches my arm with her hand, the one connected to the blue bracelet. "You're coming tonight?"

I glance up at her but not for long. "I guess so."

As I walk off, I hear B say, "She'll be there, Mom, don't worry." I know he's saying it to me too.

After ten long, silent minutes of air-conditioned Lark time on the wet Dayton streets, I pull into the Brighton Brothers lot. I roll down the windows and turn off the car. The last throes of summer air push in wet and hot. I pull out my phone and almost call Liz, but then I have this idea that I'll call Tim, and that he'll come right over and hug me. Or do something with me that I'm not supposed to do.

When he answers, the whole story floods out of my mouth before I can stop myself—stupid cakes and fruit cups and Mom and some dude named Roger.

"Heavy." Tim laughs a little, like he's nervous.

I laugh too, because I don't know what else to do.

"Dude, what's up? You're totally spazzing out."

"I know." I watch a few drops tentatively hit the

windshield. The half-clear blue and half-cloudy gray sky can't seem to make a choice. I decide that September is turning out to be a confused month for all of us.

"You know," he says, using his philosopher voice, "things change. Change is life."

"You think I don't know that?"

"Maybe you just need a reminder."

"She didn't tell me she met someone." Some raindrops sprinkle in through the window. I roll it almost all the way up and watch it cloud with steam. I close my eyes and whisper, "She said Dad was it for her."

"People change their minds."

"Yeah, but would you do it?" I hear my voice getting louder again. "Would you just forget about the love of your life for the first hot yoga teacher that came along?" I sound angry.

"Shit, Donna, I don't know." The tone of his voice tells me I may have found something Tim's not cool with—this conversation. "You could skip dinner tonight. We could go hear that Irish punk band at Canal Street." He's ready for us to move on.

But I'm not. "I don't think you get this."

"No, I don't think I do." He sounds exasperated.

I feel desperate. And panicky. I think about chocolate ghosts and weird dates and my brother's wedding. Something so permanent, but with no guarantee to really last.

It didn't for my parents. I have that feeling of falling again, and I don't know what else to do right now but be honest. "I'm just having a really hard time."

I don't know what else to say, and I guess Tim doesn't either.

After a minute, he says, "Listen, I've got to go. I have class in ten minutes."

"Okay, I've got to get back to work."

"I'll call you later."

Once we get off the phone, I remember it's Friday, and Tim told me he doesn't have class on Fridays.

Inside, Mr. Brighton is talking on the phone and tugging at his white mustache. He nods at me with a serious face, and if I didn't know he plays dolls with Delia and drinks iced mochas with whipped cream and a bendy straw every day, I'd be intimidated. I head down the main hallway and take the short flight of back steps to the prep room. Descending straight into hell, I think, for treating my Mom like shit.

I wait outside the prep room and look in through the glass door.

On one of the stainless steel tables is a body that must belong to Rory Mahoney, who died yesterday at age sixty-five. Mr. Brighton has already taken Rory out of the disaster pouch, and his body lies stretched out in a white cotton hospital gown with a pastel peach geometric pattern.

This man had a wedding, I think. I know because his

wife Nora will be here in two hours for her arrangement conference. How long did they have? And was it long enough? I know I don't need to be all freaked out while I observe my first embalming, so I go to that familiar place in my chest, where it's quiet and I can focus. The Dead Zone, I think, that's a good name for it.

After a few minutes I hear someone coming down the steps. " How was lunch?" Mr. Brighton asks.

"Okay." I follow him into the prep room, and we put on coats from the hooks on the back of the door. He holds out the box of gloves to me. Sliding on the gloves, I wonder what it would be like to be a surgeon, to work with a live body. And I know it wouldn't have the stillness that's here, with the dead.

Once we're all covered up, Mr. Brighton says, "Come on over and have a look."

I breathe in and notice a slight sharp odor. I fight to relax the furrows in my forehead.

"You'll get used to the smell. Just part of it. Are you doing all right?"

I nod.

Mr. Brighton says, "You can do this part. Gently close his eyes and mouth."

Rory Mahoney's skin feels cold through my gloves. For a second, I look into his green eyes. When I close them and his mouth, I feel his skin cold and hard through my gloves.

Mr. Brighton removes the hospital gown, turns the

water to a low stream on the table, and gets to work. He explains everything to me as he goes, and his voice is calm. As he injects embalming fluid into Rory's carotid artery, I wonder why being here with this body seems easier than meeting Mom's new boyfriend tonight.

Mr. Brighton massages Rory's arms and hands as pink fluid seeps into him and blood drains out from his jugular in deep red streams and clots down along his body and into the stainless steel sink at his feet. Fluid goes in. Fluid goes out. I can't see a stream of Rory's intangible parts —how smart or funny he was. And I believe they haven't gone away.

Like the intangible pieces of Dad still with me and still with Mom. But what happens to those invisibles when another warm, blood-pumping body named Roger steps into that space? *Change is life,* Tim said. Maybe, but that doesn't mean I have to like it.

After almost two gallons of embalming fluid, it's time to sew up Rory's neck. With an S-shaped needle, Mr. Brighton closes the spots he opened. He makes it look easy. I find my hands twitching slightly, trying to mimic his movements.

After poking a new opening in Rory's stomach, Mr. Brighton pulls out the organ juice and puts in the cavity fluid. When he's done, he seals Rory's stomach with a single button that'll be hidden under the smooth line of buttons on the suit Nora Mahoney gave us to dress Rory in tomorrow.

Rory's suit is navy, and without wanting to, I imagine Tim in this spot, in a navy suit. Which is yet another reason I will never be normal. I close my eyes, say a prayer, take a deep breath, and blink my eyes until the image dissolves.

Mr. Brighton rinses off Rory's body, and I recognize that he's doing his best to get Rory Mahoney ready for his last big day, while Gwen and B are planning their first big day together. While Mom seems to have forgotten about hers.

When Mr. Brighton finishes, we head up to his office. "So what did you think?" he asks.

"It was fascinating."

"It's a pretty amazing thing."

Mr. Brighton's phone rings, and when he answers he sounds so serious that I excuse myself.

A few minutes later, Mr. Brighton comes to my desk, and the color's gone from his face. Delia's in the emergency room and he doesn't know exactly what happened, but he has to go. He asks if I'll greet Nora Mahoney and start going through the checklist with her and to please extend his apologies and say he'll be back as soon as possible.

"Sure," I say, and feel like my face has turned a little white, too. I'm worried about Delia and worried about meeting with someone by myself.

"I trust you."

I nod. "You should go. I'll be fine."

I go up to the yellow room and take the arrangement

binder with me to review the checklist. A half an hour later, after I've practiced the questions, washed my face, and given myself a pep talk, I head downstairs.

With a lit cigarette extending from a holder between her lips, a woman perches on the arm of one the big lobby chairs. She wears a long white raincoat over a silky brown dress, and taps the pointed toe of one of her elegant brown-and-white spectators. Bobbed silver hair frames her made-up face, and I think she looks like a gracefully aged Hollywood starlet. "I know I'm not supposed to smoke in here, but you look like you could use a hit, too." She takes a puff and watches me.

She's right. I could use a hit of something, but I don't think that's appropriate. I offer a smile that I hope says, *Thank you, I would, but clearly I'm a professional.*

"Fine, I'll get rid of it. Just don't tell on me." She steps outside and returns a few seconds later sans cigarette.

"Okay. Mrs. Mahoney?"

"The one and only." She looks from my toes to my head and shakes her head. "If you don't mind my saying, you look awful. Maybe you should get a different job."

I'm used to dazed and weepy, which is how most people have walked in here in the last few months. But this I am not expecting. Since I have no idea how to respond, I pull out an old industry standard Mr. Brighton uses. "Let's go into the sitting room."

I'm guessing she's right about my looking awful, because

that's exactly how I feel—tired and in need of narcotics. As she chooses a cream-colored armchair in the sitting room, I hope Delia's okay and that Mr. Brighton will be back soon.

Situated on one end of the blue sofa catty-corner from her chair, I explain Mr. Brighton's emergency. I say, "So I'm happy to answer any questions, if I can. Do you, um, have any?" I open the brown leather binder on my lap to Mr. Mahoney's page.

"I've got a million of them." Nora Mahoney winks. "Here's one: what'd you do today?" She reaches for her pack of menthols and then pushes it back into her purse. She smiles. "And call me Nora."

"Okay, Nora," I say slowly. "Don't you want to talk about the arrangements?"

She looks at me like, *What the hell do you think?* I see her holding her face together, shoulders crunched up toward her neck. If I were her, I probably would want a change of subject too.

Part of me knows that talking about the arrangements is not what Nora needs at this moment. She just needs a break. And since I have a fresh assortment of distractions available, I say, "Tasted cakes for my brother's wedding, fought with this guy I'm dating, and found out my mom has a secret boyfriend. And my brother's fiancée doesn't even like cake. She wants to have fruit cups."

Nora's shoulders relax a little. "Well, you've got to have a cake. They're traditional."

"Oh." I'm not in the mood for another argument about wedding cake or anything else. And I certainly don't want to debate with this lady who's just lost her husband. I look down at the open binder and feel guilty for talking about myself. "I could help you pick some nice holy cards."

She leans back in the chair. "Tell me everything about the wedding. I'm sure Fruit Cup's got a real winner planned."

I make my voice as gentle as I can. "We really are here for you."

"I don't care about any of it," she says sharply, and closes her eyes. "I just want it done. You pick it all. Tell Mr. Brighton the medium price for everything—Rory loved averages." The edge of her voice softens into a sigh. "Now a good fight—that's what I love. Would you tell me about yours?" I can hear the *please* without her saying it. I know what it's like to need distraction.

"Average it is." I make a note for myself on Rory Mahoney's paperwork to have Mr. Brighton put together a medium-priced profile. "I told him about my mom's new boyfriend, and he didn't get why I was upset. I think I freaked him out. And he lied to me so he could get off the phone."

She laughs a hacking laugh that ends in a cough. She wipes her eyes. "Honey, there's always something wrong with them. He probably doesn't know how to do laundry either."

"That would be two things."

"And there's a lot they don't get. I've got news for you: they might never get what they don't get. Rory left me alone too much with our kids. He snored and he clipped his toenails in the kitchen."

I hold the brown binder to my chest and cross my legs. I'm not sure how this is comforting.

"He did all that, and he did other things. Every week he set out the Lifestyle section of the paper for me with an X and an O scrawled on top of it. And he'd bring home cinnamon buns from Ralph's on the corner just because it was Thursday, they were fresh, and he knew I liked the smell. He was a jackass, and he wasn't. And I loved him."

"Tim says nice things sometimes." I look down. "But sometimes I'm not sure he's on this planet."

"It's not all or nothing, honey. It's usually everything and something else."

"Were you happy with Rory?"

"That motherfucker, are you kidding?"

I almost gasp with the sudden urge to tell her not to speak ill of the dead.

She lets out a long cackle. "Oh, lighten up. I'm joking. And now that Rory kicked it, maybe I'll get myself a young stallion, just like your mother."

I notice my mouth is hanging open, and I close it. I've never heard someone talk like this about a dead person, particularly one she knew and loved. Clearly, Nora loved Rory, but she's not sweeping his shortcomings under the rug either. And I wonder how helpful it is to idealize the dead. Maybe that actually keeps people from being in real life.

Nora licks her lips and sits forward. "All right, I feel better now. Let's look at holy cards."

By the time we've picked holy cards and talked about the service a little, Mr. Brighton is back, out of breath and apologizing to Nora.

"No problemo," Nora says. "Everything okay?"

"She just burned her finger on the stove. Greta made it sound worse than it was. She'll be fine."

Mr. Brighton takes over, and I let my brain turn off for a while. I know I'll need to have my wits about me tonight.

eighteen

On the way to dinner, I stop at the Kroger, thinking I should bring something. After wandering around, not sure what to pick, I decide to get myself some tangerine gum. Next to me at the self-checkout with a bunch of carrots and some green juice is Charlie McIntyre. "Hello stranger," he says. "How's the death business?"

"Good," I say. I'm finding I can't help but smile whenever Charlie's around. "How's school?"

Charlie tells me he got asked to be the student representative on the environmental task force at UD and that he loves his classes. We both finish buying our stuff and stand past the checkout for a minute. The automatic doors open and shut a few times. I look at my watch.

"Don't tell me," he says. "You've got to go. You're on a date."

"I wish." I put the gum in my purse. "I'm going to my mom's for dinner. To meet her new boyfriend."

"That's big." Charlie looks down at his juice and back up at me. "You okay?" I nod, and before I can walk away, he hugs me and whispers, "Good luck. I'll be thinking about you."

When I walk through the door, I can still feel where Charlie whispered into my right ear. But now I also hear Barbra Streisand singing there, and I smell something reminiscent of meat loaf. I think of that condition *synesthesia,* how certain senses blend over into each other so that the sound of Barbra Streisand might taste exactly like meat loaf. In some ways, that makes sense to me. What doesn't make sense is Mom cooking meat loaf for some guy named Roger. I look around what should be familiar territory and feel like I'm at a haunted house. I wonder when the middle-aged boyfriend creature will jump out with a chain saw.

"Is that you, Donna?" Mom calls.

Before I can answer, she's out in the hallway kissing me on the cheek. I can smell her White Shoulders perfume mingled with the meat loaf. Baked onions with a floral bouquet—Mom's scent of seduction. She wears a white V-necked blouse and a long strand of pearls. Her gray silky skirt rests above her knees, revealing panty hose, which she only wears for church.

"Am I underdressed?" I ask, looking down at my jeans and sandals.

"You look just fine," Mom says. "Roger's in blue jeans too."

Behind Mom, B rolls his eyes. "Hey there."

"I know you." I hug him.

In my ear he whispers, "I like your blue jeans."

"Shut up." I pull out of the hug. "Where's Gwen? And Linnie?"

"Gwen couldn't make it. Linnie's in the family room with Roger," Mom says. "And I need to get back to the kitchen."

"I'll be in to help," I tell her.

She smiles and walks off.

I decide I'd like to stay out here in the hallway as long as I can. "So, how was the rest of cake day?"

"Gwen decided to compromise. Cake with berries." B grins at me and then stops grinning. "You didn't need to take off like that."

"Sorry. I was freaked out."

"Well, be nice tonight," B says, pushing me toward the family room. "I'll bring you some iced tea."

My stomach knots as I stand still and alone in the hallway. Should I stay or should I go now?

"Donder, come meet Roger," Linnie calls.

"Okay." I take slow steps in that direction.

In the family room, Linnie sits on our big squishy green couch. This month her hair sparkles like some kind of metallic cherry, and she's wearing it in long braids that I think make her look like Pippi Longstocking.

Suddenly, I can see Linnie as a baby, sitting on Dad's lap on our old couch, the mustard-colored one with the orange-and-brown stripes. I remember the scratchy carpet on my knees while I leaned on Dad's legs, how soft Linnie's little fist felt curled around my index finger, and how Dad's voice rumbled low through my ears as he sang *"Ciao, ciao, bambina"* to my baby sister and me.

Looking at Linnie, I miss her smaller self and our old couch, and I feel my chest tighten as I see the tall man sitting next to her, who is actually even more gorgeous than I remember. I cross my arms and study the long black ponytail with shiny silver streaks, resting against the most beautiful skin I've ever seen. Kind of coppery, kind of like a latte. He's barefoot, and his feet are beautiful too.

"Donna." Standing, he looks at me with amber-colored eyes, and holds out his hand. "I'm Roger."

I find I'm at a loss for speech, and Linnie kicks my leg with her left combat boot. I blush and shake Roger's hand. "Sorry, it's been a long day."

"No trouble," Roger says. "Come sit with us." He's so relaxed, like he's right at home.

If I were a wild animal, I believe I would growl or at least snarl, just a little. "I have been here before, you know," I mumble.

Roger nods and sits, saying nothing. He knows.

I almost sit on the floor and lean against the love seat, like I usually would, but I don't want to be lower than Roger. I grab a straight-backed chair from Mom's craft table and pull it up to the couch. As I sit, B brings me iced tea, and I wish it was whatever pale brown liquid with ice he's got in his short glass.

Once we're all sitting, and the quiet feels weird, I say, "So, you teach yoga?"

"You're welcome to come," Roger says. "I teach Wednesday and Sunday mornings at seven."

"I can't this week, but I'll totally be there sometime," Linnie says, and kicks me again with her boot, a gesture my shins and I are getting tired of. And I'm noticing something else. She doesn't seem quite so sullen. She looks, if I dare say it, like she's glad to be here. "And I'll bring Donna."

I scoot my chair a few inches away from my sister. "Sorry, I don't get up that early."

B takes a drink of what I'm guessing may be just whiskey and ice. He crunches a piece of the ice in his teeth. "So, Roger, what else do you do other than yoga?" If I'm not mistaken, my brother might be feeling a little territorial himself.

Roger pulls his legs up and sits cross-legged on the couch, flexibly folded. "I cook, I dance."

"Maybe you could give B lessons," I say. "That way he won't embarrass himself at his wedding."

Roger laughs. "I'd be happy to."

Mom comes in and sits on the arm of the couch next to Roger. "What about the wedding?"

Linnie smirks. "Roger's going to teach B how to dance."

B crunches another piece of ice.

Mom smiles. "He's a great dancer." She and Roger look at each other, and something intimate passes between their eyes. Roger touches her arm, and she blushes.

Mom and Dad loved to dance, and apparently she's found a new partner. All of a sudden, I wonder what else she's doing with her new partner. I feel dizzy, like I should sit down, but I'm doing that already.

"Awesome," Linnie says. "What's your favorite dance?"

"The tango, of course." He smiles and squeezes Mom's arm. "Although I can't do it very well."

"Then how can it be your favorite?" B asks this like a TV detective who's just trapped the culprit in a lie.

Breathing deeply, Roger moves his hand from Mom's arm and folds his hands in the center of his lap. He's not letting B get to him, a skill I wish I could acquire.

But right now I don't have that skill, and I do understand Nora Mahoney's love for a good knock-down, drag-out. I say to B, "You can't play football, but you love that."

"Shut up, Donder."

"Well, it's true."

In the background, the Streisand album has reached the duet with Donna Summer. I worry that the needle is stuck on "enough is enough is enough," but then I remember that's just the song. The wailing voices seem to be tying sturdy sailor knots in the already tense spots on my neck.

Linnie scooches forward and sits on the edge of her seat. "Roger, would you like to see Mom's picture table?"

"I'm sure he's seen it before," I say, and look at Mom. "Roger's been over before, right?"

"Yes he has," Mom says sharply.

Roger walks out of the living room toward the hallway, where Mom has a long, high table filled with stand-up photo frames of all of us and the odd people we're related to. I used to hate getting dusting as a weekend chore because it meant picking up each of those frames and running a cloth over them one by one. One Saturday morning in June, when I was about ten and grumbling to myself and my bottle of Windex, Dad said, "Hey, this is your heritage. It's okay to spend a little time on it." He was carrying a cup of coffee and had the newspaper tucked under his arm.

"But I want to read my book in the backyard."

He glanced at his paper and nodded at me. Then he walked away, and I went back to resentfully spraying and wiping.

A minute later he came back with an extra rag and started helping me. "We can get it done faster this way. I want to go to the backyard too."

It actually took us twice as long because Dad started telling me stories about Uncle Lou and him getting in trouble with Nonna. But I didn't mind.

Tonight, Mom looks at B and then at me and doesn't say anything. Her blush has changed to flush, and her lips are set, even, and angry. She follows Roger out of the room.

Linnie looks at B. "Dude, what are you doing?"

"Yeah," I say. "You made Mom mad."

Linnie turns her glare to me. "And you haven't been any better."

B snickers.

I huff defensively. "What do you mean?"

"Both of you need to stop acting like assholes." Linnie shakes her head. "Don't you want Mom to be happy? In case you haven't noticed, she really likes this guy. This is a big deal for her. So play nice, fuckers." She stomps out.

B and I look at each other. "I should not drink any more whiskey," B says.

"Yeah, you're the one who told me to be nice when I came in."

"You're right. She's right. It's just weirder than I thought."

Of course I want Mom to be happy and not lonely. But it is weird, and I don't want a new Dad. His shoes are big in my mind, and Roger's bare feet, beautiful though they are, can't fill them. My head spins. "Since you decided to stop drinking, maybe I'll start."

"That's probably not a good idea either. I'm going to get some fresh air; I'll be right back."

In the kitchen I find Roger pouring some wine for himself. I eye the whiskey bottle, but reach for the iced tea.

"So, I hear you're studying to be a mortician. That's a pretty intriguing job."

I take a long drink and tell myself I should say thank you. Instead I say, "Do you love her?"

I feel like I'm channeling Dad interviewing Dave Parker when he came over to make a model of the Amazon River with me in seventh grade. I remember Dad looking hard at skinny, oblivious Dave in this very kitchen and actually asking, "What are your intentions with my Donna?"

Dave Parker swallowed hard and said, "To not spill paint on her skirt?" Which I thought was a pretty good answer, considering.

At this point, I have higher expectations. Roger isn't in seventh grade, and he's dating my mom. He sets the wine bottle on the counter by the sink and breathes as he does it. I'm used to people answering right away, but Roger seems to pause before he says anything. The silence makes me squirmy, but if Roger can pause, then so can I.

"Yes, I do. Am I *in* love with her? I don't know." He stares at me with those amber eyes. "Is that okay, to not know?"

To say no seems ludicrous. And yet I'm not really sure. I don't know if I'd feel better if Mom was having a crazy fling or if she was totally in love again. "I don't want Mom to get hurt." Although I'm not sure my motives are that pure. I'm really worried about myself, which Roger can probably tell through some kind of yoga mind-reading technique.

"Neither do I." Roger's eyes soften. "Your mother's an amazing woman. She's kind. And beautiful. And she's got some great kids who obviously love her." Behind his yogic composure, I see something I recognize—wanting to be liked.

I nod. I realize Roger's making an effort, and I'm being a jerk. So I do something I think Roger and I can both get behind. I hold up my glass. "To Mom," I say, and we clink and drink. To Mom.

The rest of the night goes a little easier. B is his jovial self again, I decide not to say much, and we all eat what turns out to be fake meat loaf. Mom made it with something called Ground Beephe, since Roger's a vegetarian. When she spells it for me to explain it's not actually beef, she stares at me in such a way that says I might be next for the slaughterhouse if I say anything.

Even though the Ground Beephe has a bit of a rubbery chew to it, I keep my mouth shut and spoon on extra tomato sauce. I discover that Roger knows Cherokee and Japanese folktales for every occasion and tells a decent joke. Still, watching him take a bite of Mom's peach pie, made with actual peaches and which I know Dad loved, makes me want to snatch his fork and put it through his hand.

After dessert, Linnie heads to her room to call Snooter. Roger insists that he'll help Mom with dishes, so B and I decide to head out. When Mom and Roger walk us to the door, B shakes Roger's hand, and I'm not sure what to do. In our family, we hug often—to say hello, good-bye, nice to see you since you came back from your bathroom break. But I don't want to hug Roger. He should be leaving too. And yet there he is, with his arm around Mom. I've never seen anyone other than Dad in that spot, that way.

I kiss Mom quickly; I don't even hug her. "Love you, Mom" and "Bye, Roger" are all I can muster without bursting into tears.

Saturday morning, Gwen calls and asks if I'll help her address save-the-date postcards next week.

"Sure." Addressing postcards sounds like a glitter- and satin-free endeavor.

"I just need to get a few more addresses. For my cousins and your Aunt Sylvia and Roger."

"Roger—like Roger who was at our house last night?"

"Yeah. Oh, and I'm so sorry I missed dinner. I had some plans I couldn't cancel with my girlfriends."

"You're going to invite Roger?"

"B and I thought it would be a good idea. That way your mom has a date, right?"

"I barely know him."

"You'll just have to bring your own date, then." Gwen giggles nervously.

"I just don't think it's a good idea. But it's your wedding."

"I can bring it up to B again, I guess. If you think so."

"No, don't. It's fine. But I've got to go. Big test next week."

"Okay," she says. "Thanks, Donna."

"You're welcome," I say, although I'm not sure for what. For spreading doubt and my bad attitude?

An hour later, Mr. Brighton and JB catch me staring at the wall in the lobby.

Mr. Brighton says, "We're going to suit up Mr. Mahoney, and then JB's doing the makeup."

"Want to observe me, too?" JB smiles.

"Sure," I say.

In the meantime, I set up several bouquets of carnations and gladiolas along the walls of Viewing Room Two. The Brightons wheel Rory and his average casket into the empty spot.

"Nora Mahoney will be here in an hour," Mr. Brighton says.

"Then I'd better get to work," JB says. "Come ahead, sweet apprentice."

Mr. Brighton shakes his head and leaves us, closing the pocket doors to the room behind him.

JB opens his cosmetics case on one of the small flower

stands next to the casket and looks at the picture Nora gave us of Rory. "Everyone's unique, and we need to honor that." JB reminds me that we always request a picture to get the right color and shading for each person. In this photo, Rory's laughing on a lounge chair in front of some ocean.

The Rory before us is not laughing. His round face rests still, gray-and-black-speckled eyebrows curving above closed lids. But I can still see the laugh lines around his mouth, and JB's already fixed his lips into a slight grin, which he describes as "no small feat."

JB pulls out the nude cosmetic and a makeup brush. "Showtime, Rory," he says. "Let's make you pretty for the big day."

JB brushes the cosmetic onto Rory's face and bald head and sets his slight grin with lip wax and a pale neutral lip color to smooth out the skin. He pauses only to say the name of each thing he uses; otherwise, he's in his own zone and does his work like a virtuoso painter. With delicate strokes, he brushes more cosmetic on Rory's hands, covering a bruise from the hospital I.V. After a few puffs of powder from his atomizer, he steps back to appraise his work.

"How does he look?"

"Good." I'm impressed. "Really good and natural."

"Thanks, kid."

In his suit, all finished, Rory could be ready for his wedding. He could be just asleep. I touch his arm, cold and stiff under the suit, and I remember touching Dad's arm under a similar suit, that same stiffness. A slightly nauseous feeling swirls in my stomach as I see my fourteen-year-old self standing at the casket, feeling like the loneliest person in the world and being fascinated at the same time.

While JB puts away his makeup case, I carefully set the last few flower arrangements on the stands flanking Rory's casket and think about Mom and the gaping hole Dad left behind. I think of Nora, who will say a last good-bye on Monday.

When Nora arrives at Brighton Brothers, I can tell she's pulled herself tightly together, buttoned into a black suit and skirt and encased in gray panty hose and simple black pumps. She's ready for this first day of viewing. Since Rory had so many friends, Nora decided on two days of visitation, with the funeral on Monday. It seems like she's got composure stored up somewhere. She asks me to come and look at Rory with her.

In Viewing Room Two, we stand next to the open casket. "He looks good," she says. "I've never seen that." She leans in closer to the body. "Rory never smiled like that for me."

"Oh, I'm sure he did." Which sounds like a stupid thing to say as soon as I say it.

"Nope," Nora says. She looks at me, then past me, and a slow smile rises on her lips. "You know, Rory's best friend Dan died when they were sixteen. He only talked about it once, when we first met, but he told me Dan would be the first person he'd see when he died. He laughed about what a good time they'd have tearing up heaven or hell together. Which place they ended up, I don't know." She wipes some stray tears from her cheeks with a handkerchief. "But I bet they're having a ball right now."

I'm holding back my own floodgates as I think, *How beautiful*. I imagine Mom reuniting with her best friend, tearing up the afterlife with Dad. But she's not in the afterlife. She's in this life, and unlike Rory Mahoney, she has a good reason to smile now. She's going out on dates. She's got her first romance in four years. I smile for her, and I feel confused, like I'm betraying Dad.

Nora swats my arm with the back of her hand. "So, how's your love life?"

"Who knows?"

"Sounds about right," she says. "Just don't give up yourself. You're all you've got, and you only go around the block once." She blows her nose. "And buy your mother some goddamn flowers."

Rory Mahoney, 65

Cause of Death: Heart disease

Surviving Immediate Family:
• Wife: Nora
• Daughter: Jenna
• Son: Jed

Makeup: Smile rigged by cotton balls and wire in back of mouth, nude cosmetic, neutral lip putty

Clothing: Navy blue suit, pale yellow dress shirt

Casket: Standard oak package

Special Guests in Attendance:
• Tommy Mahoney, cousin and playwright in from Ireland

Most self-centered thing someone says trying to be comforting: "I could write a play about all of Rory's escapades. And you can be sure it would be beautifully written." —Tommy Mahoney

nineteen

A few weeks later, I've successfully avoided two family dinners, claiming I had plans with Tim, although I haven't actually heard from him since I called him from the parking lot. I have considered calling him to say that Charlie could give him some lessons in being supportive. It's officially October, and the air creeps in with a chill at night and smells like Halloween. The leaves on the oak tree in front of Brighton Brothers have turned a flaming red, and the brightness feels almost oppressive to me. I'm more in the mood for them to go with the season and just fall.

Which is what I feel like doing. Collapsing to the ground, letting kids jump on me, and turning into compost. Instead, school is getting busier, and so is work: just as Mr. Brighton promised, more people are dying.

Fall also means a new Players production, but at the first-of-the-month meeting on a Sunday afternoon, I tell them I'm too busy with school and work, and will have to bow out this time.

When I get back to Brighton Brothers and head to the rear entrance, I find Mom sitting on the porch swing that Mr. Brighton put in for Mrs. B at the end of the summer. I sit next to her. She says, "I'd love for you to come eat with us tonight, but I guess you have plans?"

"Yeah." I can't look at her and lie at the same time, so I do my best to thoroughly inspect my fingernails. "Study group."

"So we haven't really talked since our dinner." She looks down at her red purse and plays with the strap. "What did you think?"

By the little smile I see at the corner of her lips, I know she means Roger. "About what?"

She turns her face toward me and isn't smiling. Instead, she shoots her lasso-of-truth eyes at me, the ones she always used to get me to confess that I had not actually finished my homework. "About Roger."

"He's nice," I say, as if commenting on shoes I probably wouldn't buy.

"That's it?"

"You may have known him for a while, but I just met him."

"That's never stopped you from forming opinions otherwise," she says sharply. She looks back to her purse.

I know I could be more helpful here, throw her a bone. I should say something more, something about how he seems kind and well-balanced and interesting and intelligent, but I just can't go that deep. "He's really good-looking."

This makes her smile; we can agree on this. She twists the blue Roger-bracelet around on her wrist. "So, you know Gwen and B invited him to the wedding."

I want to be magnanimous, but I say, "They don't really know him either."

"They're not supposed to know him. I'm the one who's dating him." She pushes the porch floorboards with her Keds, and we rock a little in the swing.

I rub my temples with my fingers. I can still smell Linda's perfume from the Players meeting, and the sweetness turns my stomach. "So he is your boyfriend?"

"Roger and I are dating."

"So how serious are you?"

"Serious enough."

I put my tennis shoes on the porch floor and stop the swing. "If he's not your boyfriend, then why is he coming to my brother's wedding?"

"Donna."

"What?"

"Please don't be like this."

"You could go with Uncle Lou. I'm sure Aunt Irene would be happy for a way to get out of socializing."

"Do you know who I'd really like to bring?" I see hurt in Mom's eyes, and I see that I'm causing it. "I'd love to bring your dad, but I can't figure out how to make that happen. What I do know is that there's a breathing man who wants to spend time with me. And I like him too, God help me."

I hug myself with my arms. I want to run, but I don't know where to go. And the way Mom's staring at me, I feel like I can't escape.

"I've planned for everything in my life—family dinners, education for my children, being a good Catholic mother, my wedding." Her eyes shine bright and full and fiery. "But I didn't plan for this. I didn't plan for any of this. I'm doing the best I can, and I could use a little help here." She stands up and leaves me swinging.

I use my feet to stop it, but it still feels like I'm rocking back and forth.

As she drives away, I realize we never even said hello.

That night, I'm sitting at my desk, reviewing my embalming notes, when Tim calls and says, "Hey what's up?" like we just talked yesterday. "Want to hang out this Friday?"

I say yes quickly, wanting something, anything, to fill

the void and distract me from thinking about my conversation with Mom, which I'm actually doing as I stare at my embalming notes. I feel a little bit like a starving person, grabbing at the first food that's offered to me, even if it is a stale Twinkie. A small part of me says the last thing I need is a self-centered faux-pastry, but a bigger, louder bully part reminds me that my best friend is four hours away in Pittsburgh, and if I don't want to spend another Friday night alone, I should take what I can get. So I do.

In embalming class on Monday, Mr. Troutman describes the different kinds of postmortem blood clots, two of which are called currant jelly clots and chicken fat clots. I'm a little uncomfortable with the fact that both of these sound like they could double as ingredients for a Southern dish. At the same time, I'm also curious and looking forward to when I get to start embalming.

Sitting in class, I realize something feels familiar. I don't really know any of my classmates. I haven't spoken up much in class. Other than my being fascinated by all of the subject matter, this feels like Woodmont, where all I wanted was to disappear. But I don't want to be back at Woodmont, and I find I don't want to be invisible here. Which means making myself noticed, something that I'm not used to doing.

So after class, I take a deep breath and go up to Ned

Troutman, who is erasing blood clots from the board. When he notices me standing behind him, he turns around. "Yes?"

"I just wanted to say thank you for the lecture today."

"You're welcome." I see him searching my face as though he might find my name there.

"Donna Parisi." I say it a little too loudly, like it's bursting from my mouth. But it feels good to say my name out loud, to hear the sound of it. I hold out my hand.

Ned Troutman shakes it. "You're welcome, Ms. Parisi. I'll see you next class." He smiles and seems to stand a little straighter, like he's talking to someone important. And, I think, he just may be.

In the hallway, I see a pair of familiar tattooed arms. Jason of the Restorative Arts. "So you decided to study here," he says. "What do you think so far?"

"I think I'm in the right place."

"Nice." He grins. "Class with me next semester."

"Looking forward to it."

I feel warm and energized when I get to Social Considerations of Death and Dying, but the classroom is freezing, so I'm glad I brought my thick sweatshirt.

Dr. Landon, however, has taken off her black jacket and is sweating in her short-sleeved silk blouse. "People," she tells us at as class starts, "I'm in a full-blown hot flash, and I'm not going to try to hide it." She pushes out her lower lip and blows up under her big round glasses to get the bangs out of her eyes. She leans back against her desk. "In my humble opinion, we do too much in this country to hide from what's natural."

For the next forty-five minutes Dr. Landon speculates on what she calls the American Fear of Death, how we do everything we can to avoid it, even though it's the one thing in life that's guaranteed. She talks about how so many old people die alone, in nursing homes, with families who can't face the presence of death and dying in their day-to-day lives. She says that in her view the solution is community.

One of my classmates, a short, perky girl who looks like she could be an Olympic gymnast, says, "When I was growing up, we lived with my grandma, and I loved it. Even when my parents were busy, she always had time for me."

I wonder what it would have been like to live with Nonna or Grammy. If Nonna had been around, I have a feeling I would have gotten lots more dollar bills and sips of beer than I had without her.

At the end of class, Dr. Landon gives us an assignment that's due at the end of the semester. She wants us to carefully examine our views on death, what we bring to the embalming table, so to speak—our assumptions, our fears, our expectations, our experiences. It can be in the form of a paper, or we're free to use creative license—short films, PowerPoint presentations, songs, whatever. And we will present them to the class. Which sounds about as fun to me as a chicken fat clot.

So much for not wanting to disappear.

On Thursday, I start to make death lists to address Dr. Landon's assignment. *Assumptions, Expectations, Experiences, Fears, Questions, Beliefs.* I consider making an *Assassinations* list but guess that's not part of the assignment.

For the moment, I give up. I put on my Terra necklace and lie down. I put my hand over the metal turtle shell and look over at my nightstand, at the card from Aunt Selena. *Let the beauty we love be what we do.* I like the idea of so many ways to kneel and kiss the ground, Mother Earth. I'm just not sure which way is my way.

I wonder if it would work for my assignment to make a mobile or somehow use painted rigatoni noodles like Mom helped me use to create a DNA double helix for biology. Painted noodles would definitely make this easier. I laugh about the noodles and think of calling Mom, but I'm not sure that she wants to talk to me.

I head to Mrs. Brighton's kitchen to look for ideas in the pantry, and hear my phone from down the hallway. With a box of bow-tie pasta in my hand, I get to my phone before it stops ringing, and it's Liz, who is coming home for the weekend. I almost scream into her ear. "I have a date tomorrow night, but I can cancel it."

"I appreciate that," Liz says, laughing, "but I'll get home late anyway. Let's do something Saturday—all day."

"I'm all yours."

Friday night, after I watch Tim eat ramen noodles, we have returned to his mattress. When he buries his face in my neck and kisses my ear, I make an audible sigh and hold my arms tight around him. In the space of my sigh, I feel a sad kind of emptiness, but that bully voice reminds me that a cute guy has his arms around me and that should be enough.

He slides his hands under the back of my sweater. He breathes on my neck and whispers, "You make different sounds than Tina."

I move my hands from his back to his shoulders. "What?"

He lifts his head and looks at me. "You make different sounds than Tina does when we have sex. It's cool." He grins and lowers his head to my neck again.

I push him back up. "You have sex with your friend Tina?"

"Well, yeah."

I push him off me and roll onto my side to look at him.

"You're not upset, are you?" he says.

"No, I'm not upset." Not with Tim, anyway. At this moment I feel very calm. The bully voice is shouting all kinds of warnings and threats now, but I'm not so interested.

And fortunately, I discover I also have imaginary duct tape. "I just have some things to think about."

"Before we have sex?"

"Yes." I lie back and look at the corky ceiling of Tim's room. Doesn't look very sturdy. This house could fall down at any second, I think, and here I'd be with Tim, under the rubble. Nora Mahoney said not to give up me, that I'm all I've got. And do I really want to let myself be buried under pieces of corkboard with this guy? I imagine my epitaph: *Here lies Donna Parisi. Crushed by corkboard and inadequacy. Loving daughter, sister, with a moan all her own.*

"Are you done thinking now?"

"Yes."

"Does that mean we're going to have sex now?"

"No. It means we're not going to do anything anymore." And as I say this, I know this is true. It feels like a fog lifts out of my brain, and I can see the path clear ahead. I'm tired of not caring. I don't want to just make do. I don't want to just kind of date someone. I remember what Mr. Brighton says about being passionate about something. I know what that feels like now, for the first time in a long time, in school or when I'm working. And I know I'm not feeling passion right now.

I also notice that this time, I haven't been visited by the Anti-Sex Choir. Maybe the duct tape scared them off. And instead, I've conjured more of a doo-wop group, consisting of Nora Mahoney and Bob Brighton. And I'm singing a fairly nice lead. "Take care of yourself, Tim," I say. "I'm going home."

And it comes as no surprise to me that this is totally cool with Tim.

It's two A.M., and I still can't sleep. Looking at the wooden ceiling beams in my dark room, I feel alone. But not just in this room by myself. I feel like I'm in this life alone, that one day I could be an old person in a nursing home like Dr. Landon talked about. It's not as if I want to call Tim or anything. Letting go of him—whatever it was I had of him—felt freeing. But now it feels scary. I close my eyes, hoping that might shut out the fear.

I used to love alone time. All through high school I felt better when people weren't talking to me, but it's not so much fun anymore. I want something else, and it hurts. I think of Leaf and can hear her repeating what that other nurse said: "No one's forcing you to be here." It's true for me too. No one's making me do or be anything. If I want to be somewhere else, I've got to take myself there.

But I want so many things now, I don't know what to do with them all. I want to be a good student. I want to be in love, for real. I want things to be normal with Mom again. I want to make Dad proud.

In my mind, I hear the words again. *No one's forcing you to be here.* And this time, the voice sounds like my own—strong and sure.

It feels like I opened some kind of gate and let loose a team of wild horses, galloping around inside of me and doing their damnedest to get somewhere. And in the midst of the stampede, as I feel like I might be trampled, I remember Aunt Selena's charge. If I want to matter, if I want to make my life one of consequence, I just need to be someone amazing. Oh, that's all.

My eyes snap open, and I find that my vision's adjusted to the dark. Suddenly, everything seems clearer and more defined—the grain of wood in the ceiling, the line of the window frame, my path to greatness, if I dare to take myself down it.

So here I am, the one-and-only Amazing Donna, super-hero of freaked-out insomnia, and proud owner of a team of unruly stallions. I should totally get a cape.

Of course Liz has met someone in Pittsburgh who knows the door guy to The Garage, the club B talked about all the time in college. And Liz decides it's exactly what I need to get over breaking up with Tim and fighting with Mom.

The Garage consists of one enormous open room with a concrete floor, and does, in fact, look exactly like a garage, a big one that could use a good session with a broom and an extra-large dustpan. As we step into the room and my shoes stick with each step, I realize the floor could also use a mop and a bucket full of sudsy water.

Liz's new friend makes sure we both get the over-twenty-one red wristbands from the door guy, who, not surprisingly, also gives Liz his number. Liz does look good. She's got on dark jeans and an army-green tunic dress—a combination I'd never think would work, but one which Liz pulls off completely. I'm wearing lighter blue jeans and a V-necked purple sweater. Not bad, but not Liz.

She introduces us to the bartender, who is Derek, shirtless and decked out in black leather pants. He has a tattoo of a wide-open green eye right in the middle of his forehead, and tells us that his third eye has informed him that we are in serious need of delicious shots. Given the week I've had, I can't think of a better idea. And who am I to deny the wisdom of a tattoo with eyelashes?

"The third eye never lies," Derek says, mixing things in a silver cocktail shaker.

"What kind of shots?" I ask.

"Red Roosters." He lines up three shot glasses.

Liz grins at me; I can tell she's working to get my spirits up. She slaps her hand on the bar. "Well, cock-a-doodle-doo."

Derek winks as he pours. "Any cock'll do."

I guess I won't be making out with Derek tonight.

We raise our glasses and drink them down. The Red Rooster is actually quite a delicious bird. Then Liz orders us two Coronas with limes. "Now go shake those tail feathers," Derek says.

At the edge of the dance floor, we sit on high chairs that don't even have the foot rung where you can hook the heels of your shoes. Our legs dangle, and we drink our beers. Already, the dance floor is half full of an interesting crowd. College kids, old Dayton barflies, a cluster of leather-clad goth women, and a few transvestites for good measure. One song ends, and some sugary, boppy music starts. It sounds like candy, and I feel a strong urge to dance. "You want to go out there?" I ask, and point at the disco-ball-lit floor.

"Not yet," she says. "I think I want to watch a little while."

You have one choice, I tell myself. "Okay," I say, "whenever you're ready."

And for the first time in my life, I go out onto a dance floor alone. I feel my pulse in my neck and the strength of my legs. I find my own little space and start a little step-touch. My hips start circling with the music, and I lift my arms. Like a practiced diva, I lower them to my sides. I look left and right. And I remember that I'm not actually by myself.

Over my shoulder, I say, "Hit it" to Dad and Nonna and Grammy. Nothing to be afraid of. And I know I won't disappoint them. Or me. I keep moving and close my eyes. Behind me, I can feel swaying and hear the soft jangle of sequined fringe.

When I open my eyes, some smarmy college guy with an

ill-fitting beret is dancing too close to me, shaking his hips and giving me a thumbs-up. "All right," he says.

"Excuse me," I say, "but could you not crowd us?"

"You're alone."

"Um, no I'm not." I stand still and put my hands on my hips.

"Okay, whatever, psycho." He stomps off and tries to break into the lady-goth circle. Good luck.

I roll my eyes and go back to dancing, trusting that my dead backup singers have practiced and coordinated their routine to perfection. I'm sure they can smoothly handle such an interruption.

Someone taps me on the shoulder, and for a second I'm convinced it's Dad.

I turn, and Liz is standing there, one eyebrow raised. "Okay," she says, "I'm not sure who you're with, but do you have room for me?"

"Of course," I say. "Just stand a little to the right. And this is my ritual, so keep your clothes on." I smile. "We'll make up the steps as we go."

I have lunch with Liz before she drives back to Pittsburgh, and when she leaves this time, I don't feel quite as sad. In fact, I feel alert, my whole body tingling, as though I've really got that magic I see in Liz. And I feel like trying it out.

In the yellow room, I sit at my desk and look at the box from Tim. The wood feels smooth under my fingers, and

I still think it's beautiful and, yes, artful, even the creepy pictures. But they are all dead people. And right now, I want someone warm and breathing.

From my top drawer I pull out the laminated card Becky made for us, and look for the one number that seems most interesting at this moment, one I believe will connect me to warmth on the other end.

I take myself for a walk in the neighborhood around Brighton Brothers. It feels good to wear a scarf and thick sweater and to breathe in the crisp air. The sun is shining, and I'm not so angry at the trees in all their red and gold and orange glory.

I pull out my phone and dial the number. When Charlie answers, I let the bold trees inspire me, and say, "Hey, it's Donna. How are you?"

"Great. Wow. Hi." His voice sounds warm and animated, like soup bubbling on a stove.

"I was wondering if you wanted to go for a walk." I take a breath, and the air feels so crisp and good it makes me smile.

"Well, I have class in ten minutes. But I can get the notes. How about now?"

Half an hour later, when I get back to the parking lot at Brighton Brothers, I see Charlie leaning against his car. I haven't been inside since I called him, and my nose is cold. I grab on to the inside pockets of my sweatshirt, clutching at the thick cotton.

Walking over to him, I feel my heart beating. I feel everything in my body. I think this is what passion is supposed to feel like, and I look at his lips. I ask myself what an amazing person would do, and I know the answer.

Right there, by the Brighton Brothers "Peace" sign, I grab Charlie's shoulders and kiss him. His lips are soft, and I slip my arms around him. He tastes sweet, like spring water, and I feel his warmth spreading over me. He kisses me back, like he might be feeling some passion too. Then he pulls away.

"Nice to see you too."

I laugh and suddenly feel hugely self-conscious.

"What was that for?" he asks.

I put my hands back in my pockets and look at the leaves spread out like multicolored handprints on the concrete. "I wanted to see what it would be like."

"So, what's the verdict?"

When I look up, Charlie is smiling and his eyes are so open and clear that my nervousness melts away. I slip my hands out of my pockets and rest them on his hips. "I think I'm going to have to try again to make an informed decision."

A week later, I'm eating the whole-wheat noodles and organic pesto Charlie has made for us, using the hot pot in his dorm room and the microwave in the student lounge down the hall. Charlie eats out of his mug—he insisted I use the bowl—and the feast tastes terrible and delicious at the same time. Being here with Charlie has no resemblance to being with Tim. At this moment, every part of me feels awake—my brain, my body, and even maybe my heart.

I pick up a noodle from my bowl and slurp it from my fingers. "This is pure elegance."

"Nothing but the best for you." Charlie smirks.

My phone rings, and it's Mom. "I'll be right back," I say. I go out into the hallway, which smells like a men's locker room, or at least what I would imagine that to smell like —sweaty socks and full-throttle cologne. No one is in the student lounge, so I go in. "Hi." My voice sounds weak.

"Hi." Mom's doesn't sound a whole lot stronger. She clears her throat. "So I'm having a bridal shower for Gwen and B next month."

"For B?"

"They wanted it to be co-ed."

I sit down in the corner of the stiff, low-backed couch. "Whose good idea was that?"

"Gwen's."

I'm not sure why they call this a student *lounge*—this furniture actually seems to encourage the opposite. "Yeah, doesn't sound like something B would request."

"Not exactly."

We both laugh, and then the sound disappears like the last ladle of punch at a party. All we're left with is a big sad bowl with a faded sliver of strawberry stranded at the bottom.

"Well, I just wanted you to get the date on the calendar."

"Okay, I've got it."

"Donna?"

"What?"

"I love you."

"I love you too, Mom."

When I go back in to Charlie, tears start streaming from my eyes.

He stands up and walks over to me. "What's the matter?"

But I can't answer because I'm crying, and I don't know how to explain how far away I feel from my mom, and how much it hurts.

Lilith "Grammy" Meinert, 70

Cause of Death: Heart failure

Surviving Immediate Family:
• Daughter: Martha Parisi
• Grandchildren: Brendan, Donna, Linnie Parisi

Makeup: Dusty Pink lip cream, Buttermilk foundation

Clothing: V-neck white cotton dress, Grammy's favorite pink polka-dot scarf

Casket: Stainless steel, white velvet lining

Special Guests in Attendance:
• Grammy's long-lost childhood sweetheart, Vince Verdi

Funeral Incidents:
• Five varieties of Danish served with coffee and assorted teas

Dumbest thing someone says trying to be comforting: "Well, Martha, you just keep losing people you love." —Gilda Grant, neighbor and past president of the Kettering Knitters

Sweetest thing someone says: "You know, it's funny. I never stopped loving her." —Vince Verdi

twenty

The next Sunday, I wake up like I have every Sunday since I moved into the yellow room —feeling as though I should be somewhere. Church. I pull the covers over my head and slide my knees up to make a little tent. The sunlight pushing through the blue blanket and sheets makes a soft glow.

Church, of course, makes me think of Mom, and that makes me feel like I might just stay in bed for the rest of my life. I remember Mom sharing her hymnal with me when I was learning to read. I got so excited when I could understand the words I was singing by looking at the lyrics in the book, and Mom smiled at me as if I were the smartest, most beautiful kid in the world. Now I don't know what she thinks of me. I just know I'm not making her smile that big smile anymore.

I miss Mom, and today I realize I miss something else —church. At the same time, I don't want to go to church. So within my first ten minutes of consciousness for the day, I'm already sad and confused, and another horse has trotted up to the watering hole. Awesome.

I reach out under my tent, first for my Terra necklace and then for my phone so I can call Charlie, who sounds like he's still asleep. "Are you awake?"

"No."

"Oh." I wrap my other hand around Terra and like how the shell feels curved under my palm.

"Yes, I'm awake. You just called me."

"Sorry." I stretch out my legs and let the sheet fall over me.

"I don't mind, but whatever you want, it better be good."

I almost whisper, "I miss going to church."

"You're going to have to do better than that."

"Hey." I'm getting a little claustrophobic now, so I pull the covers down to my chin and let the sun hit my face.

"Okay, so you miss church. Call your mom. Meet her there."

"But I don't want to go to church. And Mom and I aren't so much talking these days."

"Now you've got me. What do you want?"

288

The windowpane rattles with a burst of air, and I see a bare oak tree branch waving at me. "I want something holy. Something sacred."

"How about talking to me on the phone? Does that work?"

I grin. "It's a start."

"Well, excuse me." I can hear Charlie's bed creak, which means he's sitting up now. "Maybe you could think about what you like about church, or don't like. Maybe you could start there and then make up your own holy."

In church, I realize, I used to worry, think about Dad and how things were when he was alive. I would miss him. I don't want to worry. I don't want to be sad. I don't want to be the moper B thinks I am.

And I didn't like being talked at by Father Dean or even Father Bill. Or having to repeat words I'm not sure I understood. Or having to stand up and sit down and kneel because I'm supposed to.

"Are you still there?"

"I'm thinking, like you said. Shush." I think of the quiet after Communion, of listening to the organ, or singing, or being still while Father Bill would walk up and down the aisles, swinging a big ball of incense so that the sweet smell settled around us all like a smoky blessing. I realize I've closed my eyes, and I open them. "But what about God? Where does he fit in?"

"Or she, or it. Where do you want God to fit?"

Bearded God pops into my head. "Isn't God supposed to be in charge of everything, to tell us what we can do and can't do? You know, lay down the law?"

"When I look around at all the different plants and animals and people, and the things we all make and do, I think the divine must be pretty big. Has to be. So for me, God or Goddess or whatever has to be big enough to hold everything."

I realize how tightly I'm holding on to Terra. When I pull my hand away, I see my palm full of indented little half moons from her shell. And I imagine a giant sea turtle big enough to hold me and Charlie and Aunt Selena and B and Gwen and Linnie and Mom. Even Roger fits there. "Could God be a sea turtle? A girl one?"

"Why not?" Charlie laughs. "And can she fly and have X-ray vision?"

"Make up your own God," I say, sitting up and leaning against my pillow. "Thanks so much. You've been a big help."

"You're saying good-bye? I just woke up. Just now. For real."

"I have more thinking to do."

Later that night, in between studying and Brighton Brothers chores, I'm still thinking, and I look up another number in my phone. I like Charlie's idea for making up my own holy, and I know someone who might have some ideas how I could do that.

Aunt Selena sounds delighted to hear from me, and says Charlie and I should come to dinner next week. She suggests some candles and chants I might like, and tells me, "These days are good ones to talk with your dad. In many traditions, people believe that the veil between the worlds is thin right now, that it's a good time to take care of unfinished business, to let go and help the dead to let go too."

I nod. I like the idea of letting go. "Thank you—for everything."

From down the hall, Mrs. Brighton calls, "Dinner's ready!" and it sounds so much like Mom that I get a little dizzy.

Thinking of Mom, I feel like I'm right back where I started today, confused and sad and hiding under a tent.

On Halloween morning, I get back to Brighton Brothers from an early class and find a big gift-wrapped box on my bed with a rectangular gift card attached to an oversized red bow. On the card: *Everyone's got to start somewhere. Meet us in Room 1.*

Inside the box is my very own Titan 2000. I know it's my very own because on a silver plate right below the handle, my name has been engraved.

In Viewing Room One, in front of an extra-long coffin,

stand both Brighton brothers, grinning like sphinxes. Dentist-head sphinxes.

"I assume I was supposed to bring this." I hold up my Titan 2000 and grin back at them.

"We thought it was time," Mr. Brighton says, and JB elbows him. "Okay, Joe thought it was time, and I agreed. We think you're doing great work, Donna."

I feel my face getting hot. "Thank you."

Mr. Brighton walks over and hugs me, a quick, awkward, and perfect hug. "Okay, I'll leave you two to work."

JB hugs me too, less awkward and more of a bonecrusher, but still perfect. "Okay," he says, "now I observe *you*."

We head over to the front of the room together. Late this afternoon we're holding the visitation for Abe Carter, who, at age eighty-one and six feet six, is the first since I've been here to need one of the extra-long coffins. I set my Titan 2000 on one of the flower stands and crack it open. I look at Abe's long face and all the laugh lines in it. For a minute I close my eyes, hoping to honor Abe's life and all the moments that set those lines in his face. I remind myself to love the whole person as I work.

With eyes open, I study his skin tone and notice some discoloration, so I pick a Sandy Beige concealer cream and squeeze some onto a large sponge brush. I glance up at JB, who purses his lips and nods. "I couldn't have chosen better."

I take a deep breath and get to work. I smooth the concealer onto Abe's forehead and cheekbones and chin and wonder if I am getting him ready for the afterlife, like we learned in rituals class. I imagine some underground angel, like a celestial production assistant, drifting into Abe's coffin once he's buried, and saying, into a golden hands-free device, *Yep, this one's been through wardrobe and makeup. Ready to go.*

I smile at Abe. *Don't worry. You'll be ready.*

For his lips, I choose a neutral shade with just the palest hint of red. And then I turn to his hands, brushing concealer over the hills and valleys of the wrinkled landscape there. Abe doesn't look like the kind of guy who'd ever had or would want a manicure. So painting the clearest of clear polish on his nails, I assure him that this doesn't count as a salon visit.

As I let a fine spray of powder settle on Abe's face, and step back, I remember JB's still here. I raise my eyes, just enough to check out the expression on his face. He's nodding and smiling wide. "You did it, Donna P."

Knowing I'll remember this face, I look down at Abe and whisper, "Thank you."

That afternoon, after JB and I share a celebratory glass of fruit punch that looks a little too much like embalming fluid, and after I've stored my new Titan in the prep room, we're set for visitors. Since JB says he could use a little brisk air, he wears his long black coat to handle the outside door, and I take the inside post.

Standing next to the cream-colored wall, I'm feeling accomplished, proud even, and I have that grounded, solid feeling, ready to be calm and helpful and kind. And then through the door walks Patty, followed by Jim and Becky. They look like different versions of themselves: serious faces and dress-up clothes. Patty's got on a long black coat and a silky scarf. She and Becky are both wearing panty hose and heels, and Jim's got a tie on. They look like grown-ups. I wonder if I look like one too.

All of a sudden, the ground beneath my feet doesn't feel so sturdy. I feel like I'm back at Woodmont, and I want to hide so Patty can't tell me that the navy skirt I'm wearing is so last year.

Patty opens her eyes a little wider when she sees me. "Hey. I didn't know you were still working here."

I nod. I'm not sure if I should ask about school, and I remember they're here and dressed up for some reason. "So, um, you knew Mr. Carter?"

Jim nods. "He's, well, he was our grandpa."

Becky reaches over and grabs Jim's hand. "It's nice to see you," she says to me.

Then Patty's face crumples, which at first looks like her face when she thinks something is stupid, but which I realize is something else entirely, and before I know it,

Patty is crying on my shoulder and hugging me. Or more accurately, I'm hugging her; she feels fragile.

"I don't know what to do," she says.

Something, very definitely, is happening in my heart. And it's not the need to hide or escape to the Dead Zone. I find I don't actually want to escape to anywhere, and that what I'm feeling is compassion, bubbling up from a deep well inside me and filling the empty place in my chest. The strength in my legs comes back, and I feel the ground under my feet. I hold Patty in my arms and whisper, "You don't have to do anything."

I think of Patty strutting around Woodmont like she owned the place, a feeling I never had there. But at this moment, I know I'm in my element. I know Patty and I aren't so separate. And I understand, I think for the first time, what it means to love the whole person. I don't think Mr. Brighton was just talking about dead people: he meant the live ones who come to us, too. And it turns out that I can love the whole person after all.

"But this sucks." Her voice shakes, and she sniffles.

"I know," I say. "That's why you're crying."

Patty clutches at the back of my sweater, and I let my compassion rise up, maternal and protective, and encircle us both. I stay solid, holding her like earth.

"I'm right here," I whisper into her ear.

Over Patty's shoulder, Becky and Jim look at the carpet, and after a minute, Jim says, "I need to get some water."

Patty pulls away from me and wipes her eyes with the back of her hand. "Me too." She tugs the scarf off her neck and bunches it up in her hand.

"Water fountain's just down there." I point to the end of the hallway.

"Thanks," Jim says.

"Yes, thanks." Patty glances up at me with shy eyes. She reaches out and lightly touches my arm. "Thank you."

As they head down the hallway, I feel like something has let go inside of me, and I don't even panic when, a few minutes later, cousin Tim shows up with his parents. I find that I feel only compassion for him as he says hello and hugs me. And then a little disgust as he checks out my ass. Which leads to reassurance that I was wise to walk away from that.

"I saw our lunch table today," I tell Charlie that night. We're sitting on my bed with the hot chocolate Charlie brought for us, and his arm feels good around my shoulders. I explain that Jim and Patty's grandpa died, and add that I also saw Tim.

I feel Charlie's arm tense, and he raises one eyebrow at me.

I set my hot chocolate on the nightstand and turn back to him. I put my hand on his waist, and I can feel the edge of his jeans, just above his hip. "I still can't believe I wasted my time with that." I kiss him. "You are clearly the superior choice."

"Then," he says, smiling at me like he's up to something, "you won't mind attending a little party with the superior choice."

I'm hoping for some kind of event right here that involves taking our clothes off, but it turns out Charlie wants me to go with him to his family's version of Thanksgiving, one they call the Harvest Festival, so as not to dishonor the Native Americans. "Beware," he says. "The festival has the highest concentration of hippies in the Dayton metro area. It can get a little scary."

"But you'll protect me, right?"

"You've got it."

"Then I'm in."

"Thank you," he says, and kisses me softly, just a brush on my lips—an activity I've decided won't ever get old.

On the day of Gwen and B's shower, Mom has the house decorated like its own harvest festival. The house is crawling with cornucopias and Gwen's equal-parts perky and athletic friends. A lot of B's friends are here too, holding cans of beer and looking awkward. Uncle Lou and Aunt Irene have Linnie cornered, and I'm sure Uncle Lou is pestering her about Snooter. And there, in all his godlike glory, is Roger, looking like a model in jeans and a white sweater, with his arm around my mother.

I look across the room at them, standing in the corner of the living room and talking with a very animated Gwen.

Part of me wants to run over and tell Mom about all the good things happening. About class and work and Charlie. But Roger feels like a force field I don't want to penetrate. Going over there would mean that I think it's okay.

I realize I'm not standing by myself anymore, and see B. He looks toward Mom and tells me, "You're hurting her, you know. And she's the only parent you've got left."

This, I decide, is why bridal showers are usually just for girls. That way, stupid brothers or stupid yogic boyfriends can't come and ruin them. "Why don't you mind your own business?"

"This is my business. She's my mom too." I must be the only one who gets this tone from B; otherwise he wouldn't have so many friends.

By the grace of God or Sea Turtle, Uncle Lou comes over and reaches up to slap his hand on B's shoulder. "What the hell is a guy supposed to do at something like this?" He's got on a pumpkin-colored suit jacket and a tie with a cartoon turkey and the words, *I'm For Dinner* written below it.

"How'd you get out of the house with that tie?" I ask.

"I put it on once I got here." He winks. "I think I look pretty snappy."

"That you do," B says, and shakes Uncle Lou's hand. "If you'll excuse me, I'm going to see if Mom needs help setting food out." With the word *Mom*, he shoots me an accusing glance and walks off.

"Who put the bug in his boxers?" Uncle Lou asks.

"Guilty," I say.

"Yeah, you look guilty." He pulls on his turkey tie. "So, how's funeral school?"

"Good," I say. "I really like it."

Uncle Lou takes a step closer to me and looks around, like he's checking to make sure we're not being watched. "So Irene tells me she heard from your mom that you've seen my sister."

"Aunt Selena?"

"Yeah, that one." He shifts his weight from foot to foot. "So how is she?"

"She's great. She has this beautiful little house in Yellow Springs. You should go visit her."

Aunt Irene sees us and makes a beeline in our direction.

In a very low voice, Uncle Lou says, "Tell her I said hello, would you?"

I nod, and feel sad for Uncle Lou. And Aunt Selena.

When Aunt Irene gets to us, she hugs me and then turns her eyes to Uncle Lou. "You look like the cat that ate the canary."

"Speaking of which, I'm starving." Uncle Lou strains his neck toward the kitchen. "Where's this food your brother was talking about?"

After food and before presents, Mom catches me on the way out of the bathroom.

For a second, we look awkwardly at each other. There's so much to talk about, I can't think of anything to say.

She hugs me and touches the sleeve of my sweater. "You look nice. I love that dark green on you."

I look down at my sweater and khaki skirt and remember something I can ask her. "Oh, you know, I was wondering if you had a dress I could borrow. I'm going to a party. A harvest festival thing." I neglect to mention that it happens to be on the same day as Thanksgiving, when she'll likely expect me to be here instead.

Her eyes seem to get brighter, and she smiles. "Oh, I know just the one. Same color as your sweater. Let's go take a quick look right now." Mom's not one to leave her party guests, so I know she's excited I'm asking her for something. And it's a relief to discuss something easy. She takes me downstairs to the Wild Youth closet.

I say prayers of thanks as she slides several sparkly pantsuits to the side, and I breathe in the cedar smell of the closet, where I used to stash myself behind long plastic coverings and shoe boxes when B and I played hide-and-seek.

"You know," she says, "I saw Bob Brighton at the Kroger, and he told me you're doing a wonderful job."

"Oh."

"I told him I wasn't surprised." She smiles at me and slides the plastic cover off a dark green, knee-length dress with a flared skirt. "How about this one?" It has a scooped neck and the fabric looks a little like snakeskin, but it's shiny and ripply, like water. It's perfect.

"I love it." I reach down and pull out the skirt to see how far it stretches.

"I wore this to my first New Year's Eve party with your dad. We danced the whole night. The skirt's really good for that."

I let the skirt fall. "Are you sure it's okay for me to wear it?"

Mom looks at the dress and takes a breath. She hands it to me. "What good is a dress if no one's wearing it? It's been shut up in here for too long." She puts her hand on my cheek. "It's okay to give it some new memories."

I want to reach up and touch her hand, but I can't. Instead, I make my voice cheerful. "Thanks, Mom. This'll be great." I slide the plastic back over the dress. "Let's get back upstairs. We don't want to miss them opening presents."

"No," Mom says, slowly closing the cedar doors to her wild youth.

Abe Carter, 81

Cause of Death: Stroke

Surviving Immediate Family:
• Sons: Paul, Greg
• Daughter: Laura Plintz
• Grandchildren: Jim, Patty, and Tim (ex-boyfriend)

Makeup: Sandy Beige concealer, Pure Sand cover-up cream, Neutral Glow lip color

Clothing: Hunter green wool fisherman's sweater

Casket: Extra-long birch special

Special Guests in Attendance:
• Becky Bell

Funeral Incidents:
• I comfort Patty.
• I survive brief, creepy hug from Tim.
• On the way out, Patty lets me know that I look better in brighter colors.

twenty-one

Mom calls the day before Thanksgiving and says, "We're doing dinner at four."

Out the window of the yellow room, the bare tree branch waves to me as the light fades from the sky. I feel a little sick to my stomach as I say, "Oh, actually, tomorrow's that party I told you about. At Charlie's parents' house."

"Charlie? Are you two going out?"

"Yeah." I press my hand onto the cold glass. "I've been meaning to tell you."

"Honey, that's great. You should come by after the party."

"I think the party goes late." Which sounds as lame as it feels to say.

"Oh." Mom sounds disappointed, and I feel like a jerk. "Should I save you some stuffing?"

"Yeah, that would be great."

"We'll miss you, Donna," she says. "You know that, right?"

"I know." From the corner of the window, I feel a tiny draft of the winter air. Stepping away from it, I put my hand in the pocket of my sweat pants and wonder when the heat will kick on.

On the afternoon of Thanksgiving/Hippie Harvest Festival, I'm waiting for Charlie and watching PBS on the little TV that JB donated to me and the yellow room. Some classically trained British actor narrates a special about crocodiles, and the low voice and ambient noise help my shoulders relax. I don't want to be nervous about the party or meeting Charlie's parents, and animal shows tend to comfort me. In the two years before he died, Dad and I watched them together.

It started late one Friday night when I was twelve and counting sheep couldn't stop me from worrying that no one would ask me to dance at my friend Jenny's boy-girl party. From the bedroom I shared with Linnie, I heard the distant TV buzz and wandered down the hallway toward the blue light in the living room. Dad was sitting in his paisley pajamas on a corner of the couch, and turned when he heard me step on the creaky floor spot in the doorway. "I can't sleep," I said, hoping I wouldn't get into trouble for still being up.

"Me neither." Dad held out his arm to me. "Might as well sit down with me and the cheetahs."

I curled up next to him, even more wide awake with the prospect of just me-and-Dad time. As we watched the sleek muscled cats run in slow motion, Dad made tsking noises. Maybe he wanted to run that fast too.

"Why can't you sleep, Daddy?"

"Well," he said, eyes on the TV, "your dad didn't get a raise at work, and he should have."

Something fragile in his voice made me nervous. I scooted an inch closer to him and clutched at a soft piece of his pajama top. "What are you going to do?"

He looked down at my hand and then put his own over it. I liked how big his hand was and how it felt warm on my fingers. He turned to me and smiled, like he just remembered something. "I'm still going to do my job. And I'm still going to be good at it."

I nodded. "I bet you're the best bridge seller they've got."

Dad laughed and squeezed my shoulder. "Maybe I should work for you. Got any friends who need some steel beams?" We settled in with the big cats until we started to doze off.

I think Dad would have liked this crocodile special I'm watching now. Even with those stubby legs, they can actually run pretty fast on land.

When the phone rings, I know it's Charlie downstairs. At the back door, he stands all lanky and handsome in a brown jacket over a thin cobalt sweater. "Damn," I say, appraising him and smiling. "Let's stay in and make out to nature specials." I take his hand and lead him back upstairs.

"That does sound like a better idea."

"Maybe we can harvest and then make out." I smile.

In the yellow room, I grab my jacket and purse and go to turn off the TV. I pause to hear British Actor Man explaining how crocodiles let out this noise called a bellow. He describes it as their own unique cry, a deep rumbling, like building thunder. He says they must do it for no other reason than it's their noise, something that identifies them just as them, and not some other creature.

My mind jumps back to that night watching the cheetahs with Dad. Around two A.M., when he tucked me back into my bed, he whispered, "The only person who needs to believe in you is you." He kissed my forehead. "And you've always got me in your corner."

I wonder now if Dad just needed to say those words out loud, if that night he was reassuring himself as much as he was me. I look at Charlie, and my chest feels full—my corner has turned out to be really well staffed.

"Ready, Super Croc?" Charlie asks.

"As I'll ever be."

Outside, the air smells like snow. I remember I haven't eaten anything since breakfast, and my stomach growls. Or maybe it's the sound of my own distinct bellow, rumbling up from the center of me and demanding to be heard.

On the way there, Charlie tells me that his mom and dad, who he calls Erin and Gabe, are really excited to meet me. I'm looking forward to meeting them too, even if I feel a little intimidated. Charlie's told me that Erin and Gabe are mega-smart and always learning something new. Like when Erin learned how to ice-skate a few years back, and not just circle-round-the-rink skating, but things like double salchows and leaps and spins and stuff. And she's actually pretty good. And while she skates, Gabe grows herbs in the kitchen window and cans things they plant in the backyard.

Once I learned how to make pot holders out of multi-colored pieces of panty hose, but that doesn't seem quite on par.

When we arrive, Charlie's parents' house is already buzzing with people, and Charlie leads me through them for a quick tour. Gabe and Erin have outdone themselves. Every room holds at least one candlelit table full of food and drinks—brown rice risotto with asparagus, butter-nut squash soup, pumpkin bread with maple sage butter, Crock Pots full of hot spiced cider. But my favorite spot is the enormous backyard, twinkling lights lining the trees and shed, and in the middle, a blazing fire pit with little benches all around.

Erin wears a bulky wool sweater and an orange corduroy skirt down to her ankles. Her hair hangs in one long braid, and she hugs me tight as soon as she meets me. "We're so glad you're here. I'm sure you miss your family, but I hope you'll feel really welcome."

"Thank you," I say. And even though I do feel welcome, even though the Harvest Festival might be the most beautiful party I've ever been to, even though we all sing around the bonfire and listen to Gabe play guitar, and Charlie stands behind me with arms circled around my waist, I still can't help but feel sad. And then angry with myself for feeling sad in the midst of so much joy.

When Charlie drives me back to Brighton Brothers, he says, "What's up? Was it my dad's singing? It can be a little dorky."

"No, I loved it."

"Or the stuffing? I know other people don't usually have nuts and berries in theirs."

At *stuffing*, I start to cry. "Mom makes really good stuffing," I say between tears.

"You want to stop there? It's still early, and I don't mind."

"No!"

Charlie pulls in next to the hearse at Brighton Brothers

and puts the car in park. He reaches into the backseat and hands me a napkin.

I wipe the tears from my cheeks, and the napkin smells like french fries—I guess even environmental studies majors sometimes fall prey to fast food.

"Donna, you're making yourself miserable. And you're probably making your mom miserable too. Is this Roger guy really that bad?"

I blow my nose into the napkin.

"Don't you miss your mom? Haven't you said that to me about a billion times?"

"Yes."

"Then why don't you make up?"

"I just want things to be how they used to be."

"That's not possible," he says softly. "Maybe it's time to move on."

"Maybe you don't know what you're talking about." I reach for the handle and open the door. Cold air pours into the car.

"I'm on your side here."

"It doesn't sound like it." I get out of the car and slam the door. Once I'm inside, I wait to hear the car pull out. I wait a while. I should go back. I feel angry and sad and embarrassed. Then I hear the car start and the sound of the motor fade. And all I'm left with is sad.

twenty-two

On Friday, Charlie doesn't call. Mom does call and leaves a message that she has stuffing waiting for me. Mostly, I stay in the yellow room and stare at the walls.

That evening, I can't sit still any longer. I'm mad at myself. Frustrated that I've probably really pissed off Charlie, that I missed Thanksgiving with my family, that Dad isn't here to make it all better, that Dad isn't here at all, that he's not ever coming back. And that even with so many good things happening, I still feel so painfully stuck.

I have to do something, so I pull out my Chapman books and notebooks. Homework is a good distraction. Right on top are my notes on the project for Dr. Landon, which is due next week. I have no idea how I'm going to get from one page of handwritten notes to turning in a polished final project in seven days. And now I have something new to worry about. Great.

Then I remember I might know something about getting from one place to another. I have a flash of something that Kirsten said in that class last spring about how rituals can do just that, and I realize I got so mad at Charlie yesterday because he's right. I have to move on.

I remember what Aunt Selena said about the veil between the worlds, about letting go. I wonder if it's still thin, if I can still talk with Dad. And at this moment, I know very clearly what my final project will be.

The next morning, I wake up to my alarm at six. I slip on my Terra necklace, bundle myself into flannel-lined jeans, a T-shirt and sweatshirt, and my winter coat. I wrap my neck in my purple scarf and slip on my gloves. I take the paper grocery bag I've prepared and walk softly down the steps and out the front door. The cold shocks the skin on my face, but it feels good. In the dark sky, stars glow clear and bright. I warm up the Lark and drive a route I know well, winding around to the spot I usually visit once a year with Mom in April.

I park, grab my bag, and walk up the little hill to the gravestone. A light wind sends a chilly ripple through my coat, and my body feels more charged and alert with each step. My eyes have adjusted to the dark, and it's not actually that hard to see when I get there. I run my hand over the round edge. *Domenic Parisi, beloved husband, father, brother, and friend. Rest in Peace.*

I set down my bag and find a stick. Into the ground, I start to trace a line. The earth resists, hard and cold, not soft like in the springtime, but I hold the stick steady, and finally, all around me and Dad's grave, I make the shape of a turtle, one that I think is big enough to hold it all.

I pull my Terra necklace out so it's resting on top of my coat, and from my bag, I take out a piece of paper. I've filled the paper with a drawing of a turtle shell, and I made a copy. One I'll save for Dr. Landon's class, and one I'll use this morning.

On each of the little sections of the shell, I've written words, what I know about death. And it's a full shell. I inhale, just a little, fighting against the cold air. "I love you, Daddy," I whisper. And then, one at a time, I rip off the sections and say each one aloud.

My father died when I was fourteen.

I like to think about death, but I don't like to feel about it.

I believe there's a heaven for people to go to.

Death must hurt.

With each piece I rip and say and drop, I feel my breath get deeper, my lungs fill more fully.

I am angry at death.

People grieve in many different ways.

Everything and everyone dies.

Death changes everything.

Once I've spoken them all, I've covered Dad's plot of earth with the little white pieces, like snow or a sheet, or a very thin veil between me and whatever's left of him there in the ground.

I know I want to end my ritual with singing, to use my own voice, the one that identifies me as myself. And at this moment, all I can think of is the Ave Maria, which makes me giggle as I start it. I sing and laugh, realizing I can only remember the first four Latin words, so I just keep repeating those, knowing I'm not any better than the lady in church that Dad and I couldn't stop laughing at. I hope wherever he is, Dad is enjoying this, that he knows I'm okay and I'm letting go, singing and laughing and crying all at once.

Behind the gravestone, I watch the sun seep into the sky, behind the hundreds of other gravestones that mark other fathers and mothers and beloved people of beloved people, behind the bare and skeletal trees. Behind it all, light is rising. Fuchsia strips pulse over a light blue palette and white brushes of clouds.

I sing until I can't sing anymore, until I drop to my knees and sob into the hard earth. And when the tears have stopped flowing, when my head hurts and I'm done, I feel warmth on the top of my head and I raise my face to see the sun creeping, like a great red-orange turtle, up and up and up. When I close my eyes, all of the sky colors are still there. The pounding in my head slows, and layers of fear slip off my heart, which now takes up the pounding, beating in my chest, steady and sure.

It's nine o'clock by the time I get home, and I fall into my bed, exhausted. It takes me a while to fall asleep, but once I do, I'm out.

When I wake up, it's dark, and I have a message from Charlie on my phone. He wants to make sure I'm okay. I call and ask him to come over. He agrees, and I brush my teeth.

When Charlie gets to Brighton Brothers, I meet him at the door in my pj's and a sweatshirt. Back in my room, I ask if he'll crawl into bed with me. He smiles and nods. Under the covers, we wrap our arms around each other, and his face feels cold against mine. "You're freezing," I say.

"It's winter out there," he says, and laughs. "You know, if two hikers are stranded in the cold and someone gets hypothermia, to save him, they both have to take all their clothes off and use their natural body heat."

I look into his eyes and see a little twinkle there, like the stars this morning. "Are you saying you need to be saved?"

"I totally have hypothermia." He nods seriously. "This is a life or death situation."

"I guess we don't have a choice, then."

We slip out of our clothes for the first time, and for a

second, I think Charlie might really have hypothermia, and I am too distracted by his icy skin to worry about being naked. "Holy crap, you're cold."

"I told you," he says, wrapping his arms around me. "Save me," he whispers into my ear. "Hold me close."

I realize that no chorus is currently offering me any guidance or rules or protests. The only one in my head is me, and I'm enough.

The skin on Charlie's arms and legs and chest warm quickly next to mine, and I feel goose bumps spreading from the tips of my toes to the top of my head. I decide right then that I will do my very best to keep us both alive.

On Sunday morning, I wake up early again, but this time I'm not alone. I listen to Charlie breathing next to me, and I smile. I watch Charlie's face and want to touch it, but I don't want to wake him.

I also want to go back to sleep, but I know I can't. I know that I started something yesterday and that I'm not quite done. I think about Mom and the pained look on her face when I left Gwen and B's shower, and the sadness in her voice last week. I think about the stuffing she saved for me, and imagine the exact Tupperware container with the blue lid she's probably put it in. I think about her face when she's looking at Roger and when he's looking at her. How she thought she had her life all planned out until it fell apart, and how hard she's working to start over. She does yoga every week; she's letting go of things and learning things, like me.

I don't want to be the person who causes people pain, and I know I have been doing just that. I don't want Mom to feel like she's lost me when I'm still right here. I want to be like my dad, who everyone couldn't wait to be around because he was easy to be with. And, I remember, because he made the effort. Dad used to take us over to Uncle Lou's on Thursday nights for Aunt Irene's homemade shepherd's pie, and over to Aunt Sylvia's for a packaged-cookie-and-instant-coffee breakfast on Sunday mornings after church. They were all so glad to see him. And that's how I want to be.

I close my eyes and go to the Dead Zone to be with Dad. And to be with myself, a version that lives up to the best parts of him. A version I can live with. In that peaceful spot inside my chest, I relax and I breathe. Everything gets real quiet, and I imagine everyone glad to see me. It occurs to me that the Dead Zone is as much about being with life as being with death. Sitting up straighter, I remember Nora Mahoney saying, "You only go around the block once." I rework it in my mind so she adds, "So do it right." That helps. I decide everyone should have a little Nora on their shoulder, smoking menthols and hacking out imperatives.

This morning, when it's so early that not much else is going on, I know what doing it right means. I write Charlie a note, slip into sweatpants, and drive out to Yellow Springs to Tranquility Yoga Studio.

When I walk in, I smell incense and see light streaming in through a big bay window. White paper cranes dangle from the ceiling throughout the room. Looking around at the five other people stretching out and chatting, I realize I'm thinking Mom might be here. Then I remember that she's probably getting ready for church right now. I wonder if Roger goes to church or not, and if it's a problem. But I know I don't have to be in charge of that. Instead, I listen to the soft guitar music drifting out of the speakers on the wall.

When Roger sees me, he smiles big. He's surprised, which seems like something Roger isn't very often. "I'm so glad you're here," he says.

"Me too."

"This will be a gentle class. I think you'll really like it. Make yourself at home." He gestures to yoga mats rolled up against the wall. "I'm going to get us started."

As I unroll a mossy green mat for myself, I'm struck by how graciously he welcomed me into his space after how snotty I've been to him. I feel humble and small. I find a spot in the back corner. Only about ten people are here now, so my fleeting thought of slipping out quietly and subtly doesn't seem so feasible.

Once class begins, I remember some of the postures—downward dog and bridge pose. A couple of times we did yoga in gym class at Woodmont, but I never relaxed into it. It seemed like something too personal to be doing with all those people I couldn't wait to get away from, so I kept my guard up. Now I'm letting myself really try each position, feeling the strain in my hips and my shoulders and knees. Roger speaks clearly and with simple confidence, tending to each student as necessary, gently helping to straighten or ease a posture. I forget about him dating my mother and see that he's a good teacher. And also a decent person.

Forty-five minutes later, we all lie in savasana, which, as it turns out, is also known as corpse pose. Roger comes around the room and covers each of us with a blanket. I think of how Dad used to do this for Mom when she fell asleep in the living room watching TV. And about all the years Mom has lived without someone to cover her. Tears drip down the sides of my face in quiet streams.

After a few minutes, Roger invites us to sit up when we're ready. He says, "Namaste," with hands pressed together at his heart center. As other students roll up their mats and begin quiet movement, I sit up and wipe my face. Roger sits down in a perfect lotus in front of me.

"That happens often," Roger says. "A reaction to the different postures. A release."

I nod and feel a tight spot in my neck. I cup it with my hand and breathe into the pain. "From trying something new."

"Or letting go of something old."

I raise my eyebrow at him. "Don't get all philosophical on me, Roger."

He smiles.

"I love my dad," I say.

"I know you do." Roger stands.

I say, "And I love Mom too."

He nods.

"I'm sorry." I hope he knows I mean it. "I'm sorry for how I've been acting."

He holds out a hand and helps me to my feet. "Thank you."

I put my palms together and hold them at my heart. I smile and bow my head to him. "Namaste," I whisper.

When I raise my head, Roger looks into my eyes. He moves his hands to his own heart and bows back to me.

Roger invites me to go to Mom's house with him to meet her after church for breakfast, but I decide I don't want Charlie to wake up alone. Roger agrees to tell Mom I'll be over soon. Back at Brighton Brothers, I find Charlie just waking up. "Where'd you go?" he says, rubbing his eyes.

"I cried on a yoga mat."

"I drooled on your pillow." He wipes the side of his mouth. "Does that make us even?"

I laugh. "I think so."

He smiles and sits up. His hair is huge, like it belongs on some mad scientist.

"Your hair is ridiculous," I say. "And I love you." I'm surprised how easily those words come out.

"My hair is ridiculous." Charlie smiles even wider and says, just as easily, "And I love you too."

I tell Charlie I hate to kick him out, but I've got business to attend to. He gets dressed, and I walk him out, successfully avoiding any awkward encounters with the Brighton family, who appear to be out for their Sunday morning breakfast.

I take a quick shower and change clothes. I head downstairs, car keys in hand, when I see Mom walking through the front door. I'm struck how it's the middle of winter and how Mom looks just like springtime. She's got on a new pink wool coat and has a blush in her cheeks, and her curly hair hangs loose and beautiful. She's standing there, right by the door, where we stood together four years ago, dressed in black and surrounded by darkness. And I'm standing here, from a higher vantage point, seeing clearly that everything has changed.

"I was coming to see you." I walk down the steps and stand across from her.

"Roger told me. I couldn't wait. And I have something to tell you."

"What is it?"

"I asked your brother to invite Selena to the wedding."

"Really? Wow, Mom, that's wow."

"And she's coming. She didn't tell you?"

"I haven't talked with her in a few weeks."

"Oh."

I hear the clock ticking from the hallway upstairs, and the floorboards creak as I rock back on my heels and lower my feet to the ground. I see my Mom, and she sees me.

"Mom, I'm so sorry," I say, starting to cry for the second time today. "I'm so sorry."

She pulls me to her and hugs me hard, and she smells like flowers and hair spray, like Mom. "It's okay, my baby. Everything's okay. We are going to be okay. Both of us."

Domenic Parisi, 51

Cause of Death: Multisystem failure due to intestinal cancer

Surviving Immediate Family:
• Wife: Martha
• Children: Brendan, Donna, Linnie
• Siblings: Louis, Sylvia, Selena

Makeup: Pale Rose lipstick, basic foundation

Clothing: Navy blue suit, white shirt, pink paisley tie

Coffin: Stainless steel, white satin lining

Special Guests in Attendance: Terry Roma, famed 1970s Dayton, Ohio, lounge singer, and his escort Cathy (blouse on inside-out, lipstick on teeth)

Funeral Incidents of Note:
• One fight over "filthy curse words" in funeral parlor between Lou and Irene Parisi
• One great-aunt wailing and passing out: Josie Santora

Dumbest thing someone said trying to be comforting: "He's much happier in heaven, dear. God did this for a reason." —Gilda Grant, neighbor and founder/president of the Kettering Knitters

twenty-three

After the wedding, in the reception hall, I watch Aunt Selena and Uncle Lou do a shot together at the bar, the rainbow lights from the disco ball playing over their laughing faces, and feel like I must be in an alternate universe. A bizarre and delightful one.

Charlie scoops up a handful of confetti from our table and lets it fall to the ground in a sparkly shower. "Confetti is fun," he says.

"And you are easily amused."

Someone comes up behind me and grabs my shoulders. "Donnnderrrr! You should be dancing." B's face is red and damp from jumping all over the dance floor himself. "Can't waste a dress like that sitting around." He smirks.

"You're right." I stand up and smooth out my gold taffeta dress, which, as Linnie predicted, is officially and unequivocally dumb. "I'll be out there for the next song."

"I got married," he says.

"Yes, you did. And you threw a great party. Dad would be impressed."

B kisses me on the cheek. "I love you."

"I love you too. Now go shake your groove thing."

B dances off, and Charlie stands up and holds out his hand. "Shall we?"

"Yes, but first I need a little fresh air. I won't be long. Will you wait for me?"

"I waited for almost a year. I don't think five minutes is going to kill me." He puckers his lips, and I kiss them.

Outside the reception hall, it's been snowing steadily, and I button up my long black winter coat. I feel snowflakes land on my nose and cheeks. I can't believe B is married, and I can't believe it will be a new year in just under an hour. The door falls shut behind me, and the music fades to a distant beat. I put my hands in my pockets and look out into the night sky.

Next to the parking lot, a long field stretches like a big white sheet cake, and I have an urge to do something I haven't done since I was little. I walk to the edge of the field and turn around. Taking a deep breath, I let myself fall backward into the snow, stretching my arms out and flapping them up and down like wings. When I'm done flapping, it's cold and quiet and perfectly still. I feel like I could stay here all night.

But inside is my family, and inside is Charlie. Inside are warmth and light and people I love. I stand up and look at my body in snow angel form—the long legs, the wide sweep of angel wings, the powdery dent of angel butt. What makes me special. The unique shape of me. And suddenly I know what Liz meant about me and transformation, how I might have taught her that. How I've taken myself from one place to another. I can see it, right there in front of me.

I brush the snow off my coat, blow a kiss to my snow angel self, and walk back into the reception, where the music is pumping and everyone is up and clapping.

As I go to meet Charlie on the dance floor, I sense that my backup singers are with me again, Dad right behind me. And in front of me, everyone else forms two lines so that each person can dance down the aisle in between. I've always hated when this happens, forcing people into a painful spotlight, but tonight I see that it's beautiful.

Linnie and Snooter grabbing hands and running as fast as they can together. B twirling Gwen all the way down. Uncle Lou and Aunt Selena trotting through some kind of crazy polka. Aunt Irene with one of the table arrangement roses between her teeth doing her own solo flamenco. Charlie strutting so I can watch. Mom and Roger waltzing along. They look happy together.

And suddenly my backup singers aren't behind me

325

anymore. Right across from me, watching it all, I see Dad, dressed to the nines in a slick tuxedo, toasting Nonna in her fancy red dress. And Grammy in her cream-colored silky gown doing the twist.

Dad holds his glass out to me, and it's brimming with red wine. And he's laughing that enormous laugh he has, the one that makes his whole body shake, the one that's contagious with joy. He spreads his arms wide as if to say, *Here it all is. Here is my family. Here is life. And isn't it grand?*

I spread my own arms back to him, feeling how full they are, how much they can hold, smiling right back at him so he knows that I agree, and that his little girl is just fine.

Dad claps and laughs as each person heads down the aisle. And I do too.

They all dance old steps and new steps, with new partners and old ones. Some graceful, some tentative, some flailing their arms and legs like the music's taking them over. But all dancing nonetheless, using their beautiful bodies to move on through, the best ways they know how. Just like me.

acknowledgments

My deep thanks—

To all you dear creatures who have supported me and my writing, particularly those who kept me afloat while I finished the final draft of this book. I am profoundly blessed with community, and I wish I could name each of you here and sing your individual praises for pages and pages.

To my writing mentors and friends from the University of Dayton, especially the inspiring Joe Pici, in whose class I first located my voice.

To my University of New Orleans CWW classmates and teachers—particularly Joseph, Joanna, Rick, Barb, Casey, Chrys, Nicole, Parker, and Rachel—who, while weathering an incredible storm and its wake, offered invaluable feedback for early forms of this book and evolving forms of me as a writer. Special gratitude for the prowess of the insightful AC Lambeth, the astute Arin Black, and Amanda Boyden, mentor extraordinaire.

To Maya Wilcox, Stuart Rodes, and my one-woman Rock of Gibraltar, Erin Nelson, for thoughtful input on in-between drafts.

To the foxy ladies—Robin, Erin, Julie, Maya, Emily, and Sharon—who made my dream of a book shower a reality and helped me prepare for this book to be born.

To the brilliantly discerning Sarah Kiewitz and Brian Nealon, affirmation champion, for input and support on later drafts.

To the generous Suzanne Fields, for answering all of my questions and being the most gracious dead-people expert imaginable.

To Jeremy Armstrong, who for the first three years in the building of this book, was my family and offered unwavering belief in me and this work.

To Tamson Weston, exceptional editor and delightful person. I'm so grateful for the expert care you've taken with work so precious to me. And to all those at Hyperion who have lent time, talent, and wisdom—I'm in awe of your efforts.

To the fancy and fabulous Lish McBride, for wholehearted professional and personal support and for introducing me to Jason Anthony.

To Jason Anthony of Lippincott Massie McQuilkin, stellar agent, manuscript-wrangling rock star, and lovely human being. You are my hero, just FYI.

And finally to my beloved family, especially Elisa Taffe, Teresa Trombetta, and the inimitable Claramarie Wulfkamp Violi, who all know firsthand what it means to experience loss and to find joy on the other side. Thank you for being my first and best teachers.